THE QUIET LIMIT OF THE WORLD

CARLOS RAMET

The Quiet Limit of the World

Edited by Resa Alboher

Published in North America, Australia, and Europe by RIZE. Visit Running Wild Press at www.runningwildpress.com/rize, Educators, librarians, book clubs
(as well as the eternally curious), go to www.runningwildpress.com/rize.

ISBN (pbk) 978-1-960018-41-0
ISBN (ebook) 978-1-960018-40-3

To
Nancy Cirillo
Friend and Mentor

I wither slowly in thine arms,
Here, at the quiet limit of the world,
A white-haired shadow roaming like a dream,
The ever-silent spaces of the East...

Alfred, Lord Tennyson
"Tithonus"

CHAPTER ONE

1978

I left early on a Sunday morning so that I could avoid any traffic going through L.A. My parents stood on the concrete driveway in front of the one-car garage. My father gripped my hand.

"Diego—be careful, my son."

A Spaniard, he'd never lost his Mediterranean accent despite years as a cook in London and Los Angeles. His eyes darted to my car, a 1973 Toyota Celica that I'd bought used, and I wondered if he knew what had happened in my last year in college.

My mother had tears in her eyes and handed me a neatly crimped grocery shopping bag, as heavy as a sack of potatoes. I'd watched her pack salami, cheese, a jar of olives, a bundle of mandarin oranges, and warm sandwiches wrapped in tin foil.

"Schnitzel sandwiches for the drive to San Francisco," she said, "with sauerkraut and senf."

"Thanks, Mutti."

How an Austrian and a Spaniard stayed married was a family intrigue. She proffered a thermos with hot coffee. "Don't forget who you are, Diego." I choked up when she brushed tears from her eyes.

In the Spanish tradition, I would have been known as Diego Contreras Forsthueber, since the mother's maiden name is retained for one subsequent generation. I kept it simple and dropped my mother's family name—the Austrian side of me. My parents had met in England after the War and we had immigrated to the United States shortly before I started school. But even as a boy, when I was asked what "Diego" is in American, I'd reply "Diego."

"I won't, Mutti."

Before it got any worse, I wanted to shove off. I hugged her, shook hands again with my Dad, and stepped wordlessly into the car. In the rearview mirror, I saw them wave as I drove down our street of single-story homes, pick-up trucks on blocks in driveways, the weekend ritual of repairs.

I turned right onto Beach Boulevard and could hear the Sunday morning bells from St. Pius V Catholic Church, where my brother and I had gone to school and where I'd been an altar boy. My older brother Hidalgo and I were both products of an Old World culture preserved in the United States by way of family and the Catholic school system. While my father would have encouraged me to learn a trade—to be a master electrician, for example—my mother loathed the trades and wanted me to be an attorney. I chose the arts instead and moved from the church choir to high school musical theater to film school and Lit, none of which had gotten me anywhere.

I turned north towards the freeway and told myself I was leaving my town, and religion, and my old life behind.

* * *

The steering wheel shuddered when I accelerated, but my tires hummed on a dry road. A railroad yard snapped past a row of warehouses. I thought I looked good in the Celica, with my trimmed beard and Army surplus jacket. The car had a customized paint job with wide orange and white bands fanning across the front doors like wings.

Just past the iron works in Downey, I noticed a silver Pontiac Trans Am with a red thunderbird painted on the hood pull up behind me, swerve from side to side as if aiming to overtake me in heavy traffic. But almost no one else was on the road. Screw him, I thought to myself. Let him overtake me. The Trans Am must have hung on my tail for at least two miles and my heart was pounding. But why should I get out of his way? I was as good as anyone.

When he finally roared past in a blur of silver and red, I saw a hairy hand hang out over the roof and a finger point upwards. A great start to a long day, I told myself. I tried to calm down.

A cluster of office buildings drifted into view. Looping through the downtown interchange, I glimpsed the red-tile roofs of USC—the college I'd attended, though my mother always went on about how my brother was a Stanford man and I'd only graduated from USC. At least I'd graduated; I tried not to think about my brother.

Instead, I thought about Yuki, my sometimes girlfriend in college. The freeway curved north along the perimeter of the city center, not far from Little Tokyo where Yuki taught me how to use chopsticks and where, in the parking lot of the Atomic Café, we'd almost taken things too far.

But not all the memories that cut into me were comforting. I drove by Los Feliz and the exit to Griffith Park. Thick columns supporting an overpass shook past and I remembered how a year-and-a-half earlier I had almost done it in. I'd been in school most of my short life up until then, and each steady step led to the next, though I'm sure nervous breakdowns and mental instability ran in the family. My older brother had been institutionalized twice, and the third time he would have been wearing a prison uniform if he hadn't run away. For me, in my last year of college, uncertain of any prospects, spurned by one of the bridesmaids at a friend's wedding, and after eight or nine martinis, I got behind the wheel of my car.

On the freeway back to my college digs in L.A., I saw where the road divided, the turnoff to the north, the turnoff to the south, and the pylons of the overpass marking the divide. It would have been so easy just to turn the steering wheel a fraction of an inch and hit the pylon straight on at eighty-five miles per hour.

Instead, I took the north offramp and circled back around, tempted by the pylon a second time and then a third until, sobbing and yelling blasphemies, I swerved onto the turnoff south.

I travelled hard the year following college. I spent eight weeks bumming through France and Germany, working the vendage, sleeping rough sometimes when I didn't have the money for a hostel. After that night of desperation on the freeway, I told myself anything I experienced was a gift, a bonus, value-added, overtime, even moving back in with my folks. I worked a series of odd jobs that year, both in and out of the film industry, in and out of Orange County kitchens with my Dad, and tried writing a film script and a play. By the end of that summer, I'd been accepted into a graduate creative writing program at San Francisco State University.

With the thought of a fresh start, I was in a maniacally good mood as I drove up the I-5 that August. San Francisco would be my SoHo, my Berlin, my Greenwich Village. Never mind that the Golden Dragon massacre, a botched Chinatown shoot-up the previous year, was symptomatic of the City's gangland feuds; or that older neighborhoods were in decline, with tensions from displacement and rapid change reflected in the city council, escalating between Harvey Milk, the City's first openly gay supervisor, and Supervisor Dan White, a former policeman and fireman, leaving the beleaguered Mayor Moscone to mediate.

Instead, for me, a film and Lit major and recent college graduate, San Francisco was "an oasis of culture in the California desert," as the George Saunders character Addison De Witt put it in the movie *All About Eve.*

But first I had to get there in a pale green four-seater that was good on gas but had a leaky radiator. Nothing a couple of cans of Stop Leak couldn't fix.

* * *

By midmorning, I had climbed the Santa Clarita Pass and soared through the canyons near Pyramid Lake. I was my own man, I told myself. I had some modest savings, a couple of film scripts in a satchel that I might rewrite as plays, a boxful of books that I had read and reread since college: *The Sorrows of Young Werther; Immortal Poems of the English Language,* edited by Oscar Williams; *The Complete Works of Shakespeare;* and Mickey Spillane's *My Gun is Quick.*

The back seat was piled high with my clothing, photo albums from my recent trips, and framed enlargements I could use to decorate a room. A couple of large travel posters were rolled up in a mailing tube. In the car trunk was an electric typewriter, along with a portable cassette player, pots and pans and cookware my parents had given me, and a set of dishes and utensils in case I had to supply my own in whatever new digs I would find. I also kept two jugs of water in the trunk in case the radiator was thirsty.

My car chugged up the Gorman Pass and the engine seemed to cough and hesitate. I downshifted, negotiated the steep incline in the lowest gear but noticed the needle on the temperature gauge inched into the red. Even though it was eighty-five degrees outside, I turned the car heater and fan to the highest setting and unrolled all four windows. I was broiling but drawing the heat off the engine seemed to help and the temperature gauge needle hovered back into the safe zone.

Winding my way through the Grapevine was even tougher on the cooling system. Steam started to hiss from the radiator. When I crested the top of the Tejon Pass, I pulled over to let the engine cool. I waited nervously for more than half an hour, told myself I should enjoy the view from the pass, and took a few deep breaths. When it was safe, I used a thick rag to loosen the radiator cap. Steam rose slowly like tobacco smoke, but at least it wasn't a hot geyser of boiling fluid. I was able to pour in cold water from a jug and noticed the radiator was leaking again. I always kept Stop Leak with me and added two cans.

Back in action, it was time for some music and I inserted Jethro Tull's "Aqualung" into the dashboard cassette player. I kept the box of cassettes on the front seat and it wasn't all rock and folk, but Shosktakovich, Rachmanioff, Rimsky-Korsakov, Ravel, the great Romantics, some Baroque.

I drummed on the steering wheel as I shot past a dry lake near Buttonwillow. Clumps of sagebrush covered the flatlands and I thought of some of the good and bad dates I'd had in college. Most dates fizzled because I didn't know who I was, or I was trying too hard, but angrily I always told myself it was because I grew up working class and didn't have enough money.

I remembered taking a young lady from my theater class to

see Jon Voight as Hamlet. I could barely afford the tickets, let alone gas for the MG Midget sportscar I'd borrowed from my roommate for my "big date." Dinner at a Jewish deli had set me back, but it was worth it because she was pretty and she told me she liked theater. As my father put it in his inimitable way: "You spend all your money on broads. No wonder you're always broke."

"Everyone has to have a hobby," I told him. "You have your motorcycles . . ."

"My motorcycles are reliable," he retorted, which was a joke. Half the time my mother had to drive him to work because one motorcycle or the other was broken down.

I also liked to work out and burn off frustration by running hard or pumping iron. I was looking forward to a new routine in a new city. San Francisco State had a gym and I couldn't wait to hear the clank of iron weights again.

I stopped for gas in Lost Hills. Even though it was only midmorning, the young girl standing at the cash register looked tired and bored. She was cute, probably a high school student who could only get hours on a Sunday morning, and she had bright green eyes and a light sprinkling of freckles across the bridge of her nose. I wanted to see her smile and grinned: "Lost Hills? Must be nice living here."

The girl looked at me, then looked out the window. Oil derricks pumped lazily on the flat plain.

"There ain't a hill around here," she said, "but everyone that lives here is lost all right."

She didn't smile.

* * *

I grew tired of listening to music and in the afternoon, on the long drive to the Gilroy turnoff, I unrolled the windows and let the warm air rush in, rush up against my body like hands. I sang some of the songs I'd learned in childhood. I'd grown up listening to old Richard Tauber recordings and belted out in a strong baritone voice "Wien, Du Stadt Meine Traume" and later, since my father had insisted I learn the songs of the Spanish Civil War, "Si me quieres escribir." I had only the sound of the wind to compete with my voice and even sang the Andaluz exile's lament "Yo soy un pobre emigrante." The reservoir I drove past made me think of a Scandinavian lake. I'd never been to Norway or Sweden, but it didn't matter. Almost everything in my background was a cultural mishmash.

I arrived in San Mateo in the late afternoon and decided to spend the night. The San Carlos Motel was a step above a "Y-Tel Motel," where johns paid by the hour, but it would be cheaper than staying in San Francisco and I could drive the rest of the way the next day feeling refreshed. A couple from India ran the place. I paid in advance and the man took a key down from a hook on the wall and handed it to me. He poked a thin finger in the direction of the room. "Check out time is eleven. No large parties."

I thought that was amusing because I was by myself, but the last time I'd stayed at the San Carlos Motel was only a year or so before, when six or seven of us had packed into a double room—two to a bed, two or three on the floor—to save money. We had driven up from USC to attend the Stanford game. The owner of the motel gave me a second look, and whatever grim smile he had disappeared. Maybe he remembered me.

The room had thin carpeting and a small bathroom to one side. The bed looked like it sagged in the middle—maybe from overuse—and the faded pictures on the wall showed a canal in Italy. A writing desk, a chair, and a television set were opposite the bed. The room had been aired out recently.

I'd passed a liquor store on the drive to the San Carlos. It was about a block away and I walked south on Walnut Street and bought a six-pack of beer and a bag of potato chips.

When night fell, I finished the last of the sandwiches my parents had packed, ate a few oranges, and opened a can of beer. I watched television. An old movie played—*Waterloo Bridge*, starring Robert Taylor and Vivien Leigh; a black and white film that made me feel miserable. I shut off the television and was on my fourth beer. I listened to the sound of traffic and decided to write a letter.

The motel only provided a few sheets of letterhead. I'd need to be brief and started to compose a missive to my former girlfriend—the Japanese-American woman I'd gone out with the previous year. Maybe I'd mail it, maybe I wouldn't. Maybe she'd write back to me. Who knows? Maybe we'd even get back together. I started writing that I thought of her sometimes and that I was sorry things had ended badly. I explained that we had broken up because when you really love someone you only want the best for them and I knew I wasn't worthy of her. I tore that up—it made me sound too noble—and I wrote a much milder version, stating simply that I was moving to San Francisco and that I hoped she was having a good year. I tore that one up as well. The truth was, we had broken up because I was too restless, too confused, and at times too angry to have developed any kind of stable relationship. I liked her but hadn't felt any love for her until it was over.

I finished the last two beers and the potato chips. In the morning, I would drive the rest of the way into San Francisco.

* * *

The last short leg of the journey took me through San Bruno, then Serramonte, and past Daly City where houses, strung together like pearl necklaces, laced around the hills. A white and orange BART train ran parallel to the freeway and for a while I felt as if I were racing the train.

The five miles from Daly City to the campus went quickly; even with morning traffic I was at the turnoff within minutes.

I'd only seen the campus from a distance when driving through town on previous trips but made my way to the corner of Holloway and Nineteenth where I parked in a concrete structure. I handed over a tuition payment at the Bursar's Office, then swung by the Division of Graduate Studies to touch base with my advisor. A young Asian woman was in the waiting area as well. She looked at me and smiled. She was stunning, with deep luminous eyes, a pert nose, and lightly glossed lips. Her long black hair cascaded to one side, with a strand falling in front of one eye. She brushed it aside.

I wanted to ask her a question, find out what program she was in, but stood in silence.

I kept thinking how beautiful she was. She might have been Filipino or Chinese, or maybe mixed. She was dressed in a short beige leather jacket, open in the front, set off by a cream-colored lacy blouse; black jeans and jet-black shoes completed the combination.

I was about to say something when the receptionist, a young man with pimples and an Adam's apple that bobbed up and down, croaked out that she could see her advisor now.

I watched her pass through a hallway door. I waited, saw my advisor, and started thinking about everything else I had to do. Above all, I needed to find digs. I could afford another night or two in some "El Cheapo" Motel—a place more or less like the San Carlos—but before too long I'd need to find something more permanent.

I crossed campus. A few of the buildings had roofs angled like open cantilever bridges, but most of them were functional post-war buildings of poured concrete and glass. The Housing Office was in a grey slab of a building.

Along the narrow hallway a bulletin board was papered with notices: *Roommate Wanted, House for Rent, Trailer Available, Live with Family Only Forty Miles From Campus*—none of it seemed appropriate. Then, I found what I was looking for: *Large Room for Rent. Furnished. Close to Market Street, City Hall, and All Amenities.* I was curious what "large" meant in the heart of the city, but the rent was less than one hundred dollars per month, utilities included. Best of all, the notice read: *Available for Immediate Occupancy.* I wrote down the phone number.

* * *

The pinging of the Celica's four-cylinder 1.6 liter engine V-4 was reassuring, whispering to me that the pistons were moving up and down and the car was carrying me uphill. Portola curved through the heights near Mount Davidson and I could see the panorama of the City, the white skyline in relief against the Bay, the dark stretch of water fanning out in the direction of Oakland. The day was crisp and cool, invigorating, and I told myself I could be happy here.

I followed Portola to Market then turned left on Larkin, driving past City Hall and Civic Center Plaza, with its neoclassical opera house on one end and beaux-arts library building on the other. I told myself that section of the City looked like Vienna; I thought of the Hofburg and the Kunsthistoriches Museum and the Rathaus.

I knew that just east of the palatial municipal hall modelled on the U.S. Capitol Building was an encampment of the homeless, and beyond that the Tenderloin district, a mecca for junkies and runaways and prostitutes.

But I wasn't headed there. San Francisco would be my Vienna. The Vienna before the First World War wasn't a mecca for junkies but for unknown artists and intellectuals who moved silently through crowds of the well-established and were on the verge of joining their ranks. Such was my dream.

Of course, there was a problem with this fantasy: San Francisco was a hard-edged American city with pockets of decay, a long list of social problems, and little intellectual ferment other than the angry froth of politics and resentment.

Eventually, I would learn that San Francisco wasn't even one city; it was seven separate cities, each of which hated the others.

I circled back to Market and turned right on Sanchez. A short jog took me to the street I was looking for: Granger Street. I decided to reconnoiter and headed north on Granger, up a hill. The building where I might end up living was at the lower end of Granger, opposite a park. A few short blocks took me past the Painted Ladies, the famous varicolored Victorian homes. But to get there, I had to cross Haight and Page. As I looped back around and drove south to the bottom of Granger, I saw iron bars on windows, what looked like an old carpet rolled up and lying in a doorway until it moved, and brown shards of glass on the sidewalk.

I crossed Waller and the neighborhood seemed less blighted. The park was well-maintained and a young couple helped a child into a swing. I parked opposite the building and looked down the street. A laundromat was nearby, the streetcar line ran east-west a block away, and a bar and a bakery faced each other on opposite corners. The neighborhood would be fine.

* * *

A man in his mid-fifties trundled down the stairs and held the beveled door open for me.

"Diego?"

He introduced himself as Mr. Meriwether and as I followed him upstairs, he explained that he leased the top floor and then sublet individual rooms, including what had once been the living room. I knew that many of the old Victorian homes and post-war townhouses had been divided in that way. Less than a dozen years before, during the "Summer of Love," a generation of seekers had descended on the Haight to find their own version of truth, and building owners with falling property values were happy to divide and conquer and rent to them. Many of the buildings had never been reconverted into single family homes.

We reached the third floor. Mr. Meriwether wore a yellow and green silk shirt that was too tight for him. His belly bulged out and I could see a line of pink skin. He also wore thick glasses and a mop of curly blond hair that was obviously a toupee. He inclined his head toward me and apologized.

"Hearing aid," he pointed. "You'll have to speak up."

I hadn't said anything. He waited expectantly.

"Oh," I replied at last. "Can you tell me about the room?"

We were in the middle of the hallway and Mr. Meriwether stretched his arms so that he could point in both directions.

"All the bedrooms are behind me, on this side of the hallway. Three in this direction and two in the other. There's a shared kitchen and bathroom and phone privileges." He flicked his hand toward a rotary phone on a hall stand next to me. A notebook stuck out from underneath the phone. "I don't worry about local calls, but we write down our toll calls. The monthly service fee is divided and everyone pays for their own long-distance calls."

"Sounds fair to me."

"The front room is available. I'll show you."

I followed him down the hallway in the direction of the street. Where the building ended, a common sitting area with magazines and a television was to the right. A private room was to the left and Mr. Meriwether unlocked the door, then held it open.

"This is the second largest bedroom on the floor. The bedroom at the back end is larger. An Australian couple stays there. My room is in the middle, two doors away from this one." He smiled. "I don't bother anyone. I just collect the rent and keep to myself."

We stepped inside the room. On the south side, a window opened onto an alley but to the west two large Bay windows offered a view of the city street and park. Sunlight fell across a desk and chair near the window. To my left, a fireplace stood in the middle of the wall and the screen and andirons made it seem usable.

"Does the fireplace work?"

"Chimney's sealed off." Mr. Meriwether pointed instead to a set of cast-iron coils about three feet high, painted silver. "Steam radiator. It's a lot safer than burning wood."

"Yes, of course."

A single bed was against the wall opposite the fireplace and a chest of drawers faced the foot of the bed. If I ever bought a television set, I thought, I could place it on top of the chest of drawers. I looked down. I could also buy a couple of cheap area rugs—maybe with a Persian design—to cover the hardwood floor. The wallpaper pattern and the tin-tiled ceiling were old-fashioned, but so was everything else in the room. A settee, an ottoman, and a small bookcase completed the furnishings.

"Skip Spence, the drummer from Jefferson Airplane, lived here for a year," Mr. Meriwether added. "Right before they made it big."

He tilted his head to one side, probably to hear me better if I spoke. He waited, looking over the top of his glasses, smiling slightly.

"I like it," I said.

He grinned.

"Maybe it will bring you luck."

CHAPTER TWO

I set the photo of the three of us from 1967 in a prominent location, on the mantlepiece above the disused fireplace. We had helped my older brother get settled into the dorms at Stanford and then had spent the day and evening seeing the sights of San Francisco, visiting Chinatown and Fisherman's Wharf and Nob Hill.

My brother must have taken the photo because it shows my father, my mother, and myself by the green entrance gate to Chinatown. I stood between my parents, twelve years old with fair hair and blue eyes wearing a cardigan from St. Pius V grade school. I looked uncomfortable. Maybe the sun was in my eyes.

It must have been my very first time in San Francisco and I was amazed that my father still knew his way around the City. He'd been a British merchant seaman in the 1950s, docking at the Port of San Francisco and taking shore leave in the years before we emigrated. In 1967, after nearly nine years living in Southern California, he could still find his way to favorite San Francisco restaurants and points of interest.

My father, Bartolo Contreras Navarro, had lived an adventurous life, or so it had seemed to me, and a large part of me wanted a taste of similar adventures. Born in Andalusia, he was forced to leave Spain shortly before his seventh birthday. His father—my grandfather—had died in an accident with a horse-cart, and my grandmother, for the first time in her life, needed to find work outside the house. Illiterate and with only housekeeping skills, she avoided the shame of working as a maid in her hometown and found work instead in French Morocco, a short ferry ride across the Straits of Gibraltar.

My father grew up mostly in Casablanca but also in Rabat and Meknes.

When the Second World War started, he joined the British Army in North Africa and participated in campaigns near Cairo and in Crete. He was "D-Day Plus-Six" and was wounded at Malmedy during the Ardennes Counteroffensive. That effectively ended his service in the British Army; following the German surrender, he completed a culinary training program, married my mother, and worked as a chef in a number of hotels in England and as a ship's cook for the Royal Mail Line.

My mother, Irmgard Fortshueber, also led an interesting life. She was born in Austria, close to the Swiss border, and like my father was taken out of school at the age of fifteen. She always wanted to improve herself and arranged to leave Austria for England to work as a domestic servant. "At least I'd learn another language," she always said, and fortuitously left Austria shortly after the *Anschluss* when the Nazis took control. She was later taken into custody by the British authorities and was classified as a "friendly enemy alien." She spent two years at a women's internment facility on the Isle of Man, which she described as a kind of paradise except that there were no men—she meant, of course, eligible men since all but the old and unfit were serving in the armed forces.

Eventually reclassified, she moved to London where she experienced the closing air raids of the War. She remembered the Victory in Europe celebrations at Trafalgar Square, what rationing was like, meeting her husband, and raising a family in England in the post-war years before we moved to the United States. She was the driving force in the family in more ways than one, and since my father only rode a motorcycle and I was too young to drive in 1967, she was the one who made that first long trip to San Francisco and back.

I'd become more familiar with the town in later years, as a college student from USC traveling up for the annual "away" football game either with Stanford or Cal, and my drunken carousing adventures at pep rallies on Union Square or in the dives in North Beach with my college pals seemed in my mind to pale in comparison with the experiences my parents endured.

I placed a photo from my recent trip to the U.K. on the mantlepiece as well. In the picture, I stood with my back to a harbor in Scotland. Fishing boats were behind me. I wore a scruffy beard, a blue blazer and captain's cap, and a thick brown sweater. A passerby had agreed to take the photo for me.

"Liking a boat?" I thought he asked me. It was a forty-five minute ferry ride to the Isle of Skye. Then I realized he'd asked if I was larking about.

"My gap year," I smiled. "Seeing the world while I can."

* * *

In a new location, everything looked odd and familiar. For the next few weeks, I felt upbeat about everything, including getting to know the Duboce Triangle neighborhood and the denizens who lived on my floor.

In the room next to mine was Ferrano, about my age; cleanshaven with dark hair. He was well-spoken and seemed to come from a good family. He told me his father was the principal violinist for the Cleveland Philharmonic. Ferrano was also a survivor of some sixty acid trips, according to what he admitted. We would be sitting at the dining table in the shared kitchen when he would say, after a dead silence: "Motivation has always seemed to me a social phenomenon, that we do things out of a stimulus from others—do you know what I mean?" Then he would issue a high-pitched laugh as if that had answered his question.

Mr. Meriwether lived in the next room down the hallway, just past Ferrano's digs. Eventually, I learned that Mr. Meriwether's first name was "Philbus," which was one reason he wanted everyone to call him Mr. Meriwether. I was outside his room one afternoon and noticed that he had paperbacks in boxes, on shelves, and piled on the top of a dresser. I asked him about his collection and he told me he was very fond of romance stories by Barbara Cartland and World War II novels. I loved reading and asked him what he was into these days.

"This." He picked up a Signet edition from the top of a pile. "It just came out in paperback." He showed me the cover. The title was *Eye of the Needle,* and it had an image of a Nazi dagger on the front. The author was someone named Ken Follett.

"How is it?" I asked.

Mr. Meriwether glanced at the back cover and read: "'A truly suspenseful novel . . . heart-stopping, nerve-freezing terror,' according to the *L.A. Times*."

"Sounds interesting," I mentioned casually. "Maybe I'll read it someday."

Mr. Meriwether was also a collector of a different sort. He told me about his collection of back issues of *Life* magazine. And I learned, over time, that he had frequent visitors—in particular a black teenager of about eighteen or nineteen named Marcus. I'd sometimes see Mr. Meriwether give Marcus "pocket money for taking care of chores."

San Francisco had always marched to its own drumbeat. Marcus certainly looked like he was over eighteen, so my attitude was: "Whatever twirls your beanie, pal." I wasn't going to ask too many questions. I just wanted to live cheaply, earn a graduate degree, and maybe break into print with a short story or an article or two. Whatever else I was looking for, I couldn't quite articulate—a purpose, a passion, a plane ride to a place where adventure awaited at every turn? Maybe I was looking for salvation of a sort—a reason to live, a person to live for.

Karl Hamburger, a big, hulking farm boy from Visalia, a cow town in the Central Valley, was in the second-to-last room. The phone and hall stand were directly opposite his door and Karl was usually grumpy if the phone rang and he had to answer it. Karl had quit school at sixteen "to see life" and had ridden the rails to Reno and Salt Lake City. He was in his early twenties now and had lived in Berkeley, selling beaded handbags and woven belts on Telegraph Avenue. "Frisco is a lot cheaper, man. By far!" Karl beamed. He also insisted that as roomers, all of us would be welcome to anything he put inside the shared fridge. His understanding, no doubt, was that he would be equally welcome to anything that was ours. This was not a good arrangement, and Karl soon became known as the "Mooch."

The back room, facing a sunless alley, was shared by Stephen and Lisa, a couple traveling together from Australia. They said they were married, but Stephen once confessed that Lisa was his sister and that marriage was a "front" so that he could enjoy life more discreetly in places like San Francisco. Both Stephen and Lisa were good conversationalists—we often talked about books and movies and travel—but Stephen had the unusual habit of licking his dinner plate. They argued frequently—often about whether they should go to a gay night-club—and Lisa was routinely in the common room by herself reading magazines.

I was inspired in those days and read voraciously—*Middle-march, The Naked and the Dead, Paris Spleen, The Collector,* a collection of Chekov's plays, books of criticism. I wore my hair moderately long and sported a Van Dyke. And I pounded out word after word on a blue electric typewriter, hoping it wouldn't break, and hoping what I wrote and rewrote might have some value.

Mostly, it was a lot of emotional drivel, therapeutic in its own way, the wild emotions of a dream, but not worth saving.

I tried automatic writing, turning off the lights in my Bay-window room and tapping the typewriter keys in a steady stream-of-consciousness. It was all really rotten stuff, but some images from the darkened room have stayed with me: nothing but shapes and long blue forms in the night, the streetcar passing uphill, a long tube of tiny window lights inching along what appeared to be glistening snails' trails into a tunnel.

* * *

The campus was about forty-five minutes from where I lived, either by light rail and bus or by car. On a beautiful day, I might walk an hour-and-a-half to campus and enjoy the exhilarating views from the high point of Portola Avenue. Because my typing skills were so strong—I tested at a little over one hundred words per minute on an IBM Selectric—I was hired as a clerk/typist for an academic unit, the Department of Social Work.

I spent most of my office time pounding out multiple copies of policy statements such as: "Yet another dimension of preparation recognizes that the social administration of social services requires a recognition and concern for the manner in which agencies provide services and the mandate to change the operation of agencies so that they adapt to the changing environment surrounding it while continuing to provide relevant services," and I realized that if the world doesn't need another young aspiring creative writer, it could always do with a few good copy editors.

Tedious as it might be, office work gave me a routine, and my graduate classes were a place where I could dream of better things. I especially enjoyed a seminar on existentialism and modernism, taught by Yurgis Papandrakis, whose waxed grey moustache made him look like a Greek general. He would tell stories about being a young man in Greece, about sitting at a sidewalk taberna in the sun all afternoon with his friends. They would talk about crossing over to the taberna on the other side of the road, but they never did. Such was existentialism.

Walter "Walt" Wilson, best known for a prison saga called *Hard Time for Mr. Morrison,* taught a graduate novel-writing workshop. Each week, one or two students would read their drafts out loud and Professor Wilson would make some larger point about dialogue, exposition, or setting, usually by reading from published material by Dreiser, de Maupassant or Malamud to show us "how it should be done." One of the students in particular resented this approach. Eddie, from Hoboken, always seemed to know better, maybe because he'd been in the program for seven or eight years but had never submitted a thesis.

Most of the members of Walt Wilson's class were men in their late twenties or early thirties—sometimes older—but there were two women. One of them was seven months pregnant and had a beatific smile. She had been a Peace Corps volunteer in Togo and was working on a heartwarming story about helping people. Everyone liked her. The other woman in the class was Penny Clifton, from Bakersfield, who was writing a Steinbeck-like novel about the dispossessed and about grape workers in the San Joaquin Valley. Everyone liked her because she had an agent.

Rounding out my schedule was a writing/performance course taught by Ramsay O'Donnell, who had been a playwright-in-residence at the O'Neill Theatre Center. I had submitted a five-act play for O'Donnell's playwriting workshop and it had been selected for a staged reading that semester, which meant I would be part of the rehearsal process for my own play and for other student plays. An M.F.A. theater student would be assigned to direct the piece and student actors would be cast in the various roles. I would rewrite sections as needed, the play would be performed with limited props and costuming, but with the actors familiar enough with the lines that they would only need to refer to the script occasionally. It was heady stuff and I was excited about the project because it meant I might be able to rewrite it as a thesis. I was starting to believe I might actually be happy.

Early in the semester, I worked up the courage to talk to the attractive Filipino-Chinese woman. I saw her in the cafeteria at lunch and asked if I could join her. I was slightly embarrassed about the way I was dressed, in a denim shirt with the sleeves rolled up to the elbows. She was wearing a summer dress with a floral pattern. She seemed very beautiful and very young, but she was actually a year older than I was. She told me her name.

"Ramona? You're kidding me. Like in the song?"

She chuckled with obvious delight. "No, *Saloma*. Saloma Sevilla," and she pronounced the double "L" as a "Y," which pleased me.

I introduced myself and told her I was a graduate student in creative writing and worked for the Department of Social

Work on campus. Saloma explained that she worked for Yurgis Papandrakis as his secretary and was completing a master's degree in psychology. I should have been leery, because most psychology majors I knew were trying to figure themselves out —but the same could be said for creative writing majors.

"So what do you plan to do with your degree in psychology?"

"I don't know." She looked away. "I've always loved children. Maybe I'll work in a school or work with special ed kids. And you?"

Actually, I had an intense dislike of small children; I was the youngest in my family, didn't have any nieces, nephews or cousins in the United States, and wasn't around children very much. As a result, I found them to be annoying and impertinent. But that's not what she was asking.

"Write the great American novel, I suppose." I let out a dry laugh, but it probably sounded forced.

She nodded thoughtfully.

I hardly ate, I was so wound up talking to her, but she had an infectious smile and an easy laugh. Saloma told me she was from Daly City but lived close to the campus now. Like a lot of immigrant families that had originally settled in San Francisco, her family had moved to the suburbs after a generation in the States. She was Filipino-Chinese, she said, with some Spanish blood.

I told Saloma about my own immigrant background and that my father was from Spain.

"I grew up near Los Angeles," I disclosed. "We have a lot of Asian culture there. I only moved up here two months ago."

She glanced at me and smiled, revealing an even row of very white teeth. "You're very brave."

I must have looked puzzled.

"How so?"

"To make a move," she replied. "I've been uprooted twice." She picked at her food. "I can't see myself living anywhere else anymore, except here."

We seemed to be hitting it off. She was a bit shy and maybe was as nervous as I was, but I invited her to lunch for the following Wednesday.

That evening, in my rooming house, I sat with Ferrano and Karl Hamburger in the kitchen. Ferrano kept talking about life and motivation. "What is life?" he asked after a pause. "Are we ever really motivated?" He giggled. "I mean, can we even really know if we are alive—if any of this is real?" I watched Karl Hamburger swig from a bottle of milk that wasn't his. I kept thinking about Saloma. I wondered what she was really like.

I was keyed up all that week and made it a point not to swing through her building until the appointed day and time. We went to Stacks, a family restaurant in nearby Stonestown, and we talked about a lot of things. I found out that her mother was from a prominent Filipino-Chinese family that had settled in San Francisco in the 1920s. Although her mother was born in the States, her father was from Manila. They had met when he was a student at UC Berkeley.

Saloma smiled ruefully.

"I never wanted to move to the Philippines," she admitted. "I was born here and lived the first nine years of my life right here in the City."

"Then what happened?" I asked.

She shrugged.

"My father insisted. He was bored being a nobody in America. He knew everybody in Manila. He could be a big shot there with a big job in the Ministry of Defense."

"You had it made." I was thinking of my own modest background by comparison.

"We had servants and a driver and lived in a walled

compound. I went to convent schools. It was very decadent." She let out an embarrassed laugh. "Are you Catholic?"

I hesitated. I had read somewhere that under the Spanish, the Filipino-Chinese often held privileged positions as merchants and intermediaries and were largely integrated into colonial society. They had embraced the religion, the attitudes, the mores. In more recent times, they were resented for their wealth, but the Philippines overall was staunchly Catholic.

"I went to Catholic schools. Yes. Twelve years of it." I couldn't help myself and made a slicing hand gesture across my brow. "Up to the eyeballs."

"That's not what I asked."

I looked away.

"All my teachers were either Irish priests or Polish nuns. You couldn't get much more Catholic than that."

She seemed disappointed, and I said in response: "How about you? You're not in the Philippines anymore."

"We moved back to San Francisco right before I finished high school," she divulged. "My parents got divorced and my mother had to work—as a secretary. She said it's not so bad, and I agree. It's not bad. I like being a secretary."

"Why's that?" I asked.

She smiled at me. "Because sometimes you meet some very nice people."

* * *

For the next several dates we had lunch at area restaurants or sometimes drove after work to Irving Street. We poked around the used bookstores and sat out in the sunshine drinking espresso or Beck's beer. Saloma was an avid reader. We enjoyed visiting the rare bookstores, where we perused the leather-bound volumes, and then crossed over to the used paperback bins on the sidewalk. We ended up with an armful of titles such as *What Time Collects, Les Chants de Maldoror,* or Turgenev's *Fathers and Sons.* Saloma would tell me about her childhood in San Francisco, about going to Mass at Old St. Mary's Cathedral in Chinatown and never being seen in town with her mother unless they were both wearing white gloves and pillbox hats.

That part of her was very much old San Francisco. One could still catch glimpses of that era in the high teas at the fancy hotels, the ballroom dances, the women with white gloves on a Sunday, but one had to seek it out and it was fast disappearing. I was growing fond of Saloma, I thought she was lovely, and increasingly I was happy whenever I was with her.

We spent a Saturday together. I picked her up from the apartment near campus that she shared with her younger sister and drove back to the heart of town, parking on Hyde next to Russian Hill. We spent the day enjoying the fresh air and each other's company, lunch in Chinatown and then drinks later at Señor Pico's at Ghiradellhi Square. We ordered a pitcher of Sangria and Saloma surprised me when she asked me if I'd like to smoke. I had a lot of bad habits, but tobacco wasn't one of them. She lit up a Virginia Slim, puffed at it like an amateur, and announced: "I'm into feminism."

"I can tell."

Saloma was full of contradictions. I couldn't see her as much of a feminist, but she stated that by the standards of the Philippines she was a rebel. When she was seventeen, her father had arranged for her to be engaged to one of his business partners, but she had refused to get married. That was one of the reasons her mother brought her back to the States and her parents were now divorced. She was very close to her younger sister and to her brothers and sisters who had stayed with their mom in Daly City, but she was independent too.

"I'm paying my own way in grad school," she explained. "I could have commuted but it feels good to more or less have my own place."

Was she inviting me back? I was getting ahead of myself. Maybe it was the Sangria. When we left Señor Pico's, it was nearing dusk and we walked up Larkin to the top of Russian Hill. We could see ships out in the Bay, hear their horns, could see the ferries plying their way back from the tourist destinations, could hear the call of seagulls. It was growing dark and the lights were starting to come up. We stood next to my car in those full, luminous moments of indecision. I kissed her gently on the lips and could feel the contours of her body. She kissed me back and pressed her hand against my cheek.

"We'd better leave," she said.

* * *

And so it went for the next several months, with me diligently working on academic papers, trying to write short stories and chapters for a novel, seeing my play in rehearsal, and taking Saloma out, mostly for lunch. She was often distracted by families at nearby restaurant tables, especially if they had small children. Saloma would wave to the little kiddies, smile at them. Once, she even asked to hold someone's infant daughter and cooed to it, bouncing it in her arms.

Our chaste kisses sometimes lingered for a while and I tried telling myself that I had to win her trust, that she felt she didn't know me well enough. But I was becoming increasingly frustrated. The physical side of things lagged behind the emotional. She probably wanted to wait until she was married. For Saloma, it was all about having children of her own. Half the time, I wasn't even sure if I ever wanted to get married, let alone have a squawking brood. But when I wasn't with her, she was never far from my thoughts.

If I was frustrated by Saloma sometimes, I derived satisfaction from my classes. I enjoyed Walt Wilson's novel writing class. Most of his criticism was of the mixed variety, usually along the lines of "this is the way Saul Bellow would have handled it." Sometimes his criticism was more pointed, as when he told Eddie from Hoboken that his story lacked a moral compass, any sort of guiding intelligence, and was one-hundred-and-fifty pages of disconnected incident and blood and guts. Eddie leaned back in his chair, smirking, and looking thoroughly self-satisfied. He fancied himself a boxing expert, had published a sports article or two, and worked part-time in a boxing gym. But Professor Wilson had obviously disliked Eddie's narrative *The Big Punch-Up*.

In general, Walt Wilson had high praise for two types of material—work that was very good and work that was very bad. One graduate student, Serge Freemantle, had been in the fiction-writing workshop for several semesters. Serge was in his late twenties, trim, with wavy sand-colored hair that was cut short for the time—that is, didn't fall much below the center of his ear. He said he was retired and lived in Mill Valley. He was writing a suspenseful narrative about a young man in his twenties, with sandy hair, who had started smuggling marijuana out of Mexico as a teenager. Things had escalated and the business had gotten better and better, not only with harder drugs but with speed boats, helicopters, and low-flying Cessna airplanes making "cargo" drops. The hero of the story had become so wealthy that he could retire in his mid-twenties and buy a spacious home in Mill Valley.

Professor Wilson often started the class with a reading from the drug-runner's draft. As Wilson pointed out, it was well-paced, descriptive, had gradually deepening characterizations, and was commercial—a principal goal for any of us in the class.

A bald-headed man with long fringes hanging from his temples was writing a novel about a gnome, from the gnome's point-of-view. When it was his turn to present, he did so in a soft monotone. He mumbled. For an hour-and-a-half, he read out loud the saga of the gnome, who lived in a tunnel in the ground, mole-like, guarding his treasure and only poking his head above ground on rare occasions. His classmates were starting to fall asleep. Even the former Navy chaplain's eyes glazed over, as if he had heard one too many battlefield confessions. Professor Wilson appeared to be taking notes, but his pen moved in lazy circles.

I don't remember when eye contact started, but some of us started to notice that others were nodding off. The student who was reading was intently focused on his typescript, which he gripped with both hands. His fringes swayed and his words seemed to form as physical objects on his lips, hung there, and then came out as a muttered temple chant. Someone started to snicker; another person tried to suppress a laugh with a cough. Several members of the class had broken out in a hot sweat from the effort of trying to keep from bursting out in a guffaw.

When the reading finally ended, there was a long silence until Professor Wilson started to talk about the elegance of point-of-view in D.H. Lawrence. Others chimed in with reference to social parody, a crystallization of the human experience, all the world's a stage and all the men and women merely players. I think Professor Wilson let us make our exits early that night.

* * *

In early November, the Jonestown story broke. Under pressure from concerned family members, Congressman Leo Ryan, who represented a district just south of San Francisco, headed a delegation to Guyana to investigate what was apparently the increasingly deranged and dangerous leadership of San Francisco activist and preacher/cult leader Jim Jones at his Peoples Temple Compound.

Ryan, most of the members of his traveling party, and several Peoples Temple congregants who were attempting to defect, were shot and killed by Jones' security forces as they tried to fly out from the Kaituna airstrip in Guyana. The infamous mass suicide of nine-hundred-and-nine inhabitants of Jonestown, including Jones and three-hundred-and-four children, ensued thereafter.

Because so many of the Peoples Temple congregation had ties to the Bay Area, the tragedy had a rippling effect. Two of the faculty I worked with in the Social Work Department knew someone who had died drinking cyanide-laced Flavor-Aid in Jonestown. This horrible event became the stuff of popular humor in later years, but at the time we moved in silence in the office.

I wasn't going to let distant world events get me down for too long, but as with most everyone else in San Francisco I was stunned by the news a few weeks later that Mayor George Moscone and Board Supervisor Harvey Milk had been assassinated. Both had been murdered by the ex-policeman and ex-fireman Dan White, who had quit as city supervisor and whose reinstatement had been blocked by Milk and Moscone.

The chair of the English Department told me that Milk was a hero to the gay community and that if justice wasn't done the City would erupt. He asked me if I was going to the candlelight march downtown. I politely said I'd think about it. As a newcomer to San Francisco, I wasn't versed in the murky city politics, redistricting, and the machinations that had led up to the double murders. San Francisco still felt to me like a foreign place.

* * *

Toward the end of the semester, I started to see Saloma more regularly, sometimes two-to-three times per week. I took her to a production of Edward J. Moore's *The Sea Horse* at the Goodman Theater. It was a rough, naturalistic play about two people who don't think they need each other.

I walked Saloma back to the car after the play; it was raining; the streets glistened and we snuggled under my umbrella. Inside the car, we started to kiss. Saloma was more affectionate, more responsive than she'd been before. Maybe it was from the emotions churned up by the play, but she took the initiative and opened her mouth against mine.

We had a date planned for the next night, for Saturday, and I thought maybe afterwards we'd have drinks in my room. I'd wait and see. Saloma was the kind of woman who couldn't be rushed, but I wanted it so badly.

On the drive back, she was very quiet and sat about as far away from me as she could in the passenger seat. When I pulled up to her apartment, she was crying. I left the engine running and the wiper blades swooshed back and forth, forcing the rain down the sides of the windshield in rivulets.

I gave her my handkerchief. Saloma told me she didn't want anything physical . . . we were friends . . . good friends. That was enough. She said she didn't think she could ever love anyone— "but if she did—" Her voice trailed off and she rushed out of the car into the rain, ran up to her apartment.

I unrolled the window and called out to her. I muttered

something about phoning her tomorrow. She waved back at me without turning while she fumbled for her keys.

* * *

In the morning, she phoned me before I could call her. She rang about ten in the morning.

The landlord, Mr. Meriwether, knocked on my door. He lowered his voice and said there was a young lady on the phone asking for me. I approached the hallway stand and the phone, thinking things weren't going the way they should.

Saloma told me she needed to break our date, that something had come up.

"What's that?" I tried to sound mildly curious and to keep an inquisitorial tone out of my voice.

"Oh, my sister wants to go somewhere tonight. To a high school dance." She laughed drily. "We both look young. I think we can pass. It's at the Catholic high school in Daly City."

"Okay." I paused. "See you some time," and I hung up. I went for a long, angry walk up the hill to the top of Buena Vista Park, and from there out to the Panhandle and to Golden Gate Park. That was just like me, getting involved with someone who was immature. I wasn't any great shakes in the maturity department, but what was Saloma going to do—wear a white blouse and a tartan skirt? I'd had enough Catholicism to last me a lifetime. From the age of seven to seventeen, I attended Mass every day; as an altar boy assisting with the service, I sometimes heard the Mass four or five times on any given weekend. I didn't need her. I needed to stay away from her.

"Weave a circle round her thrice," I paraphrased, "and close your eyes with holy dread, for she on honeydew hath fed."

I knew my Coleridge.

When I was a high school exchange student in Mexico, living with a middle-class family, I was surprised they weren't devout. The father of the family, who owned a large hardware store, told me that in Mexico educated people didn't go to church—or if they did, didn't really believe. It was only the poor and the ignorant who prostrated themselves before statues, crawled on their knees up the center aisle with their arms outstretched, as if on the cross.

By the time I turned seventeen, I'd given up all pretense of either believing or attending Mass.

Walking through Golden Gate Park, past the couples on roller skates and the band preparing for an afternoon concert, I was angry at religion for standing in my way, for keeping me from Saloma. I lashed out under the false assumption that it was all about the Catholic Church, about religion, but I realized years later that it was more about the Philippines, about her father, about what happened there. My poor darling, if only I could go back in time. But we're stuck living each moment, never knowing what comes next. Instead, I cursed her and told myself we should stay away from each other. No good could come from this, and she too should weave an ever-widening circle away from me, for I had also sung of Mount Abora and played a dulcimer and had a vision in a dream that vanished.

CHAPTER THREE

I started hanging out at Buchanan's, a bar in the Inner Sunset frequented by graduate students and other denizens. The felt wall coverings and clown pictures—sad clowns, insane clowns, happy clowns that all looked like Emmett Kelly—and the Christmas lights that were twinkling year-round, gave the place the feel of a down-at-the-heels salesman's dive with a daub of the bohemian.

The owner, "Buzz" Buchanan, was almost always holding court. "I'm the king here," he would say. "I am the place. I'm king," and he would pour drinks on the house and regale the listeners at the bar with stories about his combat experiences during the Korean War.

Some published writers hung out there. I met the Beat poet Gregory Corso, who was bunched up in the corner looking surly, but maybe was just wary of autograph seekers, and Gina Berriault. She was no longer teaching at San Francisco State but still gave poetry readings around town. I was introduced to Leonard Gardner, whose novel *Fat City* I admired. But mostly,

Buchanan's was a place where barflies competed to buy each other drinks and to talk about the "fights."

As often as not, I was at Buchanan's with Eddie from Hoboken. He knew a lot of people from the East Coast who had moved out to San Francisco, and a few weeks before Christmas I sat at a corner table with Eddie and two women he had known in D.C. during the protest movement. Amanda was tall and slender and wore a sack dress with an acorn and turquoise-pebble leather necklace. She was from Western Pennsylvania and had done a year of college. Frannie looked a bit older. She had dark, wavy hair that didn't seem to have been combed in a while. Her fingernails were long and dirty and some of them looked chipped. She had a nice smile and seemed intelligent. She told me she was from Baltimore.

We ordered a pitcher of beer. Eddie held forth, his Trilby hat cocked at an angle: "The best skittle-bowl bars in all of Western Pennsylvania! Tremendous!" Eddie always seemed to speak in hyperbole. Everything was the best, the greatest, the most fantastic. He didn't lack for opinions and argued with Amanda about the modern novel while I discussed Sophoclean drama with Frannie. We were across the table from each other, at angles; there was a lot of cross conversation and it was hard to hear. Then Eddie blurted out: "I can't read Jane Austin. It's too bourgeois. Pig literature!"

We did shots of bourbon and Eddie demonstrated the art of the Hoboken boilermaker when he dropped his shot glass into the beer stein. The concoction started to fizz and Eddie guzzled it.

He said his pal Kupinski was having a party at his crib in the Haight and we should head over there. It was a short taxi ride, and we bought a couple of six packs at Buchanan's, then went back for a bottle of gin. We were riding high by the time we got to Kupinski's. His pad was a fifth-floor walk-up and we were all laughing by the time we struggled up the last set of stairs. I met Birdman inside and a guy named Stringer. Birdman wore a Confederate Army cap with the crossed rifle insignia on the front and grey Confederate trousers with a yellow stripe along each outer seam. He had a parrot on his shoulder and fed the parrot peanuts from his mouth.

I got into a conversation with Stringer because he was showing everyone his scrapbook with yellowing newspaper clippings from some of the great prize fights. On the black construction paper pages, he had pasted articles on Jersey Joe Walcott and Primo Carnera, Marcel Cerdan and Jack Johnson. I told him my father had been in a boxing club in Casablanca and had known Marcel Cerdan.

"He was one of my Dad's heroes." I sipped from a can of beer. "So was Carlos Gardel. Both of them died in plane crashes." I tried to think of something profound but drank more beer instead.

Stringer nodded. "That's a bummer, man. Buddy Holly, the Big Bopper, Otis Redding. What a bummer."

My beer can was empty, and Eddie passed by, handing me a plastic cup full of gin. I looked around. A couple of black chicks with Afros moved rhythmically to some good vibes from the stereo. Pink Floyd's "Dark Side of the Moon" woofed off the speakers. Everything was cool.

In the corner, the coal of a doob was dancing merrily as a joint was passed around. When it got to me, I took a couple of hits but I was happier drinking gin. It was getting late and the party was breaking up, so the four of us headed a few blocks over to Amanda's place to keep things on a roll. Amanda's third-floor apartment smelled of cats; she seemed to have at least four of them clawing the couch and carpet. She also had an upright piano and plenty to drink. I was swilling vodka at that point and watched Amanda fall against the piano bench, spill her drink, laugh and spin around to flip open the keyboard lid.

She started to play. "Any old tune," she announced. "You name 'em, I play 'em."

My perceptions were becoming warped because it seemed to me she played quite wonderfully on a piano that must have been out of tune.

Frannie encouraged me to sing. I was in voice, I told myself, and belted out, in my strong baritone, "Galway Bay," "Mr. Tambourine Man," and "I'll Take You Home Again, Kathleen."

I needed to take a piss and Eddie joined me out on the balcony. We stood side by side, urinating down the three floors to the courtyard shared by a number of apartments, and had a little man-to-man talk.

"What do you think?" I asked. "Do you think I can score?"

He smiled. "The field's wide open, man. They're friends of mine."

"What do you think about Amanda?" I thought she was the more attractive.

"I think you've got a better chance with Frannie," he said, zipping up. I decided to see which of the two gals would stay up longer, and we went back into the living room.

Eddie passed out on the couch about three in the morning and Frannie went into the guest room about four. I stayed up singing with Amanda until almost five; we could see the sky start to lighten and the beer and vodka was gone. She stood up. I caressed her cheek clumsily. We swayed in each other's arms and I could feel one of the cats wind around my leg.

Amanda picked up the purring cat and started to stroke it. She smiled at me. I rubbed the cat's fur as well and leaned forward to kiss Amanda. We kissed for a while, the cat between us. It was the promiscuous 1970s in San Francisco and no one had heard of AIDS. I thought we might make it happen.

"Good night," she said, and I sacked out in the armchair.

* * *

When I got back to my room that afternoon, I slept for a few hours and woke up from a vivid dream. I was in high school but had my adult height and build. My father came home lurching like an Irish lout and threatened the family. He wanted to fight me.

I lay awake and stared at the patterned tin tiles on the ceiling. I had forgotten how bad it had been when we never knew if he would come home. I remembered my mother always worried about money, and then the arguments between the two of them; he had smashed up a picnic table he had built for the family, incensed because my mother wouldn't give him any more money that day to buy booze.

He drank because he was tormented by memories of a country he'd left early, because he was a bomb-happy combat vet, and because he'd lived in various countries saying he'd never felt a part of any. "Mi tierra es la tierra de emborrachar," he would say, hoisting a glass. "At least I have that."

Then, he would try to make it up to the family, working an extra job at night, mostly to pay the attorney who was trying to get him off a D.U.I. He maintained that he only got caught because he rode a motorcycle, and everyone could see him.

"Everyone sees me when I'm drunk," he used to say in Spanish, "but nobody sees me when I'm thirsty."

No wonder I was trying to get away and avoid commitments. From what I'd seen of family life, it just burned you.

* * *

I flew down to Southern California for the full two weeks of Christmas break. The first Saturday back, I joined a group of friends from my hometown—some couples, some singles—for a night out. We started with shots and beers at the Corner Pub in Stanton, then drove in three different cars to 183rd Street in Cerritos because the Sidesaddle Inn had a buffet dinner and a dance floor. We closed the place. I'd been dancing all night with a woman from the group, Marilee, who made it very clear the way we slow danced and the way she rubbed her hand along the back of my neck that she was going to drive me home.

Before she drove me to my parents' house, we made a detour to her apartment in Tustin. "Now, this is all your idea, isn't it?" she kept saying.

I was surprised that a woman of thirty-two would be nervous about sex, but her nervousness went away as soon as we stepped inside her apartment.

She dropped me off at my parents' house at five a.m., just as my father was leaving for work on his motorcycle. We nodded to each other in the driveway. The few hours with Marilee had straightened out my thinking for a while, but then there was family.

My mother was always trying to introduce me to a "nice girl," preferably German. She had lived in England longer than my father had and in many ways was thoroughly Anglicized. Most people, when they first met her, thought she was British, and it was only in her later years, when she moved into her nineties and beyond—passing away at the age of one hundred and three—that her Austrian accent came through very distinctly and she pronounced "shrimp" as "Schrremp." She was always very determined to get ahead, and if higher education was denied her in Austria, she could always take night classes in England or America, advancing over the years from a secretarial position in an import/export business, to ad setter, layout artist, and eventually graphic specialist. Above all, she was determined to hold the family together, and while I found her to be annoyingly persistent in those days in telling me I needed to settle down with a nice girl and be a lawyer, like some of my friends, I grew to love her dearly, especially during the last twelve years of her life when I took care of her.

* * *

Having flown down for the Christmas break after my first few months in San Francisco, I asked my mother on my fourth day back if I could borrow her car.

"Why don't you drive me to work," she suggested brightly, "and you can use the car the rest of the day. Besides, I'd like you to stop in the office to meet one of the student workers."

When we reached the campus and the side entrance to the graphics center, I told her I wasn't interested in meeting anyone and would stop inside the office some other day.

"Really?" My mother looked disappointed. "I wanted you to meet Annamaria. She's a very nice girl."

"I'm sure." I gave her a tight smile. I wondered if she was majoring in German. "Maybe some other time. I have some things I want to do."

I drove to Anaheim to see a Navy recruiter and we talked about different programs, but everything in one configuration or another added up to a six-year enlistment. I had to figure out what my next step would be when I'd finished with the master's degree program, but I wanted something that was a little more short term.

I'd already talked to a Peace Corps representative in San Francisco about teaching in Mali or Senegal, both Francophone West African countries. The Peace Corps gig would only have been for two years, but it seemed to me there were less arduous ways to improve my French.

I drove back to my parents' house for lunch. My Dad was in the garage straightening bent nails. He held each nail by its head with a pair of pliers, placed it against the top of the vice, and tapped the shaft of the nail with a hammer until it was straight.

I asked my Dad what he thought about the merchant navy. I said I knew someone who told me he could help me get my seaman's papers. Maybe I could sail on the Mateson Line.

My father looked up from what he was doing. In Britain, once he'd completed his chef's training, he'd found an outlet for his restlessness and recklessness and desire to escape the confines of our family by serving as a ship's cook for the Royal Mail Lines, sailing primarily to Argentina and the Panama Canal, up the Pacific coast to San Francisco and Vancouver. He missed the sea, and another of his great regrets was that he had to give it up when we immigrated to the United States. The British ships were "wet," but he couldn't support a family in the United States on a British merchant seaman's wages, and the American ships were "dry."

He seemed neither to approve nor disapprove of my interest in sailing on the Mateson Line. He said simply: "Whatever you do, don't sign with a Panamanian or Ecuadorian or Libyan ship that needs men. There's no life insurance and no accident compensation if you get hurt. Also, they dismiss you miles from your home port."

He went back to straightening nails.

"Try to sail with a British or Norwegian captain. Don't sail with a Greek."

* * *

Jimmy Carter was the President, and long lines of cars snaked around the gas pumps. A twenty-five-year-old man was stabbed to death in an altercation at a gas station in Fremont, and I found myself one afternoon in San Francisco arguing with a blonde woman who forced her car in front of mine. It took hours to get gas, if any was left, and I'd usually go to the Chevron station at the corner of Guerrero and Sixteenth and ask, the day before I wanted to fuel up, what the hours of operation would be.

The attendant once told me: "We'll pump gas from four a.m. to six," and when I got there at three-thirty the pumps were idle and would be all day. The attendant called me a liar when I confronted him.

My head started to spin, I saw white swirls in front of my eyes, and I was afraid I was going to bash the attendant against the pump.

Another time, I waited in line for three-and-a-half hours and filled my tank just before the pumps were shut off at eight in the morning.

I was ready to drive my car into the Bay, with me inside, and forget about everything. Maybe I was desperate to be in some heavy relationship with Saloma or someone like her. Maybe I thought a great passion would give me a reason to live, but I tried not to think too much about her. I was too torn up inside. If it hadn't been for progress in the graduate program, I don't know how I'd have hung on, but Ramsay O'Donnell told me that if I revised my play in his workshop in the fall, he would recommend it as my thesis. Walt Wilson, from the novel writing class, and Yurgis Papandrakis, the existentialist, agreed to help me select the three major authors for my exams, and the graduate committee approved the proposal for a qualifying examination on Hendrick Ibsen, John Steinbeck, and John Fowles.

I had completed much of my formal course work and had room in my schedule to take on more hours in the Social Work Department. I also had time in my schedule to brush up on foreign languages. I'd always known some German and a bit of French, so started taking formal classes. That was another means of escape, linguistically and imaginatively. I could see myself in a foreign country rather than in the kitchen of a San Francisco rooming house, eating from a can of tuna to save money, and listening to Karl and Ferrano bullshit about life.

My parents may not have agreed on much, but they spoke in unison when it came to the importance of learning more than one language. My father used to say that knowing another language was the first sign of an educated person; my mother that knowing a second or third language would open doors. And I was eager to head outside and to some foreign land. I'd been locked up and secluded for too long, cloistered, and was ready to bust out or break up something.

I attended the Haight Street Fair in early May and marched down the blocked-off street with a lot of hippie hangers-on in a time warp—American flag patches on the buttocks of their jeans, ponytails and tie-dyed shirts, beads, and bandanas—until we reached the stage at the far end and listened to a punk rock band.

I wasn't into the punk rock scene; I wasn't even sure why I was at the Haight Street Fair. Sid Vicious and the Sex Pistols had played at the Winterland a few months before and anarchy was in the air. The screeching sound made me angry and when some wild dancers pogoed in front of me, and some skinny kid with flailing hair and a scruffy beard crashed into me, I caught him with my elbow full force in the solar plexus. I heard him grunt and expel air like a cushion. He doubled over but didn't go down. A swift kick that landed on the point of his ankle dropped him as his girlfriend screamed. The circle of ecstatic dancers pogoed faster and faster, and I slipped through the crowd and into a park.

* * *

The final week of the semester, after Walt Wilson's novel writing class, Rory Fontaine asked me if I could give him a ride back to the Castro since I'd have to pass the gay district on my way back to Duboce Park. Rory was from Oklahoma, very fit and openly gay. His goal was to write the great gay novel.

I didn't mind giving Rory a lift, though increasingly I was starting to think that a car in San Francisco was a liability. It was almost impossible to find a good parking place downtown, and I'd already been ticketed a couple of times for parking in the wrong zone. Car insurance rates were high and renting space in a small house garage cost as much as rent for my room, so I parked each night on the street.

Each month, my car seemed to pick up an extra dent or two. My trunk had been broken into, but nothing stolen since I didn't keep a set of ratchet wrenches or other tools. My radiator sprung a periodic leak, which I'd plug with a can of Stop Leak. To make matters worse, a guy with a car was expected to give everyone rides home after the bars in North Beach closed, or give a lift to a classmate after the semester ended.

I should sell my car, I told myself, and just take public transportation.

When we approached the corner of Castro and Market we could already see large crowds on either side of the street chanting: "Gay Revolt Now!" and "No Justice!" Dan White, the former city supervisor who had assassinated Harvey Milk and George Moscone, had just been given a sentence of manslaughter instead of first-degree murder, and the crowd was growing larger, with people sallying into the street to hurl chunks of asphalt at passing cars.

I could feel a surge of adrenaline, a pounding in my temples. Rory jumped out and I floored the accelerator, narrowly missed a trio of protestors who lurched in front of my car. Part of me wanted to bowl them over. I wanted to see them flying in different directions, their legs in the air as they spun over the hood or under the chassis. But I sped off into my neighborhood.

The night of May twenty-first was long. I kept thinking I'd hear someone pounding on my door as the police searched for the man who had tried to run over three protestors. Instead, I heard sirens from the direction of City Hall, sirens from firetrucks racing down Market, and later glass breaking in the Castro as the police retaliated for the violence and smashed the windows of gay bars and shattered business signs.

For weeks, there'd been ugly incidents—knifings in the Tenderloin, fires deliberately set in North Beach strip clubs by anti-sex trade activists chanting: "Take Back the Night." The City was always about to explode.

In the rooming house a few weeks later, I saw the Australian couple, Lisa and Stephen, in the common room sitting cross-legged on armchairs opposite each other as they ate Ramen noodles from bowls. They were a matched pair, both thin and angular with mousey blond hair and an earring plugged into one lobe—Stephen's on the right and Lisa's on the left. I doubted that anyone really took them for husband and wife; their profiles were nearly identical.

They sat transfixed, watching television.

The newscaster, David Brinkley, was hosting a special

report on the recently-signed SALT II agreement. I sat on an ottoman and watched for a while.

The dapper David Brinkley, with his crooked smile and trace of a North Carolina accent, explained the outlines of the U.S.–Soviet agreement intended to limit the number of nuclear weapons held by each side. The agreement appeared to be controversial since, according to its critics, it did nothing to restrict an entire class of weapons.

Brinkley then discussed in detail the number and kind of weapon each side already had, their range and destructive capabilities, which cities would be targeted and how long it would take for them to be obliterated. At the conclusion of the program, Brinkley turned to the camera, gave his crooked smile, and wished everyone a hearty goodnight.

"Thanks a lot," I said. Lisa turned to me, her chin on her knees, the empty noodle bowl on the armchair seat.

"Won't be easy to sleep tonight."

Stephen was positioned similarly as he hugged his shins and rubbed his chin thoughtfully against his knees.

"Not bloody likely. What else is on?"

Lisa aimed the remote control and flicked to PBS. An art critic discussed Raphael's paintings: his frescoes commemorated the great classical thinkers meeting on Mount Parnassus, the blind Catullus dictating to his loyal student.

"The colors were muted and harmonious; the figures balanced and aligned," the critic noted. Yet it could all go up in a big bang, along with the rest of us. What was the point of living? I wondered, but I didn't want to go down that path again. I was starting to feel better about some things; it had taken me a while to reach a plateau, maybe even ascend tentatively. I was desperate not to reverse course.

* * *

In the rooming house that summer, there wasn't much relief from the heat. With the Bay windows open in my room, I could hear the neighbor's television set most evenings—reruns of the Dick Van Dyke show, punctuated by canned laughter at predictable moments. I could hear a husband and wife arguing, buses passing by, glass breaking from a bottle fight followed by high-pitched laughter as the neighborhood children ran away.

In the kitchen, I could smell all the other dinners from all the other floors and from the adjoining building. The kitchen window opened on a common airshaft, and the odor of different meals from different cooking styles sometimes mixed into something aromatic, sometimes something foul.

Some evenings, the summer heat let up before bedtime. The air would start to move and feel a few degrees cooler. On a Sunday night, I would sit in the neighborhood laundromat an hour or so before it closed, thinking it might be cooler and less crowded then. The space was often too warm, even at that hour, because of all the countless dryer cycles and the lingering heat of the day. The machines I used would spin round and round and I would stand by the doorjamb, hoping for a breeze, hoping to see something unfamiliar. Instead, I saw a city quieting for a moment; a streetcar that slipped from the Twin Peaks Tunnel and down the hill, clicking past the row of dark houses.

* * *

Ferrano's birthday was in August and he'd received a check from his family. He couldn't wait to spend it, he told me.

"Eighty bucks! We should go to some of those places you know about," he declared. "North Point?"

"North Beach," I corrected him.

I'd been feeling stuck in time for the past few weeks. Something was missing in my life. I dreamt I was swimming in a circle, searching for Saloma in the middle of a vortex, trying to save her. Her hand reached out to mine; she tried to save me, then disappeared before our hands touched, and when I woke up from the vivid dream I was covered in sweat and was crying. I dreamt something similar on several different nights, but always with the same ending—with me reaching out to find she wasn't there. I started to grow restless again, uncertain what I was going to do, where I was going, wondered about the next change of scene.

I'd thought of taking the train to Vancouver, just to get away, and to spend time in a city that might be saner. Then Ferrano told me about his birthday present. He wanted to do the town, get drunk, wake up with a king-sized hangover that he'd earned. I'd been paid that week, I told him, and we could buy each other drinks. I was in a half-crazed mood anyway, maybe from the heat, maybe from boredom, maybe from a sense of loss.

We started drinking at O'Flaherty's, ordered a pitcher of green beer even though it wasn't St. Patrick's Day, and signed our names on souvenir baseballs that were placed in a fishbowl. I paid for two shots of bourbon and then Ferrano did the same. When we hit the next bar, "New York, New York" played on the jukebox and Ferrano asserted he'd always wanted to try a Manhattan because he'd never been there. I explained to him what went into the cocktail and he joked that the sweet vermouth sounded good and I should like the bitters because I was a bitter guy. The bartender made it with rye whisky in an old-fashioned glass.

With our second Manhattan, I asked Ferrano if he was buzzed.

"Buzzed, man. I feel like I've scaled the Empire State Building. No wonder they call it a Manhattan. I feel sky high."

We staggered out onto the sidewalk. I tried to get my bearings, figured south was to my right in the direction of a fire hydrant and some parked cars. A neon sign in the shape of a cocktail glass beckoned and I waved to Ferrano to follow me when a reveler lurched from the revolving door of the Delmonte, holding a quart cup of beer.

He wore an Oakland Raiders cap, a ruffled shirt, and tight jeans. He was about my age and size but wore a cocky grin. Laughing, he flung the quart cup at me; the beer flew in an arc across my face and the front of my shirt.

I was enraged. Drunk as I was, I barreled into him, caught him by the shirtfront and spun him toward the fire hydrant. I had the advantage of momentum and blind fury. I drove him back into the fire hydrant and slammed him down. He yelped in pain as the fire plug jammed into the seat of his pants.

He lashed out at me, but I'd already thrown a hard punch that connected with the side of his head. He toppled from the hydrant, fell backwards and landed with a dull thud that knocked the breath out of him. I saw the back of his skull hit the asphalt and he rolled over on his side.

"Oooh," Ferrano cooed. "That was vicious."

It was over in a matter of seconds. Bright spots danced in front of my eyes and my heart pounded.

"Beer Boy won't bother us for a while." I caught my breath. The front of my shirt was soaking wet and my hair felt gummy with beer. I was tempted to kick him a couple of times for good measure. I looked down at the form on the street. He lay in a fetal position and was moaning.

Ferrano and I pushed into the next bar. It was thronged with partiers and we had to work our way slowly to the corner section where we called for a drink. I was glad the bar was crowded in case the cops were looking for me. My pulse raced, I could feel a throbbing in my temples, and I worried that at any moment a policeman would grip my shoulder. My right hand hurt. I hoped I hadn't broken a knuckle. I hoped I hadn't killed Beer Boy.

"Man, you really laid that dude out," Ferrano uttered. We called for shots of whisky with beer chasers. "You think he's okay?"

"It'll be a while before he insults decent people again," I said smugly, but I was worried that he might not get to his feet.

I gulped down the whisky and half a glass of beer. I looked at my companion curiously.

"So, Ferrano," I asked. "Do you have a first name?"

"Yeah, Dave." He mulled it over. "It's in the Bible. King David. Have you heard of him?"

I humored Ferrano.

"I think so," I smiled. "Sure."

"I never liked the name Dave or David. Just call me Ferrano."

* * *

An hour later it was my turn to lie on the sidewalk, or the street, to be exact, with my head on the curb. We had gone to a Tiki bar for Mai Tai's and I realized we hadn't eaten anything except a basket of fries.

On the way to the Tiki bar, Ferrano had sniffed the aroma of marijuana smoke coming from an alleyway where a man and a woman huddled, as if embracing. Ferrano stopped. He walked up to them.

"I hope I'm not intruding," I heard him say. The man had a scraggly beard and the woman wore her hair in braids. "But I believe I smell the sweet scent of a doob. Do you mind if I have a toke?"

They looked at each other and at him as if he were an

apparition, then must have decided he was harmless or at least wasn't a narc. The man handed over the wet joint and Ferrano lipped it eagerly, drawing deeply on it two or three times.

"Thanks, man." He let the smoke out slowly. "There's a place for both of you in heaven."

There was a place for both of us at the Tiki bar, at a table in the corner, where I promptly passed out. When I woke up, the room was spinning. Ferrano was talking to a woman with tattoos about the universe, whether or not it's real and do we really live in a galaxy. I lurched into the alleyway where I expelled the contents of my stomach. I staggered out to the street and lay sprawled across the hood of a car, hung on until everything stopped spinning. By then, I was lying on the street with my head against the curb. Ferrano stood above me, upside down, asking: "What is life? Do we even know if we know what we know?"

* * *

The next day, when I walked gingerly down the hallway of the rooming house in the afternoon, I overheard Ferrano in the kitchen talking to Karl.

"You have to watch out for this guy," Ferrano said. "He's like two people. When he's sober, he's the brainy type. When he's drunk, he acts like a dockworker."

I heard Karl grunt, move to the refrigerator, open the door.

Ferrano added plaintively: "I swear, I swear to you Karl, so long as I live, I'll never drink that much again."

Sure, I thought to myself, until the next time he has eighty dollars in his pocket—which, judging by past habits, may not be for a while.

I entered the kitchen and pretended I hadn't heard anything.

* * *

I ran a lot. I ran through Buena Vista Park, down the Panhandle, and into Golden Gate Park: past teenagers swilling Budweiser and breaking the bottles on a bench, lovers on the lawn, sunbathers, picnickers, an old Mexican couple, the "Jesus Loves You" truck, volleyball players, the Hari Krishnas with their shaved heads and flowing robes drumming and chanting by a storefront, a Jamaican steel drum band, a bagpiper.

It was a good thing I liked to run and walk long distances. The transit strike affecting the BART subway system entered its second month. The labor dispute was either a strike or a lockout, depending on which side you asked, and while management and a non-union group kept some of the trains running, the reality was that during the hot summer days the bus system was the main alternative. I didn't always want to drive to campus, and on days when I took the bus, it was stiflingly warm, overcrowded, slow, and I typically felt disgusted, annoyed, and nauseated by the time I reached my stop. It was all I could do to keep myself from shoving people out of the way when I got off the bus.

In the meantime, I put in my days with the Department of Social Work, but I needed to get something better for next year, if only a three-quarter-time job and a temporary arrangement, something to tide me over to the summer when I'd search out a change of scene. I'd heard that the Federal Government paid better for clerk/typists, and there were plenty of agencies in town.

I drove out to Orinda on a Saturday in August when the heat was eight-five degrees in the City and over a hundred in the East Bay. Chloe, from the office staff, was house-sitting for a rich friend, and Dr. Leming, the Chair of the Social Work

Department, said he would host a cook-out extravaganza if we could use the house.

Maybe the heat put me in a foul mood, or the long drive, or the sight of three-story suburban homes, or the Marxist sentiments I hadn't shaken free of. "Decadent," I kept muttering to myself for most of the party. The home of Chloe's friend came complete with swimming pool, wraparound deck, and jacuzzi. A distillation of the California "good life," I told myself—the sunbathing around the pool, the daiquiris on the deck, cigarettes and joints smoked to the nub in the spacious den.

One of the secretaries, Zoe, wore pink shorts and a red tee-shirt that read: "Liberation!" but it was unclear what or whom she wanted to free. Most of the other women wore summer sundresses and sandals; the men, Bermuda shorts and short-sleeved cotton shirts. Dr. Leming wore a Hawaiian shirt with images of long-board surfers; Dr. Morales a Guayabera. I was the only man at the party in a blue work shirt, with the long sleeves rolled up just below the elbows, and dark chinos.

Dr. Leming stood by the grill, rolling a joint and licking the paper with shiny lips. He turned the sizzling ribs, the corn in husks, the vegetable skewers. He tossed thick ribeyes on the grill, sloshed bar-b-cue sauce on top of the meat and swirled the goo around with a brush. Dr. Karen Russell, an assistant professor of Social Work about my own age, lay on a chaise lounge, browning her long legs. I could hear the adenoidal voice of Jackson Brown crooning from the stereo, the Eagles, Linda Rondstadt, all the pablum of the California country sound. In the stifling heat of the late afternoon, everything seemed to be held in abeyance. Dr. Morales stood swaying slightly by the pool, a contented look on his face, a joint in one hand and a beer in the other. The sun started to set; the rich green colors of the dry hills stood out, and Dr. Russell stretched her arms out languidly and held them there.

"Debauchery," I muttered to myself, and couldn't wait to get back to The Barnacle, The Fremont, Cheap Charlie's Saloon—all the dive bars in North Beach I prowled with Eddie and his East Coast pals. I saw the Orinda scene as fundamentally depraved, degenerate, when throwing a punch at some yahoo in North Beach was worse, when getting sick in an alleyway, then lying on the street with my head against the curb for half an hour until the world stopped spinning was no better. I hadn't yet joined the ranks of the great middle class, nor had gotten used to hosting large lawn parties at my vacation home on Lake Huron. I still saw myself as working class—my parents certainly were, and had instilled in us a keen and myopic European sense of the limitations of class. I still reveled in the image of myself as a rebel, a waterfront type, authentic. I hadn't yet made the longest journey to the respectable middle class.

And yet, despite all my anger, I had crossed the threshold with my bachelor's degree and was nearing completion of a master's. That summer, I wrote two book reviews for *Elegiac Studies* and a review of a theater production, for which I was paid. Professor Walt Wilson suggested I contact an editor he knew at a travel magazine and I freelanced an article on "Hollywood Haunts and Hangouts" —hack work, but the most money I'd ever earned from my writing. And I saw an ad from the public television station for short films that could fill gaps in the programming, especially late at night. I queried and submitted the eighteen-minute film I'd made in college set in the First World War, *Caporetto*.

CHAPTER FOUR

In the fall, the rhythm and pace on campus quickened with fresh faces and returning students, earnest master's degree candidates, and hangers-on. A woman with a guitar sang folk songs from a grassy knoll, and a young man with wavy blond hair that fell like a mane and covered his collar pirouetted as he caught a Frisbee. Strains from the marching band wafted from the practice field, and I saw Saloma on campus more than I would have wished.

I stayed busy with the pressure of preparing for my qualifying exams. I was often in the Library to take notes or to check out an armful of critical works on Ibsen, Steinbeck, and Fowles, but once a month, I cleared my mind by doing something cultural—listening to a symphony concert in the park, watching an opera from the student standing area, visiting an art museum on free admission day, or attending an open lecture. At the Poetry Center, the prominent African-American novelist and San Francisco State alum, Ernest J. Gaines, read from an unpublished story he called "The Revenge of Old Men." I admired Gaines' work, especially *The Autobiog-*

raphy of Miss Jane Pittman, and took comfort in his admonition to the aspiring novelists in his audience to continue reading and writing, even if it took ten or more years to become any good.

The cultural outlets kept me sane as I tried to balance studies and work and dispense with thoughts of failure. And doing things off-campus was a way of avoiding Saloma. But at the university, the chance of seeing her increased.

I sometimes saw Saloma in the cafeteria chatting with two or three undergraduates. They were all smiles—one wore red suspenders, another a purple "Gators" sweatshirt, the third with round "John Lennon" eyeglasses and long hair parted in the middle.

Sometimes, I saw her leaving the Psychology Building escorted by an assistant professor everyone knew on campus as "Red Roy," both for his shock of vibrant red hair and for his politics. Most days, he rode a bicycle to work; when he walked across campus, he invariably had a satchel on his back and a thumb tucked under the shoulder strap. He could be counted on to organize protests—the most recent one a campaign in support of the Iranian students who congregated near Braddock Grove with signs reading: "Death to the Shah!" and "Islamic Republic Now!"

I didn't want to dwell on memories of the few times I'd gone out with Saloma and when I saw her on campus smiling at another man, I told myself I didn't care. She was entitled to her happiness. I had two models for my comportment with women —one very Austrian, the other very Mediterranean. I either tried to behave like Captain von Trapp in *The Sound of Music* or like Alexis Zorba in *Zorba the Greek*.

I played the role of Captain von Trapp now when I told myself Saloma was her own person and I was happy for her.

I played the role of Zorba when I told myself it was the

1970s and I wasn't going to sit idle. I could get drunk and carouse in North Beach anytime I wanted.

I routinely repeated my litany of bromides, but it didn't seem to help.

The first time I noticed Saloma spent time with the Frisbee player, I was on my way to Lenny Levinski's Craft of Fiction class. Crossing the quad, I saw the man with the golden mane flip a Frisbee in a three-way game of catch. First, he sent the disc soaring into the air and his buddy, a gangly undergraduate with a French beret, leapt gazelle-like to catch it. When it came sailing back to the man with the golden mane, he spun into the air and snagged it behind his back.

Saloma stood a few feet away, entranced. When her admirer landed, he tossed the Frisbee gently to her. She gamboled in the direction of the disc and dropped it. They both guffawed stupidly and he put an arm around her.

I'd seen enough and didn't want to become obsessed. Why wouldn't other men pursue her? She was beautiful, and just about any straight male under thirty would be interested. Some of the hoary-headed senior professors probably eyed her up and down as well. She could make her own choice and I wished her good luck. Her latest beau was attractive, if you liked the druggie look. He wore a bead necklace and an embroidered shirt, open almost to the navel, and tight-fitting bellbottom jeans. No doubt, he probably thought he looked like Jim Morrison.

Late the next night, after class and before I drove home, I hurried up the steps to the Library to renew five books that were almost overdue. The revolving door was turning and I was about to enter the panel when Saloma and her beau spun out arm in arm, tittering. As they passed by, they said "hi" quickly. I gave a short wave. Up close, he wasn't much to look at, with a wispy blond beard and a few moustache hairs. I wondered what program he was in. Saloma liked them young, but up close he looked like a teenage David Cassady.

Increasingly, I saw them together, and I considered changing my work hours, finding a job off-campus, or changing my schedule in some other way. I was tired of running into them in the Bookstore, or seeing them eating sandwiches together on the grassy knoll, or watching them get into a car together right when I was leaving campus.

I worked out a lot that semester, running and lifting weights in the campus gym. Sometimes, I headed downtown with Eddie from Hoboken to the boxing club where he worked. In the gym, I'd drumroll the speedbag or slam a few thudding punches into the heavy bag while Eddie held it. I imagined using Mr. Frisbee's face as a speedbag or driving a couple of body blows into his ribs, but I knew I wasn't going to charm Saloma by beating up her boyfriend.

* * *

On Friday afternoons, if the weather was nice, bands performed in the quad. On a Friday in late September, I watched a rhythm and blues band set up near the front steps of the Library. A crowd gathered. Students sat on stone benches or on the grass. A faculty member with bushy muttonchops and holding a briefcase paused momentarily and walked on.

I saw Saloma sitting on the grassy knoll by herself. I walked over and sat next to her. She acknowledged me with a slight dip of her head. She leaned back on her elbows with her legs stretched out and her beige leather jacket and a cream-colored blouse. Black jeans sheathed her legs and her jet-black shoes pointed at the band.

I was nervous sitting cross-legged in my Army surplus field jacket and corduroy trousers. I was also slightly annoyed. I wanted her to look at me and smile, but she ignored me. I told myself I didn't care and watched the drummer tighten a wingnut on his crash cymbals. The lead singer, a skinny African-American who looked like he could belt out the Delta blues, tied a red bandana around his neck and rolled his short sleeves above his shoulders. The bass guitarist checked the amps and signaled to the keyboardist.

I wasn't interested in the band or the music. I wanted to say something to Saloma, maybe tell her how I felt, how much I'd missed her. I felt throttled by emotion, angry at myself for being unable to say anything.

At last, I blurted out inanely: "These guys will rattle the windows."

Saloma didn't reply. She didn't move, and her shiny shoes remained pointed at the band.

Her silence was galling. I was tempted to say something nasty, but settled for sarcasm.

"Where's the rock star today?" I asked.

She looked at me quizzically.

"You know. Mr. Frisbee."

"Oh, him. He's just a friend."

I tugged at some grass in front of me.

"Has he figured that out yet?"

I yanked out a clump of grass.

"You're still mad at me," she said.

The lead singer pressed his lips to the microphone and called: "Check, check, check." His voice reverberated across the quad.

"I could never stay mad at you for very long." I paused for as long as I could. How did I feel about her? I'd whispered it at night, when I was alone. I'd yelled it in my car, driving back drunkenly from North Beach. I decided just to say it. "I love you, Saloma."

She looked away from me. She still leaned on her elbows, her legs stretched out. She hardly moved.

"I know that."

I waited for her to say something else. Love couldn't just go in one direction. But with Saloma, maybe her quiet acknowledgement that she understood was enough.

I looked up so she wouldn't see my emotions. There wasn't a cloud in the sky.

"I've missed you, Diego. You used to be fun. Now, when I see you on campus you always look so sad."

I stood up. I tried to say something polite about enjoying the music but my words caught and I turned from her. Tears had welled in my eyes and I kept my back to her as I walked toward Hutchinson Hall.

* * *

Karl Hamburger pounded on my door. When I opened it, his big head filled the door frame. He looked hungover, with bruise-colored bags underneath his eyes.

"Some chick's on the phone." He jerked his thumb at the hallway. "She wants to talk to you."

He probably didn't appreciate being woken up at ten a.m. on a Saturday, but to wake Karl the phone had probably rung a dozen or more times. I'd been listening to Shostakovich on my cassette player and reading Baudelaire.

I walked down the hall. Lisa and Stephen came out of the backroom. They both wore cut-off shorts and tee-shirts emblazoned with the Australian flag. They waved cheerily as they trotted downstairs.

I picked up the handset.

"Hello." I held the mouthpiece a few inches distant and kept my tone noncommittal. It might just be someone from the office calling about extra hours or someone from the Library letting me know a book was overdue.

"Diego?"

"Yes."

"It's Saloma."

I didn't say anything. It wasn't like her to phone. Maybe she just wanted to tell me to go away.

"How've you been?" she asked sweetly.

"Since yesterday? About the same. And you?"

I heard her breathing and envisioned her gripping the phone on the other end.

"I've missed you, Diego."

I didn't know what to think or what to say. My knees felt weak and I wanted to sit down. "You were always so kind," she went on. I looked around. There wasn't even a stool in the hallway—probably Mr. Meriwether's way to keep phone conversations short. "You always made me feel so special."

I was afraid to say anything. I was afraid that whatever I would say would be taken the wrong way, but I blurted out: "Would you like to go out sometime? Maybe we—"

"No," she said, cutting me off. "You were always taking me to places—to dinner and shows. Why don't you come over next Saturday at five? I'll cook. I make a great chicken adobo."

Now, I really did need to sit down. I tried to keep from sounding too joyful.

"I'll bring the wine."

* * *

Mid-week, I planned to take the streetcar down Market to buy new clothes, but by the time I reached the downtown area from campus Market Street was cordoned off. I could hear sirens and gunshots and a cacophony of shouts and yells. I ducked into

Shaughnessy's bar near my rooming house. The television was on; the bartender and patrons craned their necks to watch the local news bulletin.

A sniper identified as Chief Cherokee of the S.L.A./W.O.O. was holding hostages on the sixteenth floor of the State Compensation Building at Ninth and Market. More than thirty rounds had been fired from a high-powered rifle, slamming into the street. Police negotiators were talking to the gunman, who claimed he had nitroglycerin. It was unclear how many hostages he held, but two had been released so far.

I sat at the bar, transfixed. I heard the sirens outside and then on the television set after a slight delay. The bartender dried a glass, nodded to me, and I indicated that he could pour a short one.

A man in his thirties with his necktie undone and rubbing his face tapped me on the arm.

"Buddy, I just came from there." He exhaled sharply. He was sweating and his hand shook as he gripped a tall glass of beer. "Holy Cow." He let out a low whistle. "I just got off work, see?—and was headed for the BART station when the shooting started. People were running and screaming every which way. I ran down Hayes and didn't stop until I got here."

He drank half his beer and clunked the glass down on the bar.

"Man, this place is still the Barbary Coast, the Gold Rush, Vigilante Days. Nothing's changed."

* * *

Chief Cherokee was captured the next day when he and his final hostage fell asleep. I saw the television news coverage in the common room of my rooming house; Lisa, Stephen, Karl, Ferrano, Mr. Meriwether and myself crowded into the small parlor. We watched as the doors of buildings in the downtown area flew open and throngs streamed out, whooping, applauding, and yelling.

Mr. Meriwether clicked his tongue. "Some of those folks were stuck for almost twenty-four hours."

More craziness in the City, but I figured it would be safe to head down Market before too long.

* * *

I rode the streetcar on Market, past the peep shows and adult bookstores, the Triple X movie theaters advertising "Annette Haven & John Leslie in Anna Obsessed," until I reached a store blaring disco music. A canvas banner hung from the awning: "Sale! Must Close Tonight!" It was a gimmick. The store closed every night at ten, as did several other large clothing stores on Market with similar signs and similar loud music.

I went inside.

I bought a polyester shirt with a King Tut design and a pair of light blue flared trousers. The merchandise was cheap in every sense of the word and probably wouldn't hold up when laundered, but some new duds could make me look sharp for an evening or two. A denim jacket would set the combo off nicely, so I bought one as well. I charged the new clothes and maxed out my credit card.

The afternoon I was to see Saloma, I trimmed my beard and moustache, showered, splashed on some Old Spice cologne, and dressed in my new threads. Our date was for five p.m. She lived in a townhouse off Arbutus, but I had already arrived by four-thirty and drove around for a while, out by Lake Merced and to the ocean, then back to her neighborhood.

I parked.

I'd seen Saloma to her door before and was familiar with

the layout of her type of apartment: living room, dining room, and kitchen on the main floor, with the bedrooms upstairs. I'd brought a mixed bouquet of fall flowers—sunflowers, rust mums, and orange roses—and two bottles of wine—a Chianti and a Bordeaux, my excuse being that I didn't know which wine would go better with chicken adobo.

I rang the doorbell and Saloma's sister, Ezzie, answered. She gave me an unsmiling look.

"Saloma's getting ready upstairs," she said by way of greeting. Ezzie looked a bit like her elder sister, but more severe, with dark, narrow eyes. Her hair was cut short and she wore a black leather jacket with a short jeans skirt and sneakers. She gestured for me to come in and put the wine on the small dining table. I kept the flowers in my hand.

"Why do you want to get involved with Saloma?" her sister asked me. "She has more hang-ups than an art gallery."

Ezzie obviously didn't like me, and I didn't care. She wasn't going to frighten me away so long as Saloma wanted me.

"I'm going out. The apartment's all yours." She slammed the door.

This was the farthest I'd ever been inside Saloma's apartment. We usually had our goodnight kisses just inside the doorway. I stood awkwardly in the living room for a few minutes, idly looked at the furniture, the wall hangings, the curtains. A family portrait was on the wall. Saloma had told me she had three brothers and two sisters. They were all in the photo, in their finery, along with pater and mater familias. What did she need me for when she had so many ties? But she had told me she felt freer living away from home. She *had* moved away, if only five miles away and to an apartment she shared with her sister, but everyone had to shake off the shackles of family at some point.

She seemed to be taking a long time, and I looked more

closely at the portrait. Saloma was probably about fifteen or sixteen years old in the picture, already strikingly beautiful, and wore a high collar and black lace shawl. The photo was taken in a foreign setting, probably in some opulent banquet hall in Manila. Everyone looked prosperous. "Now, I'm a secretary in an office," she had told me. Saloma was alluringly Old World in certain ways, but she also wanted to be modern.

Her apartment was comfortably furnished, but not with the bronze sconces and carved tables from a banquet hall in Manila. The furniture looked like the type I had grown up with —a cloth-covered armchair and matching couch, a television set with rabbit ears on a stand with rollers.

I felt guilty looking around the apartment, as if I didn't belong. A guy like Eddie would tell me she was bourgeois—or wanted to be again. But it wasn't all bad. I could smell simmering spices in a sauce: oregano, paprika, sage—whatever it was, if I could get over my jitters, I'd be hungry.

When Saloma came down the stairs, I admired the way her long black hair was pulled to one side, with a strand falling across her brow.

"Hi, Saloma. I brought these." I held up the flowers like an offering as she descended, step by step. She wore a touch of makeup on her cheeks and a pale sheen of lip gloss.

"They look beautiful!"

She wore a traditional Filipino dress. Her low-necked blouse was embroidered in a lacy design and had bell sleeves. The blouse was set off by a striped wraparound skirt parted at the knees; as she came down the stairs I noticed that her calves were firm and shapely. She wore woven sandals with a pattern that matched the striped skirt.

I had trouble swallowing. "*You* look beautiful." I added: "You *are* very beautiful, Saloma. I'm honored that you invited me here."

I presented her with the flowers and she beamed. She asked me to wait a moment while she put the flowers in water. I watched her enter the kitchen and snip off the stems, fill a vase with water from the kitchen faucet and insert them.

"I also bought you something special," she called from the kitchen. "Would you like a Beck's? For old time's sake?"

I grinned. She remembered our book-buying expeditions and sitting at a sidewalk restaurant near Irving, drinking Beck's beer and espresso and chatting amiably.

"I'd love one. I brought some wine. I should open it to let it breathe."

We sat in the living room and chatted for a while, awkwardly at first. I asked her about her family. She smiled and got up. She brought the portrait down from the wall and showed me.

"That's me when I was sixteen."

"You look like a Spanish princess."

She ran her finger across the image. She smiled and said: "Thank you," then added: "I wasn't very happy then." She went on quickly: "That's my little brother, Eusebio. We call him Yo-Yo."

I'd noticed that Filipinos gave each other nicknames that sounded like ones used by English schoolboys.

"And who's that?" I pointed to the image of an elegant woman who looked like an older version of Saloma.

"That's my mother," she smiled fondly. "And those are Esteban and Silvio, they're twins. You know Esmerelda—Ezzie. And that's my littlest sister, Marta." She looked about six in the photo. Saloma resumed: "She's a junior now in high school in Daly City."

I noticed that Saloma had skipped over the image of a middle-aged man who must have been her father.

"It looks like a nice family," I put in.

She threw her head back and laughed lightly. "What's the quote from *Anna Karenina*? 'All happy families are alike; every unhappy family is unhappy in its own way.' And you're an only child?"

"I have an older brother," I said pensively. "But we don't talk about him." I gave a wan smile and repeated what she'd recited from *Anna Karenina*: Every unhappy family is unhappy in its own way.

We both chortled at that.

"I'll get the appetizer," she said, and when she returned from the kitchen she served lumpia, finger-like eggrolls with a red chili sauce. We drank the beer out of water glasses.

"We had a lot of fun buying books together," I mentioned, then paused. "Did you ever find anything unusual in one of those used paperbacks?"

"What do you mean?"

"Oh, like a personal dedication from somebody who's probably long gone. I found a bus ticket once from the 1950s. Someone must have used it as a bookmark all the way from New York City to here."

She smiled, brushed the strand of hair away from her eye.

"Do you remember that cheap edition of *Madame Bovary* I bought?" she asked. "It was stamped A.S.E. —Armed Services Edition. Inside, it had a Marine Corps captain's name and naval station address at Hunters Point."

"When was the book printed?"

"Nineteen-forty something. Early 1940s. I wondered sometimes what happened to that captain. Did he read the book before shipping out to Guam or the Philippines? Did he make it back?"

I tipped my beer glass in a salute, took a sip.

"That's what I love about you, Saloma. Your imagination."

"I'm too sentimental sometimes. Let's eat."

* * *

We enjoyed chicken adobo in a garlic peppercorn sauce sprinkled with sliced green chilis and bay leaves. She served white rice and a fresh salad, and I watched the wine level in the bottle descend. It wasn't long before we'd finished the Chianti.

We laughed a lot, talked about some of our experiences together, joked about some of the campus characters we knew. I teased her about "Red Roy," her anarchist friend.

"That blowhard?" she quipped. "He teaches Abnormal Psychology and uses personal examples."

We both chuckled in merriment.

When the meal was finished, I told her it was fantastic. I'd never enjoyed Filipino food as much and had learned something, not only about Filipino cuisine but about attire. Her blouse was called a camisa and the wraparound skirt a tapis. The traditional dress brought out her natural beauty.

We had started on the Bordeaux and were both happy and flushed, probably a bit drunk.

Saloma started to fan herself, squirmed in her seat. She looked uncomfortable.

"Are you okay?"

She giggled.

"That's the problem with traditional dresses. They're always a bit tight."

I gave her an impish grin.

"Do you want me to help you loosen it? I'm very good at that," but she recoiled when I tried to take her hand.

"What's wrong?"

Her face darkened and her lips were pursed.

"Look, I know you think I'm a goody-two-shoes," she said at last. "You think I've never been hurt?"

She got up from me and moved into the living room. I

followed her but was afraid to touch her in case I offended her even more.

"I'm sorry."

"I'm sorry too, Diego." She rubbed her eyes, then turned to confront me. Her face was taut, her mouth a grim line. Saloma was young and beautiful and could be vivacious, but in that moment I saw old tired eyes, haggard with unhappiness.

"If I thought I could ever be physical with anyone again, I'd love you the way you want. Relationships are complicated and I don't want to get things more messed up than they've been."

She sat down heavily on the couch and her eyes brimmed with tears.

"Maybe I'd better go."

She shook her head "no" and I sat next to her. I took a deep breath.

"You think I've never been hurt?" she asked again. "I gave up on religion for a while. When my cousin—six years old—I loved him as if he'd been my own—died, I hated God. I hated the Church. The Church doesn't have any answers."

"You don't have to say that, Saloma, just because you know I don't believe."

"I don't know what I believe. I still go to church. Tick, tick, tick, says the biological clock. My problem is I love children too much and want some of my own. If I didn't love children so much, maybe I'd just be a nun."

I sat back on the couch, exhausted from the conversation. Now I knew what her sister had meant. And I thought *I* was complicated.

"We're just drunk," I said. "Maybe we should call it a night."

But she shook her head and laid her hand on top of mine. We sat there for the longest time in silence, like an old loving couple, holding hands but motionless.

* * *

I continued to see Saloma, but on her terms, and if I was confused about a lot of things I was calmer whenever I was with her. We spent a lot of time together. The evenings would end with long kisses and with caresses that seemed almost fatherly. But mostly we went out to lunch together, to El Zocalo in the Mission or to Sirkander's near Golden Gate Park. Sometimes we'd spend a Saturday afternoon book-buying, and at The Green Apple she once picked up two used paperback copies of *Anna Karenina* because she said it was one of her favorite novels. In the evenings, we might watch an old movie at The Lido or The Strand or take in a foreign film.

There was no pressure to have sex, and maybe that was a relief to me because there was no pressure to perform and we could forgo the first clumsy awkward night of less-than-satisfying sex and be at peace together.

We sometimes walked along Embarcadero, down near Pier 45, to watch the fat sea lions sunning themselves lazily or to listen to the keening of the seagulls. Saloma was a gentle person and I cared for her deeply; too much, really, and in her presence near Fisherman's Wharf and the cable car turnaround, I thought how different the experience was from some of my grimmer nights in North Beach. We were only three blocks from the Sundowner, where I often had too many with Eddie and his pals. Too many nights I'd staggered out into the alleyway, lucky I wasn't rolled. I'd hinted to Saloma about some of the dives I'd frequented in North Beach, but she seemed to know.

We were on Columbus, passed a pizzeria where a woman in a striped apron silently pounded dough and started to hand-toss the lump into a wider and thinner wheel.

"Are you hungry?" I asked.

"Why don't you take me to one of those joints you go to with Eddie?" she teased me. "You know, with sawdust on the floor and men passed out at tables."

"You've been talking to Eddie," I replied.

"He's in the same grad program you're in. He takes classes from Dr. Papandrakis," she went on. "He stops in the office and likes to talk big."

"That's Eddie."

"He told me all about you," she laughed, flashing her bright smile. "Things I never knew."

* * *

We found a table in the sidewalk dining area of Columbus Ristorante. The waitress came over and we ordered calamari and a bottle of Sangiovese Bianco in a bucket of ice. I was outgrowing my concerns. I started to feel that I was an adult—a balanced, stable one at that. In the corner park across the street, a young couple photographed their infant playing with a rubber ball and I could hear chimes from the carillon at Saints Peter and Paul. We enjoyed the fried squid and half a bottle of wine.

Then Saloma lit up a Virginia Slim, threw her head back and blew out smoke. "Everyone on campus knows about him." Her hair fell to one side and she smoothed it back before facing me. "He tries to play the hard guy but he's just a pill head."

"Eddie?" I wasn't in the habit of defending him. "He's more of an alkie, but yes, he's into drugs."

She stubbed out her cigarette in a metal tray. She hadn't even smoked a third.

"I'm not into drugs," I responded, "if that's what you're getting at."

Her gaze remained steady. I tried to read her eyes. Did I see affection? Caution? Concern?

"Eddie's good for a laugh," I added defensively. "Sure," I fell back unintentionally on my Englishness: "I've hoisted a few with Eddie and the lads. That's all."

"There's a lot I don't know about you," she said lightly, and smiled. "Who are you?"

I coughed, lifted the bottle from the ice bucket and refilled our glasses.

"You sound like a psychology graduate student now—" I placed my fingertips next to the corners of my eyes and squinted, as if peering into the gloom. "—trying to shrink my head."

I straightened in my chair, put on an air of seriousness.

"Okay. Let me think for a moment. I've got it! 'Oh, I'm just a scribbler with too much drink in him who falls in love with girls,'" I quoted, then said: "Joseph Cotton in *The Third Man*."

"I know. You took me to see that movie. Twice," she said laughing. "It's a beautiful film."

"Would you like to see it again?"

She chuckled even more freely this time.

"Your whole life is an old movie."

* * *

We finished the Sangiovese and an order of olives and cheese and felt comfortable in the late afternoon sun. We walked through Chinatown, arm in arm, down Grant, and passed the Buddha Lounge and Jade Café, a gift store and a crowded corner where hawkers sold fresh vegetables from crates. We spoke about our lives after graduate school. Saloma told me she was thinking about entering a doctoral program, maybe in child psychology. I said that I'd be done with my master's degree in December but didn't plan to graduate until May. I'd thought about a doctoral program, looked at a few, but didn't think it was in the cards.

"So what will you do?"

I shrugged. "It's a good life, if you don't weaken. Who said that?"

"John Buchan," she answered quickly. "He wrote *The Thirty-Nine Steps*. Seriously. What are your plans?"

"I don't know." I hesitated, thought it through. "I'm scheduled to sit for a civil service exam as a clerk/typist. If I land something in the new year," I went on, "I'll probably just work part-time and take a few more classes in German and French. I'll try to get some writing done," I added, almost as an afterthought.

She held my arm firmly and stopped walking so that I was forced to stop too. She looked at me.

"And then what?"

"And then what?" I echoed. "Good question." I smiled, but the corners of my mouth felt tight. I bit my lip and said nothing.

We walked on, still with arms linked, and crossed Pine. We passed a Chinese bakery, an herbalist, a lion statue by a bank.

"I wish I could tell you," I said at last. "My mother's always nagging me about what I'm going to do next."

"And you said . . .?"

This time, I was able to chuckle softly. "I told her I'll probably go back to flipping hamburgers or driving a truck, or maybe I'll work as a carnie or on a fishing boat."

"How did she take it?"

"She was hurt."

"Your poor mother."

"I know."

We reached Bush and passed through Dragon's Gate, the main entrance to Chinatown not far from where the photo of my family had been taken so many years before.

I stopped and Saloma put her arms around me. She looked into my eyes. I knew what was on her mind, and it wasn't marriage. She was as afraid of that institution as I was, equally unable to overcome her barriers, step over the rubble in her way.

"Your mother probably thinks you're wasting your life, Diego."

I kept quiet, could feel the muscles in my jaw tense.

"Everyone says you have talent," Saloma went on. "I heard Dr. Papandrakis say you're one of the best critical thinkers in the program. Why don't you talk to him about doctoral programs?"

I moved gently from her embrace and took her hand. We continued down Grant holding hands, swinging them as we walked.

"I already have," I murmured. "He said I should consider Comparative Lit because of my background and languages. But I don't know. I need some time off." I felt her soft hand in mine. We walked in step down the sloping sidewalk. We reached Sutter.

"Saloma, I've been in school most of my life. Like you, in my own way, I've been sheltered. I just want to get some experience, kick around a few years, see life. Maybe I'll go back and earn a doctorate one day."

She moved closer to me. I held her tightly and leaned back against a lamppost, letting her body fall against mine. We kissed tenderly, open-mouthed, our tongues explored lovingly, indifferent to the passersby, to a shouted comment from someone in a car.

When the kiss ended, she moved her head back and studied me.

"All that local color you're trying to pick up in North Beach —isn't that just a veneer? Isn't real experience anywhere?"

CHAPTER FIVE

I phoned her on Wednesday.

"I've been thinking about what you said, Saloma."

There was a long silence on the other end.

"We talked about a lot of things."

"Yes, we did." I moved the mouthpiece away slightly, then spoke into it. "I probably *will* do a doctorate one day—not right away—but I've looked into some programs."

"Yes—"

I hesitated. "There's a doctoral program at UC Santa Cruz I might want to check out. Comparative Lit, cross-disciplinary, cross-national." I paused. "They emphasize creative writing and criticism."

"Sounds interesting. Sounds like something you'd really like."

I listened intently, trying to detect a note of happiness in her voice. Then, I added as casually as I could: "You know, they have doctoral programs in psychology. There's one with a concentration in developmental psych...children's, infants'..." I let my voice trail off.

Now I did hear happiness in her voice.

"I know. I've read about it. I've seen the catalogue."

"Say—" Again, I tried to make myself sound nonchalant. "What do you think about driving down there one Friday, when we're both off? We could take a look around."

"I'd love it."

"Then it's settled. We can take my car."

* * *

I pulled up to her apartment the following Friday morning at nine a.m., as agreed. Her front door opened even as my car still rolled to a stop and she walked toward me, lovely in the morning light against the fall colors. She was dressed in a short tweed riding jacket with a velvet collar, a cream-colored blouse and a dark brown skirt with scenes of a fox hunt. Her brown boots ended just below the knee.

"You look beautiful." She sat next to me and I kissed her lightly on the lips. "Very sophisticated."

"Like a doctoral student?" she smiled. "You don't look bad yourself."

I chuckled. It was going to be a wonderful day and I was glad she admired my look. I'd put on a dark turtleneck sweater and a tan corduroy sportscoat with leather patches on the elbows, brown salt and pepper trousers with a crease, and thick-soled walking shoes. All I needed was a pipe, I told her, to complete the look. But then again, I didn't smoke.

I shifted into first, then cross-shifted into third as we made our way down Lake Merced Boulevard, eventually connecting with Skyline and Pacific Coast Highway. The road ran parallel to the beach, separated by steep bluffs. Initially, we couldn't see the ocean because of the haze, but as the fog lifted and we sped down PCH we glimpsed the ocean to our right shimmering and cut by jagged rock formations. At that hour and on a winding road few cars passed us.

We talked about our day.

"We can check out the campus, walk around, maybe meet with the graduate coordinator," I remarked.

"I'd like to visit the psychology department."

"Of course!" I was in a jubilant mood, elated. "We can have lunch later—maybe in town."

As I drove, I started singing the Sinatra standard "Somethin' Stupid." When I got to the part about being together in a cozy bar and then spoiling the romantic mood by stupidly blurting out words of love, I pronounced it STOO-PED. Saloma's relaxed laugh sounded gleeful and carefree.

"Why does Frank Sinatra always pronounce it 'stoo-ped' instead of 'stew-pid'?" she asked, still chuckling.

"Because he's from Hoboken."

"Like Eddie."

"Like Huntz Hall and the Dead End Kids."

"Poor Eddie."

"Poor all of us, when you think about it."

* * *

We made our way through Moss Beach, El Granada, and Half Moon Bay. The small beach towns, with their clapboard houses and corner grocery stores, their bicycle repair shops and fruit stands, made me think of the Southern California beach towns I knew so well: Laguna Beach and Capistrano and Dana Point.

"You know," I told Saloma, "I grew up in a town only sixteen miles from the beach. We'd drive straight down Beach Boulevard—in those days you could get there in half an hour—and spend the day at Huntington Beach."

"Were you a surfer?"

I grinned.

"No, I did some body surfing, but that's a good way to break your neck. I did a lot of SCUBA diving in college, all up and down the Southern California coast."

"I didn't know that. Do you still dive?"

I gestured to my right. The shoreline curved now and the coast was even rockier.

"I haven't gone diving here, no. The ocean's beautiful in this area, but too cold."

We drove on. The waves seemed to cover the rocks like a hand and then draw back. We were together, almost no cars passed, and I felt happy.

"What about you? Did you go to the beach much in Manila?"

She gave me a rueful smile. "The only time I went swimming was in our pool. It was too dangerous to go to the beach."

I glanced at her.

"You don't understand how poor the Philippines is. There are tent cities in Rizal Park. People come up to you all the time if you're not accompanied. I was almost always with a chaperone or an escort."

"A guard?"

She didn't say anything and the road moved us temporarily inland, away from the shore. Columns of sweet-smelling eucalyptus trees and fields of bright orange pumpkins flickered past.

"Our driver carried a gun—in a shoulder holster. He wore a light jacket over it, but just about anyone on the street could see the grip sticking out. I guess that's what he wanted."

We whisked through a fishing village called Pescadero and passed a lighthouse on a rocky point. The road ran straight for a dozen miles then banked into a steep incline. I downshifted into first to climb the hill when I heard a violent hiss like water rushing down a mountainside.

"What's wrong?"

"We're okay," but my foot trembled on the gas pedal. I was transfixed by the sight of the temperature needle moving faster and faster into the red zone.

"We'll be okay," I repeated, "once we level off. Once we start to go downhill."

My car shook as if rattling on a log road. I had a taste of pennies in my mouth and could sense Saloma's fear. Something banged hard against the bottom of the hood, burst in an explosion of steam. Saloma yelled something. It sounded like a muffled scream, but the engine whistled so loudly I wasn't sure.

I'd reached the top of the hill. The steering wheel was rocking in my hands and I managed to shift into neutral and coast downhill. We were enveloped in smoke and steam and what looked like rusty raindrops splattered across the windshield. With the engine out, the power steering was gone too and I struggled to maneuver the car to the side of the road, then brake hard.

"Get out of the car," I told Saloma. "Stand over by those trees."

She rushed over to a cluster of pine trees twenty yards away. I removed the ignition key, got out of the car and opened the hood. Hot, rusty fluid had sprayed everywhere and steam jetted from all corners of the radiator. I swung around, my eyes searching for Saloma. She had turned her back to me and was staring at the ocean. I walked up to her and she moved away. Her arms crossed in front of her, she headed down the beach.

"Saloma," I called and caught up with her. I gripped her shoulders from behind. The waves thudded into the sand, withdrew. "It's not a problem," I lied. "We'll just let the engine cool and I'll add some water. It's not a problem. We'll drive to the next town and get the engine fixed."

"You planned this," she sobbed. She shook violently and I tried to comfort her. "I knew I shouldn't have come."

"Saloma."

"I don't want you. I want my mother."

"Oh, Jesus Christ."

I let her slip free of my grip and watched her rush away in tears, shaking as she walked down the beach. I sat down on a log, stuck a stick in the sand, drew patterns. I listened for the sound of passing cars but didn't hear any; only the rushing of the waves. It was unlikely anyone would stop for an overheated car on the side of the road, and I hadn't seen much traffic except the occasional stake-bed truck driven by a farmer hauling squash. Saloma wandered back a half hour later and was calmer now. Her eyes were still wet and red and her hair fell in disarray. She brushed it back with her fingers and tried to smooth it in place.

"I'm sorry," she murmured. "I'm such a baby."

"No, *I'm* sorry," I said. "I'm an ass. I haven't had the car checked since I moved up here. I wanted to save money."

We both let out a light laugh, breaking the tension. She sat on the log next to me.

"Are you cold?"

She nodded.

I put my arm around her. She placed her head on my shoulder and we watched the waves roll in.

"What's she like?" I asked. "Your mother?"

I could hear Saloma's gentle breathing, the soft inhalation and exhalation almost in rhythm with the waves.

"She's very nice," she said quietly. "She wrote poetry when she was younger and played the piano. You'd like her. And yours?"

"You'd like her too," I answered. "She's very religious. Two of her sisters are nuns."

Saloma looked at me.

"No, seriously. In Austria. My mother came from a large family. Only her eldest brother could go to college." I shrugged. "He became an attorney. Everyone else had to work in the textile industry or go into the Church. But my mother didn't want to become a nun. She said she was too rebellious."

"I'm glad of that," Saloma smiled, and put her head back on my shoulder.

The engine would be cool by now, I thought, and I could add water to the radiator, but I wanted to give it a bit more time. Despite everything, I felt at peace sitting with Saloma, with the grey expanse of sand in front of me, the rollers sloshing foam across the strand, the occasional seagull gliding with the wind, effortlessly.

"Have you ever been to Southern California?" I asked.

"I've been to Disneyland once," she said softly. "And we saw the Queen Mary."

"Disneyland," I mused. "My father worked at the Disneyland Hotel for three years." That was the longest he ever worked anywhere, and it was when we first arrived. I wanted to say something, but let it go.

"That must have been nice."

"Yes, we'd get free tickets to the Park sometimes. And your father? What's he like?"

"Oh . . . I'll tell you all about him some time."

* * *

Saloma stood a few feet behind me, watching, as I approached the car. I'd left the hood up and the engine had cooled sufficiently. Regardless, I used a thick rag from the car trunk, covered the radiator cap and tried twisting it open with both hands. No such luck.

"Is it stuck?" Saloma asked.

I wanted to say something sarcastic but walked in silence to the trunk instead. I grabbed the tire iron and went up to the radiator.

"Nothing a little expert know-how won't fix," I wise-cracked, banging on the radiator cap to loosen it.

I was able to twist it open with the rag. No steam came out. Everything must have gushed from the coils. The radiator was coated inside with an inky sludge. To make matters worse, the radiator only took half a jug of water, which told me it must be clogged with metal flakes and chips.

"Is everything okay?" Saloma asked sweetly, but there was a tension in her voice. "Can I help somehow?"

I cocked my head to get a better look. "Everything's okay." I wanted to say something reassuring. "At least the heater hose looks fine."

The worn rubber hose was clamped tightly on either end but the cracks that ran like wrinkles were worrying.

We got in. I turned the key. Nothing. I tried again and the starter made a whirring, grinding noise. I pressed the gas pedal slightly and the engine roared to life. I let out a deep breath and turned to Saloma with a smile.

"We're in business," I said.

"Nothing like a little expert know-how."

She tried to be amusing to ease our stress, but I hoped it wasn't gallows humor. The car ran smoothly for the first mile and we passed a road sign that read: "Davenport 5 mi." I didn't tell Saloma that already I could see the temperature needle edging upwards, hovering in the red section of the gauge. After another mile, it was completely in the red as I snaked through a series of hairpin curves.

The road straightened, then sloped downwards like a

chute. At the bottom of the drop, sandwiched between the ocean and the hills, a cluster of buildings formed a horseshoe.

"Civilization!" I quipped. I don't think Saloma thought that was funny. A steady hissing, then whistling, screeched from underneath the hood and Saloma stared stonily ahead.

"What's that?" she cried.

We were almost there. If anything blew, we could coast into town.

Something blew.

It sounded like a gunshot or a firecracker and the car shook. A cloud of steam billowed in front of us. I drove through a blanket of hot fog. The heater hose must have burst, but when the mist cleared we were on a gravel parking lot in front of a building.

* * *

"There must be a mechanic in this town," I insisted when my heart stopped pounding in my throat. I rubbed my palms on my pant legs. "Are you okay?"

Saloma had her eyes closed but nodded "yes." She staggered from the car. We were in front of a saloon. The sign above the door read "Whalen's B & G." Weathered pier pilings and white mariner's ropes marked the wooden sidewalk that fronted the building. An overhang shaded a bench and three concrete steps led to the front door.

I moved from my car, popped open the hood and left it ajar, allowed what was left of my engine to cool and said to Saloma: "Are you ready?"

Again, she nodded "yes."

We went inside.

The Animals' "House of the Rising Sun" played from an oblong jukebox with slowly flashing lights. As my eyes adjusted, I noted the faded linoleum floor tiles, the mismatched tables and chairs, and the skittle bowl table. In front of a long bar, a man wearing a striped Mexican blanket vest sat at a round table drinking from a long-necked Bud. He smiled at Saloma, exposing a gold-capped tooth.

I went up to the bar. Saloma moved next to me. A woman in her forties was on duty. She wore a beaded headband and wristbands, each in a different pattern. She was seated behind the bar and her large breasts rested like elbows on the bartop.

"Is that your car?" she asked.

"Yes."

"You'd better get it fixed."

"Is there a mechanic nearby?"

"Bill 'll be back soon. He can probably fix it."

A sailfish hung above the bar, its broken snout reattached with surgical tape. Three coconuts, carved into comical faces, sat on a shelf below a sign that read: "The Regulars Club." A stack of old magazines was on the bar in front of them. When the Animals stopped singing about *"the ruin of many a poor boy,"* the Jody Miller version of "House of the Rising Sun" came on, with her strong voice wailing out the same lyrics.

"Jimi likes that song," the woman mentioned, indicating the lone drinker with his long-necked Bud. "Listens to it over and over. But he's harmless."

I glanced back and the man smiled affably, raising the beer bottle in salute.

I turned my gaze back to the woman.

"When did you say the mechanic—Bill—will be back?"

"Hard to say." The woman stood up and her breasts flopped underneath her tee-shirt. She wiped down the counter.

"Bill lives in a commune back in the hills. Has a wrecking yard, works on demolition derby cars. Usually comes in around this time."

"Great. How will I recognize him?"

She started to wash beer glasses in a sink beneath the bar, and as she pumped them two by two on brushes prodding from the soapy water, the cannon balls beneath her tee-shirt swung heavily. "Wears overalls and a ponytail. Always has his kid with him and a dog. Bill drives a converted bread van. Still says 'Webers' on the panel. You can't miss him."

"Thanks."

I sat with Saloma at a square table away from the jukebox and Mr. Jimi Longneck. I asked Saloma how she was holding up. She gave me a faint smile.

"I'm fine," she insisted. "At least it's not boring. I'm not just sitting in the office looking for things to do." She lit a Virginia Slim, puffed nervously. "I should have brought something to read. We could be here a long time."

"The lady at the bar said Bill should be back soon."

"Do you really think he can fix it?" She stubbed out her cigarette.

I looked around the room, at the sailfish, the coconuts, the man with the beer.

"I think Bill is probably a hippie marijuana farmer who hides out in a shack in the hills." I shrugged and took her hand. "But if he has a wrecking yard and works on demolition derby cars, he can probably fix it."

"And if he's a hippie, he probably doesn't care about money. You can probably just pay him with a case of beer."

"We'll see about that."

* * *

An hour passed and we heard the Geordie rendition of "House of the Rising Sun" and then the Animals again and Jody Miller probably for the third time.

"We might as well drink a few beers while we're waiting," I suggested.

"Sure," she smiled. "A little something to steady the nerves."

I stood up.

"That's what they all say."

She looked at me expectantly.

"I'm not ordering Beck's," I said in response. I might as well order Belgian ale brewed by Trappist monks.

She took out a small beige pill and swallowed it. "This will calm me down even faster."

"What is it?"

"Prescription."

Mr. Jimi watched me walk up to the bar. The woman was restocking the bar-b-cue chip rack and I asked her what kind of beer they had. She told me Bud, Lucky Lager, and Hamms.

"Hamms is fine."

She opened a small refrigerator and handed me two tall blue cans. "Running a tab?"

"I might as well."

I waited.

I wondered why she had washed the beer glasses if she wasn't going to use them, but I didn't want to make a fuss.

When I returned to our table, Saloma questioned: "Hamms?"

"From the land of sky-blue waters," I quoted from the advertising jingle.

With our second round, we started to feel more at ease. We shared a bag of chips, eating them desultorily, when Mr. Jimi sauntered over with his beer, gave us a big smile, then straddled a chair one table away from us. He rested his arms on the chair's back.

"Hey, bro," he called lightly. "Couldn't help overhearing

your conversation with Flo. You been waiting a while." He nodded toward Saloma and grinned. His gold cap looked like a kernel of corn stuck between his teeth. "Is this your old lady?"

Before Saloma could say "we're just friends" I cut her off with a hand signal.

"Yes, this is the missus. My wife."

"Pleased ta meet ya." He stuck out his hand. It was rough and callused. "I'm Jimi."

"We're Mr. and Mrs. Smith," Saloma declared. "That's Smythe with a 'y' and an 'e.'" She spelled it out for him: "S-M-Y-T-H-E."

He looked puzzled.

She seemed to frown in thought, then brightened. "Mr. and Mrs. Pendelton J. Smythe."

She forced a smile. She was becoming inventive, and I tensed slightly.

"Yeah?" The man put the beer bottle to his lips and sucked. "And I'm Jimi Hendricks. Heard of him?"

Saloma might have gone too far.

"Sure," I said slowly and tapped my can against his beer bottle. I gave him a conspiratorial wink. "We're all just joking, right?" I laughed drily. "Because you don't look like Jimi Hendricks."

The man leaned forward.

"I *am* Jimi Hendricks reincarnate. He died in 1970. I know that. But I've come back as the Jimi Hendricks for 1980. Can you believe it? Next year is 1980 and the world's gonna end in 1980—forty years after 1940, the year I was born."

He wasn't just harmless; his brain was fried. And the world might end for him in 1980, the way he was flying.

"I'm a musician, see? Played all the clubs in L.A. Ever heard of the Brown Derby?"

"You bet," I reassured him. But the Brown Derby was a restaurant with celebrity pictures on the wall, not a nightclub.

"Well, I played the Brown Derby and Chassen's and all them swanky clubs. But that's not what I wanted to talk to you about. You been waiting a while. I can fix your car. I've been a race car mechanic, see? If I can just cop the tools, man. If I can just cop the tools I can fix anything."

"We'll wait for Bill," I smiled.

"Just think about it," he persisted, standing up and pointing at me with the beer bottle. "Just think about it in case Bill don't show."

He ambled back to his table and put more coins in the jukebox.

And so it went that long afternoon, waiting for Bill to show, listening to different versions of "House of the Rising Sun" and drinking Hamms from cans. We ate the lunch special, zucchini burritos with a bowl of salsa on the side and watched Jimi Hendricks dump his burrito into his bowl of hot sauce, cut it into pieces with a spoon, and slurp from the bowl as if it were stew.

He lurched to his feet, then staggered to the men's room.

Saloma looked at me and shook her head in disbelief.

"And they say people in San Francisco are strange? Where did he say he comes from?" She hesitated. "L.A.?"

"He left L.A.," I commented, "and moved up here." I didn't want her to get the wrong idea about people from L.A. "Why don't we get some air?" I suggested.

Saloma picked up a magazine from the pile on the bartop and waved at the woman tending bar. "Okay? We're going outside for a while."

"Sure, hon. You can keep it for all I care."

I pushed the bar door and screen aside and enjoyed the late October sun. I could smell dry leaves and moist soil, pine needles from the trees behind us. We sat on the wooden bench in front of the building, side by side. The bench wasn't very long and our bodies pressed against each other, comfortingly.

Saloma thumbed through the magazine. "*Argosy*. Do they still publish this?"

I looked at the cover. A shark with open jaws and fang-like teeth thrust a huge head out of the waves. May 1978, the cover read. "They did eighteen months ago. Why don't you read to me?"

She flipped the pages. "I can't read this stuff."

"It's not Tolstoi," I replied.

Then, she said: "Okay."

I closed my eyes. Saloma cleared her throat.

"*Shark Attack. By Coleman P. Coleman.*"

"I wonder if he sells mustard," I joked.

"Hush. *I woke up dead. I was inside a bright, shiny casket with bronze handles. A pipe organ played long notes and a woman screamed.* Who writes this nonsense?" I heard her put the magazine down. "How does he know what the casket looks like if he's dead?"

"You're too logical. Read a bit more."

"*A cement grinder roared and flames licked the casket. A woman screamed.* He already said that."

"It's called 'artful repetition.'"

She closed the magazine and I heard tires crunching across the gravel parking lot. I looked up to see a white delivery van with the word "Weber's" on the side, still visible underneath a coat of spray paint.

"Alleluia," I sang out.

"Don't be so sure."

We got up.

The driver stepped through the open cab doorway, followed by a boy of about eight or nine and a small mangy dog. The driver was dressed in bib overalls and yellow rubber boots, a plaid shirt and a painter's cap that read "Sherwin Williams." His grey ponytail hung to the middle of his back, but his beard was cut shorter—no doubt to avoid getting it tangled in a fan belt.

"Hi."

"Hiya," he called.

Saloma bent down to the little boy. He was dressed the same as his father, sans ponytail, beard, and painter's cap, and his mousey brown hair was cut straight across his forehead.

"What's your name?" she asked.

The boy petted the calico mutt, its bones visible beneath the thin fur.

"Jupiter." He ground the toe of his rubber boot into the gravel.

"That's a nice name," she said gently.

"Yeah . . ." He tugged on the dog's collar. "Come on, Raymond!" he coaxed. "Let's go play!"

So the boy's name is Jupiter and the dog's name is Raymond, I thought and shook my head, but I had other things to worry about. I introduced myself to Bill and explained the situation. He said he'd take a look at my vehicle but needed to have his lunch first and a couple of beers. He needed to feed the boy and the dog, he went on. He called for them and the three went inside.

We waited an hour. We counted three cars whoosh north and then a truck and a van. Jimi Hendricks pushed the bar door open and stumbled out. He stood still on the sidewalk, swaying to regain his balance, then looked to his left and his right before heading past us down the street.

"Night all," he said with a clumsy wave, even though it was three in the afternoon. We watched him stagger down the road, weaving in his striped Mexican blanket vest past the post office and the bank.

Bill came out. Jupiter and Raymond ran off behind the building.

"I'll take a little look-see," Bill announced.

He picked up a rag from the truck cab and wiped his hands, then unloaded a large red toolbox that had served as a seat for the boy and the dog. He thrust the hood of my car fully open and started banging with a wrench. Saloma and I stood a few feet away, trying not to crowd him. Every so often, he grunted or let out a low whistle. He unscrewed the radiator cap and ran his finger inside.

Bill straightened and wiped his hands on the rag.

"Bought this car used, did ya?"

He shook his head and looked down the road.

"Whoever sold it to ya put so much Stop-Leak in the radiator it's completely gunked up."

I didn't say anything.

He looked at me expectantly.

"Can you fix it?" I asked.

"Sure, but it'll cost ya. Can't rebuild a radiator like that. Gotta replace it. I'll need to replace the thermostat and heater hose, radiator hose. Got a cuppla smashed up Novas in the yard that I can strip."

"What about the radiator?"

He put his hands in his back pockets.

"I can pull a radiator outta a Chevy Nova and make it fit. Probably. But it'll cost ya." He scratched his cheek through his beard. "A hundred and a quarter if ya leave it with me. You can pick it up maybe in a week."

I felt the blood drain from my head and my knees turn

spongy. I looked at Saloma. The corners of her mouth had turned down and her lips were a thin, taut line.

"How will we get back to the City?" I asked Bill.

"Cars pass by here all the time." Bill pointed to the road. "Going south, too. You can probably hitch a ride. It's nine mile to Santa Cruz. The Greyhound will run ya back to Frisco."

I turned to Saloma. Tears had welled in her eyes.

"What do you think?" I asked gently. "Depending on the bus schedule, we'd be back around dinner time."

She blinked the tears from her eyes and her face turned implacable.

"I can probably pick the car up in a week," I added. I thought of Dr. Leming, who owned a beach condo near Santa Cruz. He might give me a lift the next time he drove there.

Saloma looked at Bill.

"What's the alternative?"

"I could fix it today—maybe by sundown—for one-seventy-five." He looked at me. "Overtime."

So much for paying with a case of beer. I only earned a little over a hundred dollars a week. Things would be tough for a while. And so much for saving money by skipping routine maintenance on a vehicle. I felt like a complete fool, especially because I'd drawn Saloma into this mess.

We agreed on the price. Bill grinned broadly and pumped my hand. He suggested using his bread van to tow my Celica to the wrecking yard. I asked him how we would all fit on the front seat—the tool box—of his van.

"Oh, I can't take the two of you. Just the car. It's private land up there." He paused. "Real private."

I got the picture and was relieved I hadn't agreed to leave my car for a week or more. And now that I could see things clearly, I certainly wasn't going to let him disappear into the high country and hide my Celica between the redwoods and the marijuana plants. For all I knew, Bill ran a chop-shop in the hills.

"Can you fix it here?"

"Sure. I can bring the radiator back. But it'll cost ya. Round trip . . . Gas ain't cheap." He pretended to write in the palm of his hand. "Say . . . An even two hundred, signed, sealed, and delivered?"

I was being fleeced, but I didn't have much choice. I nodded my assent and Bill hopped in the van, whistling to Jupiter and Raymond, who came running from behind the building and leapt into the van.

Bill started up the motor and waved.

"See ya! See ya soon!"

He backed the van out of the gravel parking lot and headed north. A puff of black smoke coughed from the tail pipe.

* * *

Saloma and I walked the two blocks to the Wells Fargo Bank. I didn't say much on the way, but she took my arm.

"Don't worry, Diego. Things will work out." She stroked my forearm. "I know they will. And if you're a bit short this month, I can lend you some money."

"Thanks." I was hesitant. I put my arm around her and gave her a squeeze. "You're a pal. But I think I can manage."

I wrote and cashed a check at the Wells Fargo Bank, then walked back with Saloma to Whalen's. Inside, we sat at the same table as before. We shared a can of Hamms but asked for glasses this time. The jukebox was silent. Two women in tank tops and shorts played skittle bowl. As we waited for Bill to return, we could hear the clatter of pins being bowled over, a whoop of delight or a groan, and then the sound of the pins being reset.

Saloma read her copy of *Argosy* magazine, tut-tutting every so often, then worked on the crossword puzzle. Bill came back about five, sat with Jupiter and Raymond, ordered a basket of fries. He drank a Lucky Lager, the boy had a Fanta, and Flo brought the dog a bowl of milk, which he lapped noisily.

I couldn't see how Bill would get the job done by sunset, which would be in an hour and a half, but he got up, wiped his hands on his overalls, and chimed: "Time to get 'er done."

He called to Jupiter and Raymond. They followed lackadaisically.

All afternoon, I heard a banging from outside. But Bill enjoyed his breaks and came in regularly for another beer. "It's coming along," he'd say by way of progress report, or: "It won't be long now. Should have 'er tied up pretty quick."

The light outside the window started to change, shift to grey and then to a dark shade of blue. I went to the barroom door and looked out. I saw Bill had clamped a shoplight to the engine well of my car, had run an extension cord to the side of the building, and was lying underneath the engine block with his yellow boots sticking out. Jupiter stomped through a puddle, splashing mud in a wide circle. He kicked gravel at the dog, then picked up a stone and flung it at the dog's hind leg. He missed, but the dog took off with Jupiter yelling gleefully.

"Someone ought to smack that kid," I commented, sitting back down. Saloma looked away from me.

"He's only a little boy."

I tapped my fingers on the tabletop, glanced idly at the bar.

"Do you need to phone anyone?" I asked. "Flo will probably let you use the phone. I can ask how much."

Saloma smiled ruefully.

"No, maybe later. If it gets *too* late, I probably won't call."

"Your sister?"

She nodded assent.

"What's she studying anyway?"

"Public administration."

I wanted to say "she'd be good at that" but held my tongue.

"She's doing really well," Saloma went on, apparently happy to have something to talk about. "She's already presented a paper and may go to another student conference later this year. That would be exciting for her."

"It would be," I agreed, and realized we'd probably end up eating dinner at Whalen's.

When Flo passed by, I lifted my hand slightly to get her attention. "What's the dinner special?"

"Zucchini burritos—two of them—with salsa, rice, and garbanzo beans."

"Sounds yummy. Two orders, please."

I asked Saloma what she'd like to drink and she said anything but flat, warm beer. "How about some orange juice?" she questioned.

When I asked Flo, she told me they only had cocktail mix, so we ordered two virgin margaritas. The prospect of being on the road anytime soon grew dimmer and I didn't want to fall asleep at the wheel if I drove back late.

Bill enjoyed his dinner break too and sat at a table with Jupiter and Raymond. He smiled and tipped his beer can toward me and ordered three dinner specials, including one for the dog. Now that he was in the chips, I was surprised he didn't order steak and potatoes for Raymond. I supposed Whalen's didn't have it on the menu.

"Won't be long now," he claimed, heading back outside with his companions trotting behind him.

Time passed, for the most part pleasantly, and with Jimi Hendricks conked out somewhere, we were able to listen to something other than "House of the Rising Sun." I slotted coins into the jukebox and punched the numbers for Jim Reeves'

"Ramona" and Connie Frances' "Everybody's Somebody's Fool."

* * *

It was after eleven p.m. when Bill handed me the car keys and I forked over his two hundred dollars.

He counted through the twenties. "I forgot to ask for them as fins—fivers." He looked disappointed. "Never mind. Car runs great. I checked 'er out."

And the car did run smoothly on the long night drive back to San Francisco. An illuminated gas station floated by, like a spaceship; orange street lamps glowed when we wound through a seaside town. We were both tired and didn't say much on the drive. I slipped a cassette into the player and we listened to Schubert's Symphony No. 3.

"That's nice music," Saloma said quietly.

I smiled, pleased that something was in order.

"There's nothing wrong with 'House of the Rising Sun,'" I put in, "but I don't want to hear it in my dreams."

I rested my hand on her knee. She reached over and laid her own hand on top of mine. We were listening to the Allegretto movement, with its soothing flutes and oboes, its rustic melodies.

"We can drive to UC Santa Cruz another time," I said. "The doctoral programs will still be there." After a pause, I added: "It's a good thing we didn't make any appointments."

She was asleep.

CHAPTER SIX

She woke up when we reached Daly City, maybe from the lights of houses strung like ribbons into the hills.

"We're back." She looked out the window. "I grew up here."

"I know."

"What time is it?"

"It's almost one a.m."

I exited on Serra Boulevard, then turned onto Nineteenth and steered through a series of curves.

She caressed my arm. "You shouldn't drive anymore."

I wasn't sure what she was suggesting—maybe a place on her couch. During the long day together, we had both experienced varying emotions, from fear to affection to excitement. I felt very close to her and didn't want to spoil the moment. I'd rather drive back, tired as I was, than hurt her in some way.

I pulled up in front of her apartment, parked, and walked with her to the front door. She unlocked the door, opened it slightly and turned to face me.

"It's been a long day." She hugged me, then put her arms around my neck.

"It has," I said, kissing her. I rested my hands gently on her hips. She moved closer and nestled against me. We kissed open-mouthed for the longest time; her tongue wriggled against mine.

When she broke off the kiss, she looked at me intently. "I really didn't think we were going to make it back."

"You're kidding? You're the one who said you were sure everything would work out."

"I was just saying that." We laughed. "I was terrified at times."

We enjoyed another long kiss. With my mouth against hers, I said: "I could have gotten you back on the Greyhound."

"I care for you, Diego." Her hands moved from my shoulders to my front and were pressed against my torso; I held her close. "I wanted to stay with you. Besides, you inspire a spirit of adventure in me," she smiled, and I started kissing her again. She pushed the door open and we danced in, clinging to each other and indulging in a long feverish kiss. We were just inside the entranceway, by the coat rack, standing on a small rug. She half-closed the door.

I kissed her neck and could smell her warm skin. She pressed her mouth to my ear, nibbled it, and whispered: "Please be careful. We can't make too much noise. Ezzie is a light sleeper."

"She's not the big sister." My mouth searched for hers. "You are."

"We take care of each other."

Saloma let me slip my hand into her blouse, across her flat stomach, to the base of her breast.

"I take care of you, Saloma."

I unfastened her bra and Saloma cupped her hand over my aching mound, started kneading it. I groaned with pleasure.

"Except when your car breaks down."

"Very funny," I managed to say. I caressed her breasts, enjoyed their firmness and weight, rubbed a finger lightly across a nipple. She let out a moan.

"I like you a lot, Diego." Her hand fumbled with my belt. She loosened the front of my trousers. Her soft hand explored inside and started to fondle me, freeing my member and gripping it firmly. She started to stroke me with a smooth, pumping motion.

I tried kissing her full on the mouth but she turned her head so that my lips pressed to her cheek, her neck, her shoulder.

"Promise you won't hurt me, Diego."

"No," I gasped. I spoke with my lips against hers. "No, I won't hurt you, Saloma. I promise."

Standing just inside the door of her apartment, our mouths writhing against each other, the quick movement of her hand didn't slacken. I called out her name.

* * *

"What are you doing here?" Saloma's sister asked me in the morning. I was in my underwear, lying on the couch but covered by an Afghan throw.

"We had quite an experience getting back from Santa Cruz." I rubbed my eyes. My socks and shoes were on the floor next to the couch; my shirt and pants were in a pile a few feet away on the armchair. Ezzie stood in the kitchen wearing white shorts and a black tee-shirt that read: "End Race Hate!"

"Miscegenate!" I offered, completing the rhyme.

"What?"

"Never mind." Ezzie probably couldn't take a joke. I sat up. "I'll let Saloma tell you about our trip."

I picked up my wristwatch from the end table and strapped it on. The hands showed it was already nine twenty-six. I looked guiltily at the front door. It had been wiped clean. There were no telltale stains.

"I suppose you want breakfast too." Ezzie didn't smile.

I paused.

"That would be nice. Sure."

Ezzie cracked five eggs into a bowl, whisked them angrily.

"Just don't get her pregnant."

She crushed a clove of garlic, peeled and chopped it with a kitchen knife, flicked the bits into a frying pan.

"I'm not planning on it," I responded.

"A lot of people don't plan on it."

I watched her quick movement as she diced an onion, adding the segments into the frying pan. They started to sizzle.

"The last time she was pregnant, we still lived in Manila. We got it taken care of, but it wasn't pretty."

I felt the blood drain from my head and an emptiness in my stomach that wasn't from hunger. I felt awful. I was relieved in a way that she was more experienced than I'd thought, but Saloma loved children, especially babies. Half the time I was with her she was telling me she wanted babies of her own. I wasn't sure what I was feeling. I felt sorry for her, of course; angry that this had happened to her; pained because I knew how much it would have hurt her to destroy a life.

I heard her footfall and looked toward the stairs. Dressed in a yellow bathrobe, without makeup, her hair tousled, she still looked beautiful. If anything, I felt even more affection for her in that moment. I watched her descend the stairs, tighten the sash around her bathrobe.

"Hi," she said sheepishly.

I swallowed hard and smiled at her.

"Hi."

She sat next to me and kissed me gently on the lips. I rubbed my lips slowly across hers.

"How did you sleep?" she asked.

"Not bad. On and off."

"On her and off her?"

"Only in my dreams."

She started to kiss me again and I could hear Ezzie's harrumph from the kitchen. She scraped the garlic and onion into the bowl, gave the eggs and ingredients a stir, and dumped the puree into a larger frying pan.

"Do you like your omelet spicy?" Ezzie called out. But before I could answer she scooped a dark brown paste from a jar and added what looked like slices of dry chorizo. Chopped green chilis went in as well.

"The spicier the better," I replied. I didn't have a choice.

Saloma smiled at me and rolled her eyes, as if to say, never mind my sister. She hugged me and placed her lips against my ear, whispering: "You'll grow to like her."

"Are we going to spend a lazy Sunday together?" I asked her.

She shook her head negatively.

"You'll have to go soon. After breakfast."

"Okay." I tried to hide my disappointment but she must have read it in my eyes.

"Ezzie and I have to go to a christening this afternoon at the Filipino church. I'd ask you to come, but you wouldn't fit in."

* * *

I tried keeping my mind blank until I had driven well out of sight of her apartment and had turned onto Sloat. My hands shook on the steering wheel and my breath was rapid. I decided I was too upset to drive and pulled into a parking lot overlooking the beach. I shut off the engine and got out. With the lack of motion, the stasis of the sand, it cut into me like the wire bristles of a paint-scraping brush, a few hundred pinpricks stabbing into my skin. What did she mean by that? I wouldn't fit in?

I slammed the car door and strode across the soft sand that seemed to hold my ankles in place. With whom? With her family? I was the one who was always trying to get away from family and didn't want any messy entanglements but was in the middle of one now.

I heard the roar of the surf as waves tumbled into the sand and the water fanned out. Only the day before I was sitting with Saloma on the beach, worried about a crisis of my own making, but growing closer to her in many ways. I reached the firm part of the beach where the sand lay like cement packed hard by the water it had sucked inside.

I walked in the direction of the Cliff House and started to calm down. I was overreacting and was probably responding to a thousand slights when I was growing up, when I was in college and got the sense that I didn't fit in. We had two kinds of students at USC—legacy kids, whose parents and grandparents were part of the "donor class," and scholarship kids like myself, who were told we were lucky some patron gave us a free ride.

I passed two surf fishermen in rubber waders and knit caps, casting their lines into the sea. I had brushed off the ethnic slurs when I was growing up:

"Is it Diego—or Dago?"

"Contreras? That's a funny name for an American."

"Why don't you wait a few years," I sometimes said, but never wanted to make too much of it. For me, coming from Europe and inheriting my parents' acute sense of social distinctions, the prejudice I encountered wasn't about ethnicity but social class.

In front of me, a stumbling drunk with a New York Jets sweatshirt sat down in the sand, tried to get up, slumped down again. His beard stubble also looked like sand, as if he'd gotten wet and had fallen chin down into a dune. He looked up at me, toasted with a half-empty pint bottle of Old Granddad, and bellowed at the top of his lungs: *"Tell all the gang on Forty-Second Street I'm drunk at Union Square!"*

He was a few miles from San Francisco's Union Square—even farther from George M. Cohen's Broadway and Herald Square. Everyone had problems.

I could see the Cliff House in the distance, a squat white building that looked almost like a penitentiary. None of my resentments had anything to do with Saloma—or not very much of them did. I listened to the sound of the surf, thought of our recent experiences, and started to breathe calmly, in and out, in cadence with the surf, as she had done the day before. I stood still and watched the waves come in.

Saloma wanted to be with me; we spent a lot of time together, and we'd gone on that crazy car trip. She'd overcome some of her fears, her deep-seated inhibitions, and that couldn't have been easy for her. We had enjoyed each other's bodies—not completely—but more fully than we ever had—and she seemed happy this morning, maybe because she knew she had given me great pleasure.

But she also gave me a lot of mixed signals, and I couldn't always figure her out. What did she see in me, for that matter? She seemed to see me as an adventurous rebel, a rover, someone who brought excitement into her life. But those same characteristics kept her always at a distance, holding back, afraid I might leave one day, or worse yet, stay—without prospects, without stability, without success; afraid she would be hurt.

I continued walking. Two women on horseback galloped past and then I neared a man strolling just ahead of me, his hands folded behind his back; his long grey hair fell over his collar. He paused to pick up a stone, examined it, tossed it aside. He picked up a seashell and kept it. I passed him and continued walking when it occurred to me.

Ezzie had said Saloma was pregnant when she lived in the Philippines, but she was in grade school and high school at the time. She would have been at most in her teenage years. And from what Saloma had told me about her upbringing—the chaperones, the walled compound she lived in with a guard-house at the gate, the convent schools, the gardener and maid and the chauffeur who took the family shopping, I couldn't envision Saloma carrying on with teenage boys, making love behind a bush or near a stream, or even having the opportunity, given how sheltered and insular her life was.

Saloma's pain ran very deep and it prevented her from opening up to me. A family friend, a trusted advisor, a priest, maybe someone even closer. My mind ran in multiple directions. I didn't want to see her for a while, but when I did, I wanted to tell her how sorry I was.

* * *

On Saturday, I took her to lunch at El Zocalo, a Mexican restaurant in the Mission District. Maybe I was being overly careful with her, but I didn't want to push things too far. Saloma had a fragile, vulnerable quality, and I noticed increasingly that she could be fidgety and nervous when I saw her on campus, sometimes picking at her food like a bird.

When I met her at her apartment to go somewhere, she'd check the front door two or three times and then go back inside because she'd forgotten something. At other times, she'd be completely calm, comfortable around me, and would touch my arm reassuringly.

She was very calm now, and I enjoyed seeing the way she was dressed, with a rose discreetly tucked into her hair.

El Zocalo was well known for its menudo and I suggested she order a bowl. Instead, she ordered chorizo and eggs with corn tortillas and we called for two bottles of Negra Modelo. We enjoyed the atmosphere: the ranchero music from the jukebox, the street vendor selling elote from a push-cart just outside the restaurant window, and a Mexican family having lunch. As usual, Saloma smiled and waved at the children.

When my menudo came—a big, steaming bowl of tripe and hominy soup, which I garnished with diced raw onion, oregano, squeezed lemon, and crushed red peppers—I said: "You really ought to try some."

"I've had it."

"They say it's a cure for a hangover."

"Maybe we should order some to go," and we chuckled at that.

Later, I told Saloma I was grateful for her company and appreciated her patience with me on our zany attempt to get to Santa Cruz.

I took her hand.

"I was touched that you offered to help me this month. But I'm okay, thanks. I received a small payment for an article I wrote." I released her hand and said hopefully: "I should be able to write another one next month."

"Don't worry about it," she replied, lighting a cigarette. "I have a little extra if you ever need some help."

That struck me as a generous offer; graduate students were seldom flush.

"You struggle too," I added. "You work in an office and take graduate classes."

She stubbed out her cigarette, opened up her purse and took out a small container of pills. She took one quickly, followed by a sip of beer.

"My father," she said looking at me. "He gives us a small allowance."

I must have looked puzzled.

"I thought he cut you off."

"He did, in a way. He doesn't want to see us—or we don't want to see him. But there are six of us, plus my mother, so he sends a remittance every month."

Saloma turned away from me. She looked out the window. The street vendor selling elote had left, pushing his cart to the other side of Dolores Street near the steps of the Mission. A norteño came on, with its fast polka beat and its wheezing accordion. The radio announcer rapidly rattled his DJ patter, trilling all his 'r's', even the ones that aren't sounded that way.

"What does your father do in the Philippines?"

She turned back to me, relit her cigarette.

"Oh . . . he raises horses. He grows sugarcane. He's into electronics."

"Electronics?"

The hint of a smile formed on her lips.

"I don't mean he managed a Radio Shack. He studied electrical engineering at Berkeley." She took another sip of beer. "But he made his money selling components to the PAF when he was in government."

I knew what she meant. The PAF would be the Philippine Air Force. I shook my head in dismay and tried not to express annoyance. I still prided myself on being an angry socialist. I believed in the redistribution of wealth because I didn't have any, but Saloma's politics were to the left of mine and she came from money. We'd spoken about the U.S. Presidential campaign not so long before. Jimmy Carter was up for re-election and I'd told her I wouldn't vote for him.

"Carter's inept, feckless, and he speaks like Gomer Pyle."

"That's just the European snob in you," she had said. "Accent matters."

"I'd vote for Ted Kennedy if he got in the race."

"Of course," she'd teased me. "Plummy accent. Good family."

"Well, who would you vote for?"

"Angela Davis," she had said. "She wants to blow up the capitalist system. I support that."

I found it ironic that Saloma would accept money from a crony capitalist—but with family, irony is in abundance.

* * *

We crossed Dolores Street to the Spanish mission. The small church, built in the 1770s according to Spanish design but by native labor, was dwarfed by the adjacent revival-style basilica —a kind of Hearst Castle grotesquerie. We walked up the five short steps to the hand-hewn mission door. I turned the heavy iron ring to one side and we stepped over a raised wooden threshold into the vestibule. A white-haired woman held a finger to her lips. A service was underway. She whispered that we could visit but needed to be respectful. We both nodded our agreement; Saloma dipped her fingers into the holy water font and blessed herself, making the sign of the cross.

Only a few congregants were attending the Saturday Mass. As my eyes adjusted, I admired the simple lines of the church, the whitewashed walls and decorated rafters, the ornate Baroque reredos and the intricately carved images of saints. I should have recognized most of them, but didn't, and followed

Saloma down the main aisle, past the dark wooden benches, until we were close to a side exit.

Saloma genuflected and blessed herself again, then took her place in one of the pews. I sat next to her. I recognized the stages of the Mass. The priest had begun the ritual of the consecration and mumbled some prayers in Spanish, to which every so often the few members of the congregation repeated a phrase. I could smell hair oil and unwashed clothing, incense and candle smoke. I thought I heard a baby cry but it was a young man twitching in the corner. I thought of the church in Spain where my grandparents were married and my father baptized. I thought of my teenage years in Mexico and a faith that had eroded like a desert gulley.

I glanced at Saloma. She was always so beautiful, and the red rose tucked into her hair accentuated her beauty. I yearned for her and for a simple answer but was disturbed by the simplicity of the congregants' beliefs and by their docility.

I signaled Saloma that we should exit through the side door and as we left, she paused momentarily to look back before we entered the gardens.

Saloma tucked her arm through mine as we strolled the Mission grounds.

"Thank you, Diego, for taking me."

I didn't say anything, just wished I could share her faith. It was very peaceful in the Mission gardens, with a carved stone fountain covered in ivy, an olive tree, and a Bougainvillea climbing a trellis near one of the brick columns of an arcade. The church cemetery was off to one side and I saw weathered gravestones from the previous century and a marble sculpture of a robed priest.

We sat down on a stone bench.

"I know you don't believe in the Church, Diego," she said

wistfully. "Sometimes I don't believe either. But I'm glad we're here."

Sitting next to Saloma, smelling her warmth and her perfume, the rose in her hair, I would have liked nothing better than to have believed in something other than myself, to have trusted as she sometimes seemed to. We held hands.

The church bells from the campanario began to clang, and when its ringing ended and the sound faded away, I started singing the sentimental love song "Ramona," from the 1920s movie of that name. But Saloma cringed when I sang about the mission bells above ringing out our song of love and changed the name from "Ramona" to "Saloma."

She got up and moved away from me, her body tensed as she walked down the arched corridor. I got up and followed her.

"What now?"

She turned to face me. We were next to one of the columns, half hidden by it.

"Am I just a fantasy to you?" she hurled back. "Everything you know about women is from old movies and old songs. I'm not like that, Diego. I'm not perfect."

"I'm sorry." I hesitated. "I'm not perfect either. Not by any means. And I want to get to know you for who you are."

"Do you mean that?" She stepped closer to me. She still seemed tense, with a forced smile and no laughter in her eyes. "I'm afraid you won't like me very much if you know the way I am."

"Let me find out."

I placed my hands on her hips and she pressed herself against me. I felt the round curves of her body, her shape.

We moved closer to the pillar, hoping not to be seen.

Her voice was soft, husky. "I don't want to be your fantasy."

I smiled foolishly. "I fantasize about you sometimes."

She placed her mouth against mine.

"You don't need to fantasize," she said. "I'm real."

She kissed me fully on the mouth, then gave my lower lip a gentle bite. When I flinched and kissed her back, she ran her tongue back and forth across my lips. I moaned, and she inserted her tongue into my mouth and pressed it against mine. I broke off the kiss, afraid that a groundskeeper or a priest or a church lady would wander by and see us clutching each other frantically.

* * *

My qualifying exams were scheduled for the first week in December—for Friday, December 7, 1979, to be exact—Pearl Harbor Day, and I was determined it would not be my day of infamy. I had started the semester with eight Steinbeck novels in front of me, five plays by Ibsen, and whatever novels by Fowles I had not yet read. There always seemed another work of criticism to consume, or a new Norwegian study that had just been translated, but my practice orals went well and I spent the final month leading up to the qualifying exams studying relentlessly.

Twice I thought I was on the verge of exhaustion. Money was a perennial problem, and I had to steal time from my studies to write a string of freelance articles for a bilingual community newspaper. It didn't pay much, but it was enough to keep me going. I wrote an article, with translation, on the importance of the 1980 census— "¡Cuenta con Nosotros! — "Count on Us!" was the headline—a report on the problem of stray dogs in the Potrero District, and a profile piece on Roberto Gonzalez, who was running for the Board of Supervisors.

My academic writing was more satisfying, though it didn't pay. In the Craft of Fiction Seminar, Professor Levinski praised my paper on "Conrad and Consciousness" and advised me to submit it as a graduate conference paper. And even though it wasn't academic, I was pleased that the public television station sent me a contract allowing them to screen my eighteen-minute film *Caporetto* as a filler between shows. I tried to stay up until 3:12 a.m. to watch, but fell asleep with Fowles' *Daniel Martin* in my lap. The next week, the station sent me a check for one hundred dollars and a logoed coffee mug.

I frequently saw Saloma on campus, for lunch, or a dinner date. We sometimes walked through Golden Gate Park on a Sunday, visiting the Crystal Palace-like greenhouse or the DeYoung Museum. We enjoyed music in the park, sat on folding chairs and listened to a concert band play Sousa marches, or watched a line of African-American teenagers roller-skating in unison; they bopped up and down as they held boom boxes on their shoulders.

All of life was in a single afternoon, I wanted to tell her, and our two lives seemed rolled up as one. We had grown increasingly intimate physically and at night, in my car or behind her front door or, if her sister was away for the evening, on her couch, she would let me unbutton her blouse and unfasten her bra and would hold my head to her breasts.

"Remember to enjoy them equally," she would say. "They both need love."

We would chuckle before it became too intense for laughter and our only thought was on release. Sometimes, she would pull her panties to one side and would guide my hand. She would let me wriggle a finger inside her, sometimes two, and, thrusting, bring her to orgasm. Each night, she would work me with her hand until I climaxed. It was everything and nothing, sex without intercourse, leaving us satisfied and wanting. I didn't know how much longer this could go on.

* * *

I told my parents I wasn't going to visit for Thanksgiving. I needed the time to make one last push before my qualifying exams. Instead, I would take the train down for Christmas and stay longer.

There was silence on the other end of the phone line as my mother took this in. It was the second year in a row I would miss Thanksgiving at my parents' house. She'd probably understood the first year, when I had just moved to San Francisco. Now, she repeated the information to my father. I heard him say in the background: "He must have a woman."

My mother said sweetly: "Study hard for your exams. But enjoy your Thanksgiving too. We love you."

I didn't see that much of Saloma over the long Thanksgiving weekend. It rained most of the time and I stayed in my room, studying and avoiding the kitchen philosophers—Ferrano and Hamburger—in the back. Nuclear proliferation, the Iran hostage crisis, the presidential election, Aztec drug use—they had it all figured out.

Saloma brought me Thanksgiving leftovers on Friday, and we enjoyed them in my room. Her family had prepared a traditional American Thanksgiving meal; Saloma had heated it up in the oven before coming over and the sliced turkey, giblet gravy, Brussels sprouts, and twice-baked potatoes were still warm. I unscrewed the cap on a bottle of Gallo burgundy and we drank the wine out of coffee cups.

Saloma was kind, considerate, charming, funny, delightful to be with, exasperating, pampered, spoiled, and uncertain about herself. "Do you think I'm pretty?" she'd ask, or: "Do you like me?" and I'd almost have to laugh. I loved everything about her except her nervousness and her pills. I sometimes thought there was the real Saloma, who was agitated and afraid of sex, and the Saloma on Quaaludes who could relax in my arms and almost allow me to love her fully.

On the afternoon of December 7, 1979, I sat in a small conference room with my three examiners—Dr. Gertrude Ingebore, who was originally from Denmark and had read Ibsen in the original; Professor Fred Gallagher, who was from the Salinas Valley and had known Steinbeck when he was young; and Professor Marlowe Osborne, from the English Department and an expert on contemporary British literature.

The room was uncomfortably warm with a purring radiator on one wall and a narrow cathedral window on the other. My swivel chair seemed to have a broken cylinder, and when I sat down the chair sank until I felt very small positioned at the foot of the table. I was not allowed to have notes or even paper and pencil since this was strictly an oral examination. For four hours, I parried questions, first from Dr. Ingebore, a prim woman in her forties who wore spectacles and a tweed suit. She asked me about surrealism in *Peer Gynt* versus the alleged realism of Ibsen's later plays. Professor Gallagher, who was in his late sixties and could have passed for a U.S. Senator, with his silvery hair and chiseled features, questioned me about Steinbeck's interest in marine biology and whether or not that had influenced his theory of the novel.

"It certainly influenced his theory of human behavior," I countered. "In *The Grapes of Wrath* he dramatized the idea of the phalanx, or mass of individuals that act as a single entity."

That answer took close to half an hour, and I was happy to see my examiners argue amongst themselves. I'd learned long before that three professors in a room would eat up time as voraciously as Steinbeck's invertebrates consumed food debris.

When they turned back to me, Professor Osborne, a youngish man with long red hair who appeared not to have shaved that morning, leaned back in his chair and peered at me down the bridge of his nose.

"Why Fowles?" he posited. "How can you justify the study of someone whose philosophy is so jejune? Whose works are relatively slight and, worse yet—popular?"

It was a legitimate question and one I had anticipated. I'd already had to explain the value of studying Fowles to the graduate committee, and the question had been posed during the practice orals. I argued that Fowles was worth studying because he was indebted both to the Victorian novel and to post-war existentialism and represented a compelling blend of forms.

The radiator rattled, the heat in the room felt like a wet flannel, but I sensed that the exam was going relatively well when, during a short break, Dr. Gallagher placed a reassuring hand on my shoulder and patted me on the back.

The final hour went smoothly and I had the sense that my examiners had reached their decision. We were more like four colleagues in relaxed conversation about the merits of different works and the insights provided by different theories.

I was elated when Dr. Osborne said to his peers: "I think that does it, right? I really don't have any further questions."

He turned to me, then stood.

"Allow me to be the first to congratulate you."

I felt happy, exhausted, and proud, and we shook hands all around.

I was especially gratified when Dr. Osborne presented me with the British first edition of *The French Lieutenant's Woman.*

"I am very happy to accept this," I beamed, then added as an afterthought: "I don't have many hardbounds."

* * *

Saloma was attending a wedding in Bakersfield, so I would share my good news with her when she was back. I drove to the Mission District to relax and gather my thoughts. I found a hole-in-the-wall Korean café where I could order a huge bowl of bibimbap for a couple of dollars and could feast on the fried egg and pickled vegetables, the rice and stewed beef. I washed the meal down with a couple of Jinro beers.

I felt I had really accomplished something. I'd been driving toward this goal for a long time, and with Saloma away for the weekend I was going to use the time productively—maybe type my thesis according to the university's specifications. Using my blue electric typewriter with the handheld correction tape to format a forty-page play was a painstaking process, and if there were too many corrections I had to retype the entire page. But I felt good about the project too.

My rewritten play—a kind of *The Iceman Cometh* set in the backroom of a liquor store in East L.A.—had already been accepted as a creative thesis. I hoped it might be produced at A.C.T. where some of Ramsay O'Donnell's work had premiered, but nothing came of those attempts in the new year.

Many years later, when I was long gone from San Francisco and was successfully publishing short stories, I looked back at that old play and realized characterization needed to be deepened and that the women characters in particular seemed one-dimensional. I pared down the play, extracting what I thought was dross and rewriting the female characters. I borrowed from relationships later in life, when I knew more. The play became a short story and I had good luck marketing it.

But what was yet unknown, what had not yet been lived, was of no comfort to me as I paid the Korean cook for my bibimbap and beer.

A corner drugstore stood on the other side of Guerrero Street and I wanted to tell my parents how I'd done. The Friday night traffic was heavy with cars moving steadily in both directions, but I saw an opening and dashed across the street, weaving between a sedan and a sports car and reaching the curb. Someone honked at me and yelled. I didn't care.

The drugstore was long and narrow, with barrels of candy and shelves of chocolate bars protruding and making the passageway even smaller. I passed a revolving comic book rack and large display cases with wristwatches and instamatic cameras. The druggist was behind a counter at the back of the room; the telephone booth was edged into the corner next to a pinball machine, where two Latinos in work shirts and construction boots slapped the flippers noisily. As I opened the folding door of the phone booth, I heard the metal ball of the machine careen each time through a series of rattling flaps, sounding buzzers, and clanging bells.

It was a bit less noisy with the folding door closed, but the drugstore wasn't going to win any prizes for acoustic design, I thought as I picked up the handset, dropped a coin in the slot, and dialed the operator. I gave her my parents' phone number and said I was calling collect.

My father answered. He accepted the charges.

"I have some good news, Dad. Is Mutti there?"

"She's at church," he grunted. "Novena."

"Oh . . . I passed my exams."

I could barely hear myself speak because of the clanging pinball machine. I saw the two men slap down dollar bills and shout when they racked up a score.

"What exam is this?" my father asked. "French?"

"No," I replied, suddenly feeling drained. I hadn't realized how tired I really was from the weeks of study, the anxiety, the examination itself, and the emotional highs and lows of the semester. "My qualifying exams," I explained. "For my master's. I passed."

"Oh, that's good," he uttered from the other end. "I'll tell your mother you called."

He hung up.

I stood in the phone booth for a moment and tried to sort out my feelings of surprise and disappointment. He didn't even know what degree I was working on. I thought he did, but maybe he'd already had a few too many that night. Still, I felt lost and alienated. I remembered how I'd felt a year-and-a-half before when I'd just returned to the States from Scotland and stood in a phone booth at the Greyhound station in New York to tell my parents I was okay.

"I'm okay," I told myself in the drugstore phone booth in San Francisco. "Just a little disoriented."

* * *

Why should my father have understood my world, I think now. He had once told me I would never understand what it was like for him in Morocco in the 1930s. With enough effort and travel, I might have come close, but he was right: We lived in our own cocoons, separated by language and culture and era. And yet, I knew it was important for me to try to understand.

We got on better in later years; even grew close. Not so long after I finished my master's degree, he quit drinking as a condition of having his license reinstated and was dry for almost seven years. Even in retirement, when he started having his copita again, his drinking was never quite as bad.

In his own gruff, unemotive way, he tried to be a good father, and so long as he could give me advice we got along well. But there were strains when I became better established.

"Mr. Big Shot Professor," he would say, or "Mr. Big Shot Executive."

But we traveled together, the four of us, and I took him through French Canada and on trips to his beloved Spain.

We never made it to Morocco, though we looked out across the Straits of Gibraltar once toward Tangiers. We would have taken the ferry that day, except the crossing was too rough.

It wasn't all bad, on balance. In retirement, he started accompanying my mother to Mass, but I'm not sure the Church meant much to him except a place with a community room where he could tell his stories.

He died at the age of eighty-four after a year-long illness that left him weak and angry.

CHAPTER SEVEN

A few academic tasks remained at the close of the semester before I could head south for the Christmas holiday break. I had already bought my Amtrak train ticket for the nine-hour rail journey on December 21 and had arranged for Vince Vizcaino, an old pal in Los Angeles and my former college roommate, to pick me up at L.A.'s Union station. We would have drinks at Stottlemeyer's across the tracks at Ord and Hill or grab a bite at a Mexican restaurant on Olivera Street before heading to Orange County, where Vince's parents also lived. But first, I needed to finish up the term.

In the few days remaining, I submitted a rewritten seminar paper for Lenny Levinski and the middle chapters of a flawed novel I worked on for Walter Wilson's workshop. I also wanted to spend as much time as possible with Saloma. We'd talked about her visiting me in Southern California, but she was going to be busy with Parol, the Filipino lantern festival held each year near St. Patrick Church in San Francisco, and I was going to work down south with my father at the Carriage House Hotel in Mission Viejo during the busy holiday period. The hours would be grueling, but I knew the restaurant trade and needed to see some pluses in my checkbook.

The last night of term, Eddie showed up for Walt Wilson's workshop because his typescript was being critiqued. He kept his Trilby hat as far back on his head as possible, like a monk's skull cap, and rocked his chair on its rear legs. As Professor Wilson led the discussion by comparing Eddie's work to Mickey Spillane's—unfavorably, for that matter—Eddie looked pale, his face thin and greasy and his jawline showed several days' beard growth. He coughed incessantly and left at the break, saying to a few of us near the vending machine: "See ya at Buchanan's in a few."

I felt more relaxed after passing my qualifying exam and having almost completed my thesis. As a result, I decided to stop off at Buchanan's when Dr. Wilson's workshop ended. Serge, whose novel on drug-running was also critiqued that night, normally headed straight back to Mill Valley after class. Since it was the last night of term, he said he would stop off as well.

Buchanan's was already decorated for Christmas—that is, the Christmas lights which hung year-round above the bar were on, as always, and the clown paintings on the wall looked forbidding in the glow of the holiday bulbs. Eddie was already at a corner table with a pitcher of beer and a shot glass in front of him. I sat down and asked him about his cough. He claimed he'd just taken something for it but seemed to chortle deep in his lungs.

"I find out next week whether it's strep or mono," he snorted. "I've been feeling like shit."

"You don't look well," I commented. He grimaced and

saluted me with his beer glass, then signaled the waitress to bring me an empty one. When she did, Eddie filled it for me. "Thanks. Where've you been keeping yourself lately?" I asked.

Eddie smiled broadly.

"Shit, man. I've just got back from this tremendous trip—six days of opium, acid, hash. Tremendous. But I'm clean now. That's why I showed up for class."

I noted that the critique of his work was useful, even if Walt Wilson thought the actor Robert Gray made a lousy Mike Hammer in *My Gun is Quick.*

"Always the movies," Eddie remarked. "Someone always did it before, but better, and usually in a B-movie. What did Wilson say about the femme fatale in your story?"

"Joan Crawford did it a thousand times in the movies—but better."

We laughed and clinked glasses.

Serge came in and sat down with us. He brushed back his short sandy hair and looked pleased. He congratulated me on my exams and the acceptance of my thesis.

"Thanks, Serge." I looked from Serge to Eddie, then back. "You had a good semester yourself. Wilson had a lot of positive things to say about your novel tonight. It has some strong scenes."

"I missed all that," Eddie cut in. "It must have been after break." He turned to me. "Yeah, so your thesis. Think you'll ever finish it?"

I took a sip of beer and indulged him with a tight smile. Eddie was the one who would probably never finish anything, and I had realized over the past year-and-a-half that he relished the thought others might fail too.

"It's almost done. As Serge said, it's been accepted, but I still need to type it up according to specifications."

"Think you'll get it done anytime soon?"

"The typing, maybe. But by the time I get through the graduation audit and the rest of the rigamarole, I won't be able to receive my degree until May."

"So what will you do next semester?" Serge asked.

I shrugged.

"I'll probably register for a couple of French and German classes and hang out."

"Yeah, hang out and slip the steel into that bitch you're always with," Eddie interjected.

I ignored him.

"And I start a new job in January—with OSHA—as a clerk/typist GS3." The waitress brought over an extra glass and I filled it for Serge. We clinked glasses. Eddie joined in reluctantly. "As 'Government Service Grade 3' I'll be in the big money!"

Serge and I laughed. Eddie's look darkened. He sat back in his chair and glared at me: "What's her name, anyway?" This was a strange question. Eddie knew her from Dr. Papandrakis' office.

"Saloma," I said.

Eddie leaned forward.

"Didja fuck her yet?"

"El hombre llega donde la mujer quiere," I said quietly.

"What's that mean?"

"A man arrives where the woman allows."

"Sounds like bullshit to me." Then, after a pause, Eddie asked pointedly: "No more Wilson Weekly Workshops for you?"

"Probably not. After a while you outgrow the workshop."

I knew what was wrong with my novel about an L.A. cab strike: I had made character subservient to plot, and I knew how to fix it. I'd have to stick the typescript in a drawer for a couple of years and, if I ever returned to it, jettison the melodrama and the heroics and describe people as they were. Either that, or extract a few of the more vivid scenes and rewrite them as short stories.

I drank my beer as we launched into the favorite topic of graduate students—the indifference of professors and their inability to appreciate fine work. Even Serge, whose work was almost always praised, put in that Professor Wilson always tried to find the formula.

"Find the genre and we know the piece."

"That's right." Eddie slammed down his beer glass. "Everything has to be like something else. My story is like a third-rate Raymond Chandler piece of shit."

"Raymond Chandler is a good writer," Serge pointed out. "I think he compared your story to a third-rate Mickey Spillane piece of shit."

"Yeah, right."

Eddie turned to the bar and signaled for another pitcher. The waitress brought it to our table. The beer slopped over the brim and foamed down the sides. Eddie offered to refill Serge's glass but he placed his palm over the opening.

"No thanks." Serge shook his head gently. "I know my limit."

"Yeah?" Eddie tried to suppress a cough deep in his chest. His skin was a pasty yellow and his beard stubble stood out against it. "Well, I know my limit too."

He called to the waitress: "Shot of bourbon. Make it two!"

Serge and I looked at each other.

Eddie leaned forward. Sweat had broken out on his upper lip and his cheeks were sunken.

"Diego? You just passed your exams, right? Well, I know a thing or two about your writers, and I bet it didn't come up on the exam. They were all boozers."

The waitress brought over two shots. Eddie slugged the first one down, then guzzled his beer.

"Ibsen—got drunk all the time when he wasn't working on a play. I read that somewhere. Bet no one asked you about Ibsen's heavy drinking."

"No," I said quietly. "It didn't come up."

"And what about Steinbeck?" Eddie gulped the second shot. "I don't see how anyone that prolific wouldn't have been a boozer. It's the pressure."

"Is that how you excuse it?" Serge asked, and Eddie glared at him. I thought Eddie would lunge across the table, but he slumped back in his chair. The look of hatred didn't fade, but his face was ashen and pasty.

"The horror! The horror!" I mimicked in my best attempt at an incoherent Marlon Brando. "The pressure!"

Apocalypse Now had just come out and everyone thought Marlon Brando had ruined an otherwise great movie. I knew Eddie thought the same way about the film.

"Yeah, the horror," Eddie said, laughing at himself. He looked subdued drinking his beer, but I thought I'd try to defuse the situation further by agreeing with Eddie about Wilson's class.

"Eddie's right, though, about the workshop," I asserted. "Wilson puts too much emphasis on straight-up realism, which he defines as the slow, steady accumulation of detail. He seems never to have heard of Magical Realism, or Surrealism, or Expressionism. Everything has to sound like James Gould Cozzens and be written in third person limited omniscient."

I looked at my companions. They were nodding in agreement.

"Every scene has to be comprised of action, reaction, memory." I parodied: *"He looked at the sky. It was blue. A cloud passed. It was white. He remembered the last time he had seen a cloud."*

We crowed with laughter, and even Eddie seemed relaxed. But as I drank my beer, I started to think that Chandler, Cozzens, Hemingway, Mailer were all part of a dying cult of experience. Going off to war or working on a freighter and writing about it was a step to becoming a writer in the 'twenties, 'thirties, and 'forties, but it wasn't necessarily a stepping-stone anymore. Contemporary writers—John Updike, Saul Bellow, Margaret Atwood—held university posts.

I tried to avoid the triple mediocrities for the aspiring writer —journalism, translation, teaching—but maybe the last one wasn't all that bad; or maybe I was just trying to convince myself I didn't have to seek experience, that it was nearby—just a short drive to a woman's apartment, and from there an even shorter drive to suburban bliss.

* * *

I informed the Department of Social Work that I wouldn't be returning in the new year and that I'd accepted a position as a civil service clerk/typist. The Department hosted a farewell party, with Dr. Leming presenting me with an anthology of Beat Generation poetry. Dr. Russell told me not to be a stranger and Dr. Morales said to me in Spanish that all good things come to those who wait. I also received a cash bonus for unused vacation time and sick days. I was happy about that, even though I knew the money would go fast.

I wasn't able to see Saloma until Wednesday, December 19, two days before I'd take the train to Los Angeles. Understandably, she was busy with holiday commitments, but her large family seemed to put excessive demands on her time. There was always a baby shower or a baptism, an anniversary celebration or a birthday. Worse yet, as the eldest daughter, she felt obliged to run constant errands for her mother or to spend an entire day escorting her from shop to shop, sitting at the beauty salon, or at some novena or rosary service at the Filipino church.

Still, I looked forward to being with her before my trip. We had agreed to meet at five p.m. at the corner of Market and Powell in front of the Woolworth's and by the cable car turntable.

I rode the MUNI down Market, but the streetcar was packed with holiday shoppers and tourists and we moved slowly on the tracks in the rush hour traffic. I'd dressed for comfort and for the brisk December air and wore an open Navy pea coat with an orange turtleneck sweater and light blue slacks. I decided I'd make better time on foot. I hopped off at Hyde Street, just past the Hotel Whitcomb, and walked the last few blocks, passing florist shops and newsstands and a tobacconist.

I kept an Irish flat cap folded in my coat pocket, just in case it got too cold, but I felt warm and full of life and sang "We've Got a Groovy Kind of Love" as I walked to our rendezvous.

In front of the Woolworth's a crowd had gathered and formed a wide circle. A boombox was in the middle of the circle blasting out a hip-hop version of "Apache," and three African-American break-dancers entertained the crowd with their swirling, rolling, rotating acrobatics. I watched for a while.

The cable car came clanging on its tracks down Powell and reached the round wooden turntable at the end of the street. A line of tourists waited to board. The conductor jumped out, grabbed the cable car's stanchions, and rotated the cable car and turntable. Several tourists helped him swing the car around, then took their seats or stood on the running board.

I looked at my watch. It was already five-fifteen and I was

getting nervous. I walked in the direction of the Powell Street BART station, expecting Saloma to emerge any minute. I told myself it didn't matter if Saloma was a bit late. The transit trains might have been delayed. It was almost five-thirty, and I paced back in the direction of Woolworth's.

Saloma exited from the department store's revolving door. I caught my breath. Normally, I would have thought she looked adorable in a mid-length camel wool coat with faux fur trim at the cuffs and collar, wide-leg brown trousers, with short brown boots and a leather handbag to match.

She was delightfully stylish, but her face was taut, her eyes red from tears, and her lower lip quivered.

"What is it?"

She shook her head. She seemed unable to speak. She quickly walked north on Powell and I strode next to her. I took her arm, but she shook free of me, then stopped.

"I'll be okay. I thought I was over it."

"Let's sit down," I coaxed. "Let's find a place where we can talk."

I'd planned to take Saloma to dinner at one of the finer establishments near Union Square for our last night together before the holidays, but now I just looked for the nearest diner where we could sit and she could tell me what was wrong. We walked for another five minutes, past a police car with its lights flashing, a group of cheering college students entering the lobby of a hotel, a well-dressed African-American couple strolling arm in arm. A delivery boy on a bicycle shot past and we heard the rousing notes of a Salvation Army Band play Christmas music as we turned onto Geary from Powell.

The walk, the brisk air, the lack of conversation between us must have helped Saloma calm down. She didn't seem as agitated. She let me take her arm and hold the door for her as we entered the Pinecrest Diner.

A cook in a starched white shirt and paper service cap looked at us from behind the counter. A middle-aged waitress in a checkered apron stood in the center of the aisle and called out: "Hi, kids. Sit anywhere."

I led Saloma to a window booth that looked out on Mason. I could see taxi cabs and couples headed for a show in the Theater District. *Evita* was playing and was all the rage. I envied the happy couples, but maybe they were happy only because at some point in their lives they had waded through despair.

I turned to Saloma. I decided not to say anything. She smiled wanly. The waitress set two laminated menus in front of us.

The Pinecrest Diner was the kind of place that had a single sheet menu, with vivid Kodacolor photos front and back depicting food items—double cheeseburgers with a side of fries or eggs over easy and hash browns. But as with a lot of cafés and diners in the City, they served drinks. I ordered a vodka martini for the lady and one for myself.

"It'll calm your nerves."

"I've heard that one before."

"Not so long ago, either."

We toasted when the martinis came, and I told the waitress we might order something to eat a bit later. When she left, I looked back at Saloma. "I guess you'll tell me when you're ready."

She brushed her eyes with the back of her hand. "I'm just being silly. I know I get so nervous this time of the year. It's a kind of anniversary."

"An anniversary?"

"Three years ago, in December, my little cousin Tommy got sick and died."

"Yes, you told me you were very close to him." Sometimes I

thought Saloma needed help— "intervention" the social workers and psychologists called it. I wanted to help her any way I could, but I wasn't a professional. All I could do was maybe tell her that I loved her and try to comfort her.

"I thought I was over it," she repeated.

I considered what I might say next. "You must have studied the process of grieving in your psychology classes. This is probably normal." As soon as I mouthed the words, I knew it sounded like a platitude, but went on anyway. "It just takes time."

She toyed with the pink plastic sword in the martini glass, stirred her drink, and gave me a half-hearted smile.

"We were very rich in Manila. It was sick. Almost everyone is dirt poor there. They live in the slums or they sleep in the park. But my life was being driven around everywhere, a personal servant, debutante balls. Tommy's family was very rich too, even in the States, but that didn't save him. Nothing did."

The streetlights glowed on Mason and Geary. Office workers rushed past or paused to read menus in outdoor display cases. The traffic was steady, with cars turning left or right at the intersection, all of them with their headlamps on.

"Listen, maybe we should eat something," I suggested. "Have you looked at the menu?"

"I don't think I'm hungry."

I signaled the waitress. "You really do need to eat something."

At the end, Saloma ordered a cup of soup and a half sandwich. I offered her a cut of my Swiss steak, which she accepted. We shared a carafe of burgundy.

During the meal, she told me more about her affection for Tommy. She placed a packet of Virginia Slims on the table, took out a cigarette but didn't light it. When she thought I wasn't watching, she swallowed a small beige pill, ate a piece of bread, and sipped her wine.

"Do you know, he was so cute when he was three years old, I was jealous when he had playmates—girlfriends, I called them—his own age. I told him I was his girlfriend and he'd have to give up all the others."

I thought she was going to cry again, but instead she calmed and smiled tenderly.

"I used to dress him up in tiny polished black shoes and a little tuxedo and I'd knot his bowtie for him. I told him he'd have to ask me for a date, and we'd go out together into the garden and I'd hold his hand."

Someone once told me no matter how beautiful a woman is, you'd better know what you're getting into, but I'd never been very good at following advice. Sitting with Saloma, listening to her, I felt drained. How could I compete with a dead six-year-old? I wondered if there was any room in Saloma's heart for me or for normal affection. But then she said: "I'm so sorry, Diego. I was really looking forward to spending a wonderful evening with you and now I've ruined it."

"It's okay." I managed a thin smile.

"I even got to Powell Street an hour early because I wanted to buy something nice for you at Woolworth's. Maybe a nice leather-bound journal that you could write in. But then I wandered through the children's clothing section, saw the tiny shoes, the outfits, and it all came rushing back."

* * *

Outside, on the street corner, I held her close and kissed her, as gently as I could.

"I want you to be happy, Saloma," I told her. She nodded, and I kissed her again. We walked toward Union Square and

I put my arm around her waist. I felt her head on my shoulder.

The streets shimmered with the lights of the City, the animated Dickensian figures in shop window displays, the warm glow from the rooms of the St. Francis. The beams of white light illuminated the Dewey monument in the center of Union Square.

We crossed Powell to the Square and could see the City of Paris department store, with a replica of the Eiffel Tower on its roof; Macy's in a massive white marble building and the TWA office on the ground floor. A sixty-foot Norwegian pine, decorated with ornaments and tinsel, was on the east side of the square. Benches were nearby and some blanketed shapes slept on top. A few shrouded figures huddled on the grass or paced up and down; the glowing coal of their cigarettes moved with them.

We avoided the homeless people who slept rough and headed to the west side of the square where merrymakers pressed against the encircled fence of an ice-skating rink. Skaters moved in multiple patterns—some gracefully, most skittered like colts, to the sound of a calliope playing "The Blue Danube." We watched for a while in amusement. The rink was crowded with children and young couples; many of the skaters pulled themselves along the inside railing, venturing onto the ice for a few awkward steps, then stumbled. One couple seemed adept at figure skating and moved in rhythm to the waltz.

"Can you skate?" she asked.

"Me? I grew up in Southern California. Most people in this rink can't skate either."

Saloma snuggled against me as we watched. We were content from the wine and the meal and with each other. I could feel her warmth, her body comfortably nestled against mine.

"I only went ice skating once," I told her, "at an indoor rink in Pasadena. My roommate was from Maine and offered to teach me how to ice skate. I spent most of the time on my hands and knees, and when he tried to help me up he skated across my fingers."

"You poor thing."

"I can laugh about it now," I grimmaced, "but it hurt like hell. I still have the scars."

"Show me."

I held up my left hand. Saloma touched my fingers gingerly and felt the squiggly marks that crisscrossed my knuckles and fingers. She pressed my hand to her lips and kissed the old scars, then made a sucking sound on the knuckles.

She arched her back so that her face was pressed up toward mine, and I kissed her deeply. She rubbed her lips across mine, then kissed me along the cheek until her mouth was against my ear.

"I have a Christmas surprise, Diego," she whispered. "My sister's at a conference the rest of the week. She won't be back until Friday."

* * *

We took a taxi to Saloma's apartment.

In her living room, we snuggled and caressed each other on the couch and drank Sheffield dry sherry. It was chilled but warmed us inside. I always kept a condom in my wallet, just in case, but I didn't know what would happen if there was a second act. I didn't even know if there would be a first act, but Saloma said: "Let's go upstairs and shower first."

It was the first time I'd been in Saloma's bedroom, and it bothered me initially: the lavender curtains, the duvet with a daisy and butterfly pattern, the stuffed toy animals on the dresser, the framed photo on her nightstand of a little boy in a tuxedo and bowtie, who I assumed was her deceased cousin Tommy. But when we undressed, Saloma took me by the hand into the adjacent bathroom and we showered together in the small stall. I thought she had a fabulous body, small but shapely, with round firm breasts and a tuft of dark hair pointing to her labia.

I was erect just looking at her. I washed her first, running the bar of soap down her back and along the smooth curve of her buttocks, then gently between her legs. She turned and we kissed as the water cascaded down our bodies, enveloping us. I slithered the soap around her breasts and down her stomach. My penis ached for her, and I felt her grip it.

"My turn," she said, taking the bar of soap from me.

We laughed and kissed each other in the shower stall. She lathered my chest and backside, sliding the bar of soap between my legs. She fondled me and worked her slippery hand back and forth.

"Go slowly," I told her. She used a soapy washcloth. My stiff penis was engulfed in it and I felt her grip tighten. "Not too fast. I'm saving myself."

"For marriage?"

"For when I'm inside you."

She didn't say anything but let me press my throbbing penis between her legs. I felt the coarse dark hairs and the soft flesh of her pudendum.

We dried each other. I toweled her head lovingly and enjoyed the weight and shape of her breasts. She rubbed the towel carefully around my genitals and then more vigorously across my shoulders and backside.

We fell on the bed. I was still fully erect and her hand reached out for me. I stroked her hair and kissed her.

"Are you sure?" I asked her.

She took my hand in hers and kissed the palm. "I lost control about an hour ago."

We smiled and nuzzled our faces together, then started to kiss open mouthed, our tongues in a kind of dance. I caressed her breasts, felt her thighs hug me, her legs and ankles locked around my waist. I let the round head of my penis enter her moist divide, thrust, prod. My trousers were on a coat hook, with my wallet and the condom inside. She reached down and moved my penis to one side and with a series of quick, clutching strokes brought me to orgasm. As usual, I had to content myself with ejaculating against her thigh.

I rolled onto my back and lay there, breathing heavily. Saloma's breath came in short, shallow gasps, almost in a whimper. Minutes passed. I heard tires on a road, saw the flash of headlights on the window.

"Are you alright, Saloma?"

She didn't say anything.

I turned on my side and looked at her. She neared tears.

"I love you, Saloma."

She turned away from me, curled up.

"This has to stop. I feel too guilty, Diego." After a long pause, she continued: "You should feel guilty too."

"Right, like a good Catholic," I snapped. "I don't feel guilty about loving you." I sat on the edge of the bed. "I need to get some air."

I was about to reach for my clothes and get dressed when I felt Saloma touch my back. She caressed my shoulder. She was crying. I took her in my arms and kissed her, said: "I'm sorry, darling."

"I'm sorry too," she replied.

As I held her, I became aroused and she guided me inside her. This time, *I* felt tremendous guilt. I thrust inside her but thought of everything that could go wrong. She was fragile and childlike in so many ways. She was troubled and disturbed, mercurial, unstable; I never knew what was going on with her. And what if she got pregnant? I had nothing but a pocketful of dreams; she would never dislodge herself from her oppressive family and they would never accept me—an outsider, a nonbeliever, a threadbare graduate student. But above all, I was fundamentally unreliable, restless, always looking for the next change of scene and running toward some goal I couldn't even identify.

It was enough to make a man go soft, detumescent, and I withdrew from her and rolled onto my back.

"What's wrong?"

"Nothing," I lied. "I just came fifteen minutes ago. We're both tired."

She nodded and snuggled next to me. She rubbed my chest and ran her hand down my stomach.

"Let's get some sleep, Diego. I want to wake up next to you and still be your friend."

I wasn't hungry the next morning and had slept only a few hours. I dressed in my clothes from the night before and sat at Saloma's small kitchen table. She put on a thin orange and black dressing gown in a Batik pattern and tied her hair in a bun. She made coffee in an electric percolator and I watched the dark fluid gurgle into the plastic cap on the lid. The newspaper sat on the table in front of me, folded in half. I pressed the paper flat and glanced at the headlines. It was all bad news:

EXPLOSION AND FIRE ON S.S. SAN PEDRO
DAY 47: U.S. HOSTAGES IN TEHERAN
INCREASED SOVIET MILITARY ACTIVITY ON AFGHAN BORDER

I refolded the paper and set it aside, then heard Saloma open the refrigerator and a cupboard door. "Can I help?" I offered.

She shook her head. She split two English muffins in half, then placed them in a toaster. Water boiled in a small saucepan and Saloma cracked two eggs into it followed by a shot of vinegar. I could smell Canadian bacon frying. When the toaster popped up, Saloma assembled the breakfast sandwiches, adding a slice of cheddar cheese.

She placed a plate in front of me and poured coffee into a logoed mug that read: "Safeway."

"Looks great," I said. "If these were served open-face with Hollandaise sauce they'd be called 'Eggs Benedict.'"

"I thought they were just plain old 'Egg McMuffin.'"

"Am I boring you?"

"A little."

She smiled and sat down opposite me with an identical mug of coffee and breakfast sandwich.

"You'll be busy with your Dad working in the restaurant."

"It's only for a few weeks."

"Four weeks. That's a month."

"Look, the time will pass quickly. It's the busiest time of the year in the restaurant trade. I'll be able to make some money and pay off some bills." I took a bite of the sandwich and chewed thoughtfully. "And you'll be busy with El Farol."

"Parol," she corrected me. "And it's only one night."

"And then there's Noche Buena."

"Noche Buena," she repeated. The words for "Christmas Eve" were the same in both Spanish and Tagalog.

She ate half her sandwich, pushed the plate aside.

"Listen," I said, "Maybe this is a really good thing for us. It'll give us a chance to let things cool off for a while." She looked at me, held the coffee mug to her lips but didn't drink. "Look, I like living dangerously," I resumed. "Close to the edge, but I don't want to go too far."

She got up and placed her plate near the sink, dumped out her coffee and started to wash the mug. "Maybe we already have."

I slumped in my chair. There was no taking back what had happened last night. Even though I hadn't come inside her, there had been enough residual semen on my spent penis to have impregnated her. I didn't need a medical degree to know it only took one sperm cell and one egg under certain conditions.

"I think you're right." Her back was to me and she stood over the sink. "We should take a break from each other. Let things cool."

"Saloma," I called. She turned to me. "Sit down—please."

She brushed a wisp of hair from her forehead, took the chair opposite me, and wore a thin, tired smile. I took her hand.

"Whatever happens, I'll do right by you. If you need me, I'm there. I'll find a way."

She gave a slight nod, then turned her face from me and slipped her hand from mine. She seemed to be staring at the kitchen curtain. I looked at her profile, watched wordlessly. I didn't think she was going to cry, but her lower lip trembled and she blinked tears from her eyes.

"We'll write," I said.

"Our letters will cross." She had regained her sense of humor and looked back at me with mild amusement.

"No, seriously. If anything comes up you can phone me at

my parents'. I'll give you their number." I looked around. "Do you have anything to write on?"

She pulled open a small drawer underneath the kitchen table and tossed me a book of matches. I wrote my name and parents' phone number on the back cover, then turned it over. It was from Señor Pico's where we had first enjoyed cocktails together.

The mist slid across the windows of the train and it rained for much of the journey. I watched the pattern of raindrops on the glass and the streaks formed by the wind outside. I had gotten up early to catch the 6:01 Coast Daylight and had left my car in long-term parking. For the first hour or so of the train ride, I was groggy and restless, dozed fitfully and tried not to think too much. I wasn't going to abandon her; that much was clear. The train clicked through the outer suburbs, then sped down tracks through the backside of towns, past warehouses and loading bays, grain silos and packing plants.

Would I have to get a job in one of those towns teaching English at a Catholic high school? I didn't have a teaching credential, but a private school might hire me. Or maybe I'd have to take an office job in one of those packing plants, processing orders. And for how long? There were too many differences between us for a union to last very long—a few years, maybe. In the long term, I couldn't see us making each other very happy—possibly staying together for the sake of a child, making each other miserable, as my parents had.

It was too much to think about, and I tried turning over in my seat, placing my flat cap against the window and using it as a pillow. The train lurched to a halt at the station in Salinas and I idly watched passengers board; a mother with two children, a sailor, a young man and woman with tie-dyed shirts and beaded headbands. They held stacks of pamphlets and beamed broadly. I pretended to be asleep when the young couple passed through, telling everyone about their love for Jesus, that Christ was our savior. I felt a hand grip my shoulder, shake me.

I looked up to see the young man with his scraggly beard and long hair parted in the middle. He grinned toothily and waved a pamphlet.

"Have you heard the good news?"

"Fuck off."

* * *

I talked to a young woman in the club car, Annie. She was pert and had wavy blonde hair and wore a green leather jacket and a plaid skirt. She told me she was traveling to Santa Barbara to stay with her fiancé's family for the holidays. I said I was headed to Orange County for a few weeks. Later, back at my seat, I tried reading Dos Passos' *Nineteen-Nineteen*.

An older man with a crew-cut and gnarly workman's hands got on at San Luis Obispo and sat opposite me. He related that he'd retired from Southern Pacific Railroad a few years back but had travelled all over the country.

"Best place for steak is Kansas City," he enthused. "Bar none. Best place for seafood is South Portland, in Maine. Can't be beat."

It stopped raining near Oxnard and I enjoyed the last few miles from Chatsworth to Union Station, seeing the rugged rock formations where cowboy films were shot in the 'twenties, the snow-covered peaks of the San Bernardino Mountains that, horseshoe-like, shaped the L.A Basin, and the conglomeration of dense neighborhoods on the final run into town.

* * *

"It's the Friday before Christmas," Vince teased me. "You couldn't have picked a worse time to arrive."

I'd known Vince since freshman year in high school. Later, four of us had shared a two-bedroom apartment in college. We'd done a lot of SCUBA diving together, including wreck dives off Coronado Island and a two-week dive trip to Cozumel. Now, he worked for a furniture store in downtown Anaheim and had just finalized his divorce.

"Great to see you, Vince."

We embraced and he helped me with my bags as we left the Moorish-style train station and headed to the parking lot.

He looked good; he'd put on some weight, but mostly on the shoulders and upper arms. He kept his brown hair short and had shaved off his "Joe College" beard. I commented on it.

"Now that you're in sales," I ribbed him, "you have to look like Clark Kent."

"I thought I looked more like Clark Gable," he kidded, "without the moustache."

Vince put my bags in the trunk of his Ford Capri and we drove from Alameda Street through L.A.'s Chinatown and the brightly decorated lanes of Little Tokyo, then down Broadway with its pawn shops and camera stores, past Central Market and movie palaces that advertised "Cantinflas" on the marquees.

We merged onto the Santa Ana Freeway and moved steadily for a few miles.

"We'll see how far we get," Vince said, "in this traffic. When we're hungry, we'll pull over somewhere. Maybe the Wagon Wheel in Downey. Get a couple of steaks."

"My treat," I insisted. "You drove all the way into town to pick me up."

"No big deal," Vince shrugged. "I had to call on a couple of clients in Hancock Park anyway. Show them the new catalogue."

Vince had majored in psychology and business, so it was no surprise he had ended up in sales. I mentioned that, and he joked: "It was either selling high-end furniture or tending bar. Either way—psych and business—it's paycheck time."

He turned to me as he drove.

"So you still have your goatee."

"It's a Van Dyke."

"Same damn thing," he said, cursing a driver who cut in front of us. Vince honked his horn and muttered: "Son-of-a-bitch." He shook his head. "Some things never change—bumper-to-bumper traffic on the Five—" He smiled. "You."

"I've changed."

"I doubt it. I'll bet you're still the idealist." He lifted his hand from the steering wheel and punched my shoulder lightly. "I miss your b.s. Remember all those late-night bull sessions in college? 'What is the meaning of existence?' 'What is the nature of art?' I'll bet you're still bullshitting about those things."

I didn't say anything but watched the traffic ooze like mud down a narrow creek bed. I wished it were so, that I was still thinking about frivolous artistic pursuits rather than whether I'd gotten Saloma pregnant. My palms were moist and I rubbed them on my trousers.

We had reached Commerce and were inching past the Uniroyal Factory, disguised as an Assyrian palace with carvings of winged creatures and charioteers. We had entered that section of Interstate-5 where a billboard seemed planted every hundred feet: a rugged-looking cowboy on horseback advertised Marlboro cigarettes; a picture of a sleek Cadillac DeVille hung in the air, suspended over the near-motionless southbound commuter cars.

Vince switched on the air conditioner even though it was December.

"So how's San Francisco? Must be great, huh? Ride the cable car down to Fisherman's Wharf, have a shrimp cocktail every day. See the Giants at Candlestick Park."

I thought about it. My reality was never knowing where I was with Saloma. Her graduate thesis was on "Low Self-Esteem Among Filipino-American Women," for god's sake. I lived in a rooming house where the boarders sat in the kitchen all day, where sirens kept me awake at night, and where broken glass had to be swept from the sidewalk each morning.

"Sure, it's great if you're a tourist," I told Vince. "If you live there, it's like a foreign country."

He looked at me. He could probably tell I was becoming agitated.

"What do you mean?"

"The City always seems on edge—about to blow up." I tried to laugh. "The people are strange, everyone's neurotic, and I have a girlfriend who's an emotional mess."

"You have a girlfriend?"

I told him about Saloma, the prison of family, religion, and personal history she lived in; the uncertainty I dealt with in caring for her. When I'd summed up, Vince said simply: "She sounds like bad news."

It was more complicated than that—at least for me.

"She's very beautiful and I love her," I said.

"Bad news is bad news."

We could see the Kraft Cheese factory, steam billowed from the stacks, and the exit sign for Buena Park next to the site of the closed Japanese Village and Deer Park.

Vince eased the car onto the off-ramp.

"You don't want to end up like me and Suzette. Just another statistic in California."

I knew all about that sad story. I'd been best man at their wedding three years before. Most of us had tried to talk Vince out of his wedding plans. He was twenty-one and still in college; she was eighteen and still in high school, but they had dated for two years because the two families were neighbors. The marriage had lasted less than a year.

"I was sorry to hear it didn't work out."

"Yeah," Vince muttered. He drove down Artesia past a row of wooden buildings: the Buena Park News, a Great Western hardware store, a bicycle repair shop. "At least she didn't get pregnant. That would have been a disaster."

CHAPTER EIGHT

On Saturday, my parents wanted to visit Alpine Village in Torrance for some last-minute Christmas shopping. The plaza of European-style specialty shops was an easy drive from their home but because it was in the next county, and I'd lived in L.A. during my college years, they asked me to drive.

I backed the family car—a used 1970 Buick Regal—down the short driveway and onto the narrow street. My mother always drove used cars; my father owned new motorcycles—usually three at a time, but if even one of them was in good working order, he was lucky. Typically, one of them started after a few hard kicks; the other two were generally disassembled, with various large parts lying like split cabbage heads on the garage floor.

My parents were in the back seat, which felt odd, as if I were a chauffeur. Then again, I'd driven a taxi in L.A., a delivery van, an appliance truck.

My parents were in costume for the day, like two Bavarian shopkeepers. My father wore a dark grey Trachten, or winter suit, that he'd bought on a trip to Austria. It had a high stiff collar, military style, with dark green trim. His dress hat, with deer tail and hiking badges, and alpine necktie with embroidered acorns, completed the look. My mother wore a blue Dirndl, low at the bosom in the traditional style, and a mid-sleeved white blouse with lacework at the elbows. Her hair was coiffed and puffed up high and an Edelweiss pendant hung in the V of her neckline.

I wore a light zip-up jacket, dress shirt, and slacks. I wasn't going to wear Lederhosen and a Robin Hood cap just to keep my mother happy. My father, on the other hand, who was Spanish and spoke almost no German—he could say "Bier, bitte," and "Noch eins"—had become "Germanicized"—strange, for someone who said the only job he ever really liked was in the British Army killing a lot of Germans he'd never met. Now, he and my mother were active in the German-American club in Anaheim, went folk dancing two or three nights a week, attended Oktoberfest and Sommerfest activities, and sat inside the clubhouse at round tables with a lot of German-speakers.

Almost all their friends were European immigrants, but not always from German-speaking countries or former territories. Many of the friends they met through the German-American club were Poles or Ukrainians or Yugoslavs or Hungarians. But they all had one thing in common—the attitude that everything was better in Europe; that America was no good except for the money; that they were only here because they had to be.

I drove down Eleventh Street to Beach Boulevard, past the clapboard houses where small children played in the dirt, the drainage ditch, the empty parking lot behind a thrift store. The last few years I was deeply dissatisfied with their neighborhood, couldn't wait to leave. It wasn't just that I'd gone to college in Los Angeles, spent weekends with friends who lived in leafy neighborhoods or at the beach, or had listened to the L.A. Philharmonic perform at the Dorothy Chandler Pavilion. The groundwork for dissatisfaction had been laid all the years I grew up in my parents' house, with their stories of London and Paris and Casablanca and how much better everything was outside Orange County.

Just past Orangethorpe, I branched onto the Artesia Freeway headed west. I slipped a cassette into the player for the thirty-minute drive and we listened to "Polkafest im Alpenland," Austrian folk music with lots of yodeling and foot-stomping. My parents swayed in the backseat in tempo with the music.

We were all part of "the frozen culture," and it was always the year an immigrant had left the Old Country, whether for the Greek-American grocer in Chicago who displayed olives and cheeses the way they had been displayed in his village, or for my mother, who used idioms such as "Sau Wetter"—"beastly weather"—thinking they were still current. I was an immigrant too. Whatever recent experiences I'd had in England were overlaid by faint recollections and family photographs, and the England of my imagination was always somewhere in the 1950s—at a time when the America I lived in was changing radically.

And as I drove in the fast-moving Saturday traffic listening to Schuhplattler, I thought it probably was not possible to be a European immigrant from their era, or from my own, for that matter, without being a snob of some order: a snob about culture, or refinement, or knowledge of languages and cuisine, or understanding of geography and European politics—or just the plain old-fashioned snob about money and rank, which certainly didn't apply to us. We were working class, as my parents drummed into me, and we struggled to make ends meet —except on a Saturday afternoon when we were out Christmas shopping and looking forward to a good continental dinner. It was possible to be working class and still feel superior to people.

* * *

Alpine Village was anchored by a Bavarian-style beer house and restaurant. A chapel was nearby, with an onion-dome steeple, and a Glockenspiel rose in between two rows of gift stores.

My mother bought an ornate musical beer stein as a Christmas gift "for your Papa," she whispered, and a gaily decorated tablecloth with depictions of dancing couples in traditional folk dress. My father headed straight for the charcuterie and seemed to examine every sausage and smoked ham hanging in the window. He went inside and I followed him while my mother admired the flowers outside.

The deli owner was from Belgium and my father was delighted to engage in a lengthy conversation in French about Belgian towns. He was particularly delighted to learn the storeowner was from Malmedy, where my father had been wounded. I listened for a while, then went outside to sit on a carved wooden bench with my mother. I enjoyed the mild December weather, the feel of the sun.

Then my mother started: "How is your friend?" I could guess where this was going.

"Which one?"

"The one who's in law school."

"He's in law school. He's in his third year."

"You should think about law school too. Your Uncle Ulrich . . ."

I knew the story. After the First World War, when Austria was an economic shambles, my mother's family scraped together whatever they could, sacrificed, pooled their resources so that her eldest brother Ulrich could stay in school, attend the university, and become somebody—an attorney! My mother always said that his education and law degree set Ulrich apart, made him different from everyone else in the family, better in a way. Uncle Ulrich ended up becoming the Staatsanwalt, or state attorney, for the Feldkirch regional court. Now I had to listen to the story again. I wanted to tell my mother "Staatsanwalt—big deal"—but of course it was.

"What about your other friend?" she asked when she'd concluded the tale of the trial lawyer. "The one who earned an M.B.A."

I fidgeted, inclined forward on the bench with my forearms resting on my knees and my hands folded.

"He's working for Mobil Oil. He just started as a plant manager in Long Beach."

"And what about you?"

"Me?" I leaned back on the bench, moved my elbows to the back rest, and turned my face upwards. "I'm enjoying the sun."

Next, she was going to ask me about Yuki, my girlfriend from a couple of years ago. "Such a nice girl," my mother would probably say. Instead, she persisted: "Well, I fully expect you to be settled down within a year or so and working a decent job—something we can be proud of."

I didn't want to argue. I missed Saloma and her calming effect. She would have helped shape my perspective. Saloma seemed to understand that my mother worried about me, thought I was wasting my life, and I knew that my mother had already been deeply disappointed by two men in the family: my father, who couldn't hold a job for very long, and my brother.

I lowered my voice. "You should be proud of me regardless. I graduated from college with a double major and top honors.

I'm finishing a master's degree and I'm starting to get published."

"You live like a church mouse."

My mother was Austrian but twenty-one years in England had shaped her too and the Britishism reminded me of that. I didn't want to judge her too harshly; there were other deep disappointments in her life as well; her English fiancé who was in the B.E.F. and never returned from France, a brother in the Austrian Army who was killed on the Russian front, all the years of scrimping and saving in the United States so that my brother and I could go to private schools and be educated into a better life, however that was defined. I took a deep breath. I needed to be patient with my dear old Mum; she only wanted the best for me.

And then she said: "How is that girlfriend of yours? Yuki? Do you ever see her? She was such a nice girl. Her father was German, wasn't he?"

"German-American," I responded. "And her mother was Japanese. They met during the Occupation."

"She was really very lovely."

With all my worries about Saloma, the last thing I needed was to phone Yuki and see if she wanted to join me for a holiday lunch. Fortunately, my father finally came out of the charcuterie. He must have liked the owner because he showed us his shopping bag of purchases: a jar of liver paté, four Landjäger sausages, half a smoked ham, and a chicken galantine.

"I'll put everything in the car," I chuckled, "before we have dinner."

* * *

The "Keller Room" of the restaurant was decorated with paintings of landmarks in Bavaria—the Munich Cathedral,

King Ludwig's Castle, and the Marienplatz. Two musicians played from a corner and a large group at a table linked arms and swayed to "Es war in Böhmerwald" as we entered and sat down.

I thought I was in heaven or in Munich when a young woman in an Oktoberfest beer-girl outfit came over. She wore white stockings that ended just above the knee, a very short green skirt and a brown corset laced tight with pink ribbons. A white blouse puffed out around her upper arms and her shoulders were bare except for two thin lacey straps.

She placed a drink list in front of us and her mouth broadened into an eager smile. The neckline of her blouse plunged to reveal her cleavage and much of her ample bosom. I grinned back, gazed at her oval face framed by long, flowing brown hair, her straight white teeth made whiter by a touch of pink lipstick, her clear brown eyes and a straight nose. My heart beat faster and I thought I was in love.

I wanted to quip to my mother that she always wanted me to marry a German girl and now was my chance, but thought better of it.

My father gazed at the barmaid too and smiled broadly.

"Something to drink, fellas?" She looked back and forth between us, then at my mom. "Ma'am?"

"Bier, bitte," my father let out at last.

"You wanna beer?"

"Ja wohl!" I'd forgotten he knew how to say that too. "Hefeweizen," he added.

"I'll have the same."

My mother asked for a glass of Gewürztraminer and when the beer girl left she said: "She's working awfully hard for a tip, isn't she?"

"It's the holidays," I replied.

My mother turned to my Dad. "Bartolo, don't even think of leaving her an extra-large tip. Just what she deserves."

He laughed. "We're just having fun."

But, disappointingly, the beer girl only brought us our drinks. For dinner, we were waited on by a young man in a red woolen vest with a high collar. He placed menus in front of us, then withdrew. After a few minutes, we were ready to order but my father kept studying the menu, no doubt from professional interest, his mouth slightly open, his glasses low on the bridge of his nose.

For all the years my father had been in restaurants, he didn't seem to know that in better places—or at least in places where the staff were properly trained—the waiter wouldn't return so long as someone at the table was still reading the menu.

"Dad?" I asked.

He looked up, somewhat surprised.

"Are you ready to order?"

"I have been for some time. I'm just waiting for that kid to come back."

"Why don't you set the menu down. I'm sure he'll be back any minute."

My father closed the menu, placed it on the table, and the waiter promptly trotted over.

We ordered Kassler Rippchen with sauerkraut. My father and I both switched to wine for the meal. Later, we lingered over the Apfelstrudel and ordered coffee. My mother began: "I'm not sure how much longer I'll be able to work."

I wondered what brought that on.

"Your father wants to retire."

"He does?" I turned to my Dad. "Retire? You're only fifty-six."

He shrugged. "I'll be fifty-seven next month."

We'd probably had too much to drink, and the pleasant glow from libations with a meal could too easily turn to anger or impatience. I said, without thinking: "So what are you going to retire on? You never worked long enough anywhere to have earned a pension."

My father grew defensive. "I worked three years at the Disneyland Hotel, didn't I?"

"Great."

My mother jumped in. "I told Bartolo he'll have to work at least until he's sixty-five."

"Maybe I'll be dead by then. Okay, maybe I'll work until I'm sixty. Three more years."

My mother set her fork down, pushed the plate with the unfinished Strudel to the side. "We'd lose too much money. And we're still paying off the house. Social Security at sixty is a pittance. You'll have to work until sixty-five."

He was in good health. Why not? I thought to myself.

Then, my mother played her trump card: "So long as I'm working, Bartolo, you'll have to work. You'd lose too much face if you were living off my wages."

"Okay." He looked away. He folded his hands on his stomach. He started to twirl his thumbs. The musicians still played folk songs. They sang: *"Du machts mir viel Schmerzen."*

I wanted to nudge us back into a pleasant holiday mood. We'd only be together for a few weeks; what was the point of arguing?

I looked at my parents.

"Should we have an after-dinner drink? A digestif? Okay?"

My mother said: "Alright." She would be paying, or would give my father her credit card so that he wouldn't lose face. I turned to the bar. I hoped that sexy beer girl would come over—that would cheer me up. Then, I realized what had set my mother off. Our waiter came over instead.

"Cognac all around," I ordered. "In snifters."

* * *

Sipping her drink, my mother resumed: "I'll be seventy-three when your father turns sixty-five. I'll have to work another eight years."

"I thought you like working at the university," I offered.

"Oh, it's not that. Everything's easy when you're young, like that barmaid. When you're old, you have to work twice as hard to prove yourself, to show you can still do the job. When you're young, you learn faster, you're quick to pick up new ways of doing things. People want to help you because you're fun to be around, because you're vivacious and carefree and you make people feel happy."

My mother had been an attractive woman in her youth—beautiful, judging from the photographs—and from what I'd gleaned from her stories and from visits to Austria, popular in her day.

She liked to tell the story about how she'd returned for a visit to Austria for the first time after the War, when she was finally able to, with hostilities over. She was still single; her English fiancé had been killed in 1940, and she hadn't yet met my father. She had travelled from London to Paris to Austria by train, in a brightly colored peacock dress with a feathered hat to match and never once needed to lift her bag; every gentleman in whichever country wanted to help her, just to see her smile and hear her say "thank you," and maybe to enjoy a coffee with her in the dining car.

Now, I looked at her in her Dirndl and white blouse, her jawline starting to sag, her eyes opaque and with wrinkles flaring out from the edges. My parents slid from middle age into retirement age and beyond, and I was no help to them. The holidays, the holidays, a time to brood and grow somber, to unburden ourselves and have one more little nightcap so we wouldn't have to think.

* * *

Increasingly, my father worked seasonal and part-time jobs—the Los Alamitos Race Track when the horses ran, the Anaheim Stadium when the Angels were in town, the Anaheim Convention Center during trade shows. It was a tough way to make a living—and a far cry from his days as a sous chef at the Grosvenor House in Mayfair. In addition to his temper—I once saw my father blow up at a customer who, detecting a foreign accent, asked: "So, paisano, are you from Italy or Mexico?"—there were other reasons why my father had difficulty holding a job.

For one thing, the culinary arts had changed. In the more fashionable restaurants, nouvelle cuisine was all the rage—a cooking style my father never accepted.

"Small portions on a large plate? What is this shit?" he would say. "There's nothing 'nouvelle' about cuisine. You start with the sauce. The sauce is everything."

Trained in the French cooking style in the London hotels after the War, the tradition of the exquisite sauce dated from a time when meat spoiled quickly and had to be disguised. Now, no one cared about a nuanced, complex, aromatic sauce—they wanted to taste a fine cut of meat, maybe with a simple sprig of Rosemary on top.

But for the past six weeks my father had been gainfully employed as First Cook at the Coachman Restaurant in the Carriage House Hotel off Cabot Road in Mission Viejo. He said we would stay busy over the holidays, with banqueting and events, Rotary Club Christmas parties and celebrations, even a wedding reception between Christmas and New Year. He'd arranged for the Executive Chef, a French Canadian whom I'd known ever since I'd first started working in kitchens at age fifteen, to hire me for the holidays as Assistant Cook. I'd be working almost every day for the next four weeks.

The Carriage House, a three-star hotel with one hundred and forty rooms, had two restaurants: the Coachman, for fine dining, and the Livery, a breakfast and short order café. Modest banqueting and conference facilities ran along the south side of the hotel, and kitchen staff were pulled into various duties as needed.

With every passing year, my father seemed to ride his motorcycle further and further afield for work, and the Carriage House was forty-five minutes from my parents' home. He also needed increasingly to ask favors from old friends in order to be hired, since his reputation as a hot head who was often in his cups preceded him. Fortunately, the Executive Chef, Max Manfredi, knew my father from their earliest immigrant days when they both worked at the Disneyland Hotel and later at Los Coyotes Country Club. They liked to speak French; Max had worked in resort hotels in Germany and Switzerland and had connections there. The two old cooks enjoyed reminiscing about the Old World.

During the Christmas holiday, my father woke me up every morning at four a.m. and we fell into a kind of routine: I showered, grabbed a quick cup of coffee and dressed in coveralls over checkered cook's pants and a white shirt. I usually carried street clothes wrapped in a towel so that I could change for the commute home. I shrugged into his spare leather jacket and donned a motorcycle helmet while he wheeled his one working bike, a Laverda 750, from the garage onto the driveway; he dressed similarly, but covered in a vinyl jumpsuit, and we both tugged on thick, padded leather gloves.

His motorcycle usually started the third or fourth time he kicked down on the pedal, and he twisted the throttle a few times to rev the engine. I got on behind him; the two-seater had a strap I could hang onto. Once on the freeway, he opened up the engine and we roared through the dark at seventy miles an hour; the wind forced tears from the corners of my eyes and down my cheeks.

My father had never driven a car; he said he didn't want to learn. In Europe, the Vespa had been a vehicle of choice after the War, and in his youth he raced bicycles at the Velodrome in Casablanca. But the real reason, I thought, is that he was too much of a contrarian. If most Americans aspired to own a car of the year, he never wanted to drive any four-wheel vehicle at all. He wanted to be different, and he certainly was. But in one regard, his contrarian nature was a plus; if most Americans imbibed too much over the holidays, he took the pledge and swore he would stay relatively sober, at least for a few weeks.

In December, mornings were often cold but traffic tended to be light in the predawn hours. By five a.m., we had turned off the freeway onto the Cabot roundabout, exited and rolled into the parking lot of the hotel. We parked near a wall behind the hotel; later in the day, a few other parked motorcycles would be grouped there as well. But I think our forty-five minute commute was the longest for anyone on a two-wheeler.

Entering through the backway, I punched my timecard while my father entered the storeroom/office to review orders and beverage bills. Taking a ring of keys from his desk drawer, I unlocked a series of freezers and refrigerators and moved cartons of bacon, ham, eggs, and sliced cheese to my station, then turned on a long array of ovens, stoves, and grills.

By five-thirty a.m., my breakfast set-ups were ready and Adam, the potwasher, and Rafael and Gonzalo, the busboys, had arrived. My job was to cook breakfast to order, but I'd also help prepare items for the buffet, cook scrambled eggs for the steamtable or bake strips of bacon in the oven, a more efficient, mass-production way than frying bacon in a pan.

The Executive Chef, Max Manfredi, strolled the aisles and checked with different workers. He was an effective executive chef because he understood personalities and tried to capitalize on a person's strengths and compensate for their weaknesses. My father was in charge of all the hot food items for the lunches and dinners—the soups, stews, roasts, and other hot meats—but I noticed that whenever we prepared Chicken Cacciatore, Boeuf Bourguignon or other entrees that required wines, Max assigned me the task of adding the ingredients.

He knew my father well, and they even looked alike in their white chef's jackets, red scarves, and high starched chef's hats. They were about the same age, in their late fifties, cleanshaven except for a trim steel moustache, and with short greying hair. Max was taller than my father and a bit heavier, but they could have passed for brothers.

Somehow, we got through the day, even when there was a banquet for a hundred-and-fifty people and we worked assembly-line fashion on the salads, entrees, and desserts. I felt lucky if my father only blew up at one person per day: he didn't like waiters—most cooks don't—and he could be unfriendly to the cashier and the serving girls.

Max kept him away from the front line, where cooks dealt with customers, but back in the kitchen my father cursed if he heard "some ignorant American asked for country gravy with his Duchesse Potatoes."

I got along well with the crew. Denise Dunbarton, the hostess, seemed to enjoy stopping at my station to make a provocative remark. She was from Chicago, she told me, was twenty-two years old and had worked at the hotel for three years. I told her I lived in San Francisco and would work at the hotel for just under a month.

"So you've got a woman mayor in San Francisco and we've got a woman mayor in Chicago," she smirked. "A woman can't run a big town like that. What were the voters thinking?"

Denise usually walked away after delivering her riposte or glanced back at me over her shoulder. Her ideas certainly wouldn't be too popular with the set I knew in San Francisco, but then again, it was refreshing being away from a city where expressed opinions were too reliably predictable.

Denise had an interesting face. Her nose was slightly crooked, maybe from a fall years ago, but was offset by full lips and a sensual mouth. She had a nice smile, long blonde hair that had a fresh-washed sheen, and a curvaceous figure. As a hostess, she had to wear a short skirt and her legs were long and shapely. She knew how to wear makeup too, applying foundation and highlighting her cheeks, using eyeliner and a brush to thicken her lashes. She could be foulmouthed and was a tease in more ways than one, calling me "college boy" and "chef's son."

She asked me early on if I liked motorcycles.

"It's transportation," I answered.

"That's my Suzuki 550 parked next to your Dad's bike."

I knew which motorcycle she rode—the one with the pale blue gas tank and trim; sometimes she left work at the same time we did.

She smiled slyly. "It's not as big as your Dad's Laverda, but it's fast. I'll give you a ride sometime."

The next day, she stopped by my station while I julienned carrots and gave me a mischievous grin. "So, college boy. Are you shy around girls?"

I was embarrassed and tried not to look up in case I sliced my finger. "Sometimes," I muttered.

"I'll bet that snake in your pants isn't shy."

My knife slipped and chopped the carrot into two chunks. When I looked up, she sashayed away but glanced back at me and waved.

My father seemed to notice our interaction but to his credit never said anything.

Another time, Denise asked me to go into the walk-in cooler with her to see whether a wheel of Camembert cheese had spoiled. The walk-in cooler, where items such as fruit, vegetables, thawed meats, and leftovers were stored, was always kept at forty degrees, so we each took a jacket from a hook and wore them.

Inside, I looked at the Camembert cheese and sniffed it.

"Seems okay to me."

"It's nice and cool in here," she declared. "It's always so hot in the kitchen."

"Yes."

"So tell me, chef's son. You live in San Francisco. Lots of gay action there. Do you have a boyfriend?"

I laughed drily. "No," I replied. I gave her an embarrassed smile.

"Do you have a girlfriend?"

"Yeah," I said huskily. "I think so. It's on hold."

"On hold?"

"Yeah."

"Does she hold it like this?"

I felt Denise place the palm of her hand on my crotch. My stomach constricted involuntarily and she started to knead the firm mound. I didn't move her hand away. Her lips brushed against mine and I felt her turn quickly away from me. She exited through the cooler door with her characteristic finger-wave over her shoulder.

* * *

If I had time, I showered in the cook's locker room before heading home, but I almost always changed out of my dirty cook's outfit and put on my street clothes for the evening commute. I dropped the soiled garments in a hamper since the hotel laundered and provided work uniforms.

Usually, the return motorcycle ride after work took considerably longer with the evening holiday bumper-to-bumper traffic, even though my father often edged onto the white painted line between traffic lanes and, surrounded by a mass of cars and glowing taillights, opened the throttle. Some nights, I was so tired on the ride back that the interlacing layers of traffic from freeway overpasses and Christmas lights on houses seemed to blur into a whir and disappear. The neon sign of a Taco Bell might shudder past, or an illuminated billboard advertising Diet Rite might shake by. Often, when we reached home, it was enough to eat dinner in silence with my parents, then watch an old movie or reruns of *Gunsmoke* on television before turning in.

But that day, after the incident in the walk-in cooler, I tried phoning Saloma. I wanted to hear her voice, her reassuring tones, but I couldn't get through. No one answered, so I couldn't leave a message with her sister. They must be at some family event, I assumed.

In my bedroom, the one I had slept in while in high school and whenever I stayed for a visit with my parents, I sat at the small wooden desk and wrote her a letter. I told her how much I missed her and wanted to see her and that we'd be together soon. I folded the letter, sealed it in an envelope and addressed it to her. It only cost fifteen cents to mail a first-class letter but I licked and stuck two fifteen-cent stamps on the envelope just to be sure. With my work schedule and not having a car at my disposal it would be difficult to mail the letter anytime soon.

In the living room, my mother watched *Jeopardy* and drank a cup of tea. She sat very primly, always with perfect posture, spine straight, shoulders pushed back, chin at a right angle to her chest. I asked her if she could mail the letter for me on the way to or from work.

She looked at the envelope. "Did you put enough postage on it?"

"Of course," I said. "Twice as much as it needs."

She only wanted to see the address.

"Salonpas," she mused. Then, "Sevilla. Is this the lineament strip for arthritis? Are you writing a pharmaceutical company," she smiled, "for a job?"

"No, it isn't 'Salonpas.' It's 'Saloma Sevilla.'"

"Do we know her?"

My mother could be meddlesome, inquisitive, suspicious, overbearing, and I wondered why I even wrote Saloma if the last thing I wanted was another woman dominating my life. I was tempted to take the letter back from my mother and tear it up, but then I told myself Saloma wasn't at all like my mother and I missed her, especially so close to Christmas, and when I got back to San Francisco I'd try to patch things up.

I thought quickly.

"No, Mutti," I put in. "'Saloma Sevilla' is an advertising agency in San Francisco. I'm applying for a job." I hoped that might get her off my back, then added: "It's an executive position—very prestigious."

She smiled sweetly. "Of course, my dear. I'll post it first thing in the morning on my way to work."

CHAPTER NINE

We worked Christmas Eve and Christmas Day, and with my schedule it was hard to catch up with Saloma. We exchanged Christmas cards and she included a nice note about how much she looked forward to seeing me in the New Year. We spoke briefly on Christmas Day, but she was headed for a family event near Santa Clara.

I didn't have to work on December 26 and I arranged to go fishing at the Newport Beach pier with Vince and two other friends from college. But one of our friends cancelled because he had a hangover and the other decided to go skiing because there was fresh snow near Lake Arrowhead.

Vince picked me up in his Ford Capri at six a.m. and we drove to Fullerton in the semi-dark.

"I talked to Tandoğan," Vince began. "You met him once or twice. He's the art guy at the furniture store. And he knows a lot about fishing."

Hasan "Harry" Tandoğan was from Istanbul, was in his early thirties, and sold decorative art at the furniture store. Almost everything was a reproduction but he could discuss provenance and style, artistic periods and movements, and the value of a gilded frame.

We pulled up to Tandoğan's ground floor apartment near Commonwealth and Harbor. He must have been waiting for us because the door opened immediately. He strode out, pulling a small cart with buckets and boxes on it. The morning was cold and Tandoğan wore a short, zip-up raincoat and a battered felt dress hat that looked like it was from the 1950s. He had a trim dark moustache and a pipe dangled between his teeth. As he pulled the cart down the walkway, Vince and I both got out of the car to help him.

"Ahoy!" Vince joked. "Man, you've got more gear than Ahab. What are we going after—the Great White Whale? I thought we'd be lucky to catch smelt."

Tandoğan said hello and shook hands with both of us. Vince opened the trunk and moved a large cooler to one side. We started to load the aluminum bait bucket, a short wooden club, and two five-gallon plastic tubs.

"We'll find out at the pier what's biting today," Tandoğan explained. He tapped the tackle box as Vince set it next to the cooler. "It's just the standard stuff. Extra line and hooks, bobbers and floaters, sinkers. A small first aid kit in case you hook yourself in the ass when you're casting."

"Very funny," Vince said.

"Needle-nose pliers in case I have to dig the hook out."

"Even funnier."

"We'll rent rods at the pier," Tandoğan continued, "and whatever else we need."

The handles of the cart folded down and we were able to fit it neatly into the trunk. Vince drove, I sat shotgun, and Tandoğan claimed the back seat; his arm rested on a spare cooler next to him. As we headed toward the 55, the sun came up and created an orange crease on the horizon. On the drive to the pier, we spoke mostly about the Soviet invasion of Afghanistan, which had taken place two days before.

"Can you believe it?" I wondered out loud. "Jimmy Carter claims he was taken completely by surprise. What an oaf. The build-up was covered by the newspapers, for god's sake."

"I know, I know," Vince tsk-tsked as he drove. The skyline brightened, but we hoped the fish would stay hungry for much of the morning. "The guy's always surprised about something. Like he didn't know letting the Shah into the U.S. would cause trouble for us?"

I could smell the aroma of fine tobacco as Tandoğan lit and puffed on his pipe. From the back, he observed: "In the Middle East, only the strongmen prevail. You cannot show weakness."

"No kidding," I said.

"You have to pick your despots," Tandoğan went on. "Do you want to support a pro-Western dictator who is your ally? Or do you want to let a pro-Soviet dictator take over?"

"What about democracy?" Vince protested.

Tandoğan let out a loud guffaw.

"Democracy! Hah! That was Carter's mistake. All this handwringing about human rights and the rule of law and one man one vote. Now he's lost the Middle East for a generation."

"Maybe longer," I asserted. "Even my father, who's an avowed socialist/anarchist, thinks Jimmy Carter is the worst leader of a Western power since Édourd Deladier."

"Who's he?" Vince asked.

"Munich, Appeasement, Hitler, Chamberlain. He's the prime minister who signed for the French," I explained.

"That's why he was out by 1940," Tandoğan added. "But he was considered a great hero in the First World War—the one we lost."

Vince and I looked at each other and smiled.

* * *

Vince parked at the foot of the pier, opposite Charlie's Chili, where we sometimes had a meal in the wee hours of a night of drinking. It was already daylight and the haze was lifting from the beach as we unloaded the trunk. It should be a nice day, I thought to myself, with the temperature climbing from the morning low-fifties to almost sixty by noon. I zipped up my jacket and helped set the cart on the ground and inserted the handles. We piled our gear on the flatbed—our bucket, tubs, two coolers stacked on top of each other, tackle box. Vince pulled on the handle while I pushed the cart from the back. Tobacco smoke curled from Tandoğan's pipe. He walked next to us and relit the bowl two or three times.

We passed a sign for the "Dory Fishing Fleet—estd. 1891," three beached wooden boats and a rack of fishing nets and glass floats, then headed onto the wooden pier. We stopped at a bait and tackle shed that played classical music from a radio inside. On the one hand, it seemed out-of-place. On the other, why shouldn't someone in a bait shop listen to Baroque? I heard what I thought was something by Vivaldi but also the slushing of the waves and the swirling of the water around the pier pilings. A seagull cried and I saw it glide above us.

Tandoğan did the talking because he knew what to rent. He verified that no fishing license was required because it was a public pier and that anglers were having good luck using squid for bait to catch sablefish out near the end of the thousand-foot long pier. I might not have been an expert on bait and tackle but I knew from time spent in too many commercial kitchens that sablefish—sometimes known as black cod or butterfish—yielded great tasting filets with a fine texture.

Tandoğan told us to rent stout six-foot, one-piece rods with conventional reels and use high/low rigging baited with strips of squid. We ran our lines down to thirty feet. Tandoğan pointed out that sablefish were generally caught in deeper waters, but with the warmer than typical weather, schools of sablefish were closer in. The fishing should be good.

We spent a pleasant morning leaning over the wooden rails or baiting hooks and dropping lines, talking about geopolitics and travel, books and world affairs, San Francisco and women. Vince insisted he was playing the field for the next few years; one divorce in his first twenty-four years was one too many. Tandoğan maintained that the best life was the married life. He still tried to bring his wife and three children over from Turkey. I said very little but delighted in the winter sun, the light breeze and the banter, the gentle swaying of the wooden pier, the undulation of the blue-green sea, and above all, the excitement when the fish began to strike, the rods bent into an arched C-shape, and we leaned back to reel them in. The blackish-grey fish emerged into the air, their tails swatted at nothing, their mouths agape.

Ships were at anchor, and I wanted to be on one. A tanker touched the horizon, and in the frenzy of hauling in the struggling fish, clubbing them, tossing them into the tubs of water, I lost sight of it. When I looked up, the stern and supercargo formed a bright white speck that winked and disappeared.

On the drive back to north Orange County, we joked about what great fishermen we were. Twenty-seven sablefish, mostly in the ten-to-fifteen pound range, were in bags of ice in the cooler and the tubs in the trunk of the car. We had gutted and iced them at the cleaning station at the foot of the pier and had divided them amongst us, both by weight and size.

Vince exited the 91 at Harbor and drove north to Fullerton's downtown, passing a used record store, a barbershop, a five-and-dime until he reached the two-story Fox Theater and parked next to it. We'd agreed to eat at Alessandro's, an Italian restaurant in a redbrick building abutting the movie house.

The décor in the dark dining room was a collage of knick-knacks from Italy—dusty paintings of Venetian canals, marionettes hung from wooden ceiling beams, long-nosed carnival masks, and empty wicker-wrapped Chianti bottles with candles in the necks served as table centerpieces. It was certainly kitschy but created a lighthearted atmosphere.

We sat at a round table that wobbled slightly on the plank floor and ordered a pitcher of beer. Vince filled the three glasses; we picked up the menus the waiter had left and glanced through them.

"What do you think, guys? Pizza?" Vince asked.

"Only if it has ham and sausage," Tandoğan said. I thought he was joking.

"I'm not a very good Muslim," he went on, glancing up from the menu. "I eat pork. I drink beer. I don't pray five times a day."

"You smoke tobacco five times a day," Vince put in.

"That's different."

We drank our beers.

"And guess what? I feel free," Tandoğan announced, putting down his glass. "Look at what's happening in Iran. All those guys with long beards telling you what to do, how to think. I don't need them. I just want to get my family out of Turkey to join me. And go fishing."

We toasted.

"Pizza's fine," I agreed, though I was impressed by the menu. I'd been to Alessandro's a few times in the past but I had a changed perspective. Osso Bucco, Linguine con le Vongole,

Bistecca alla Florentina—it was as good as any comparably priced Italian restaurant in North Beach.

I mentioned that to Vince and Tandoğan and they seemed pleased.

* * *

We dropped Tandoğan off at his apartment, helped him unload and get his gear and portion of the catch to the front door, and thanked him for all the fishing lore.

On the drive back to my parents' house, Vince headed down Commonwealth. We passed uniform suburban homes sequestered behind block sound walls, a vacant school yard, a Spanish mission-style church. Vince sat back, steered with one hand, and drummed his fingers on the wheel.

"Enjoyed the day, did you?" he said, turning to me.

"Great day. Couldn't have been better."

"You meant what you said about lunch?" he asked, probably because I'd spent a lot of time around restaurants or because I'd been living in San Francisco. "You really thought that place was good? As good as any pizza joint in Frisco?"

I thought about it. I didn't want to tell Vince that only people who weren't from San Francisco called it "Frisco," but responded: "Alessandro's isn't a joint. It's a nice place and about as good as a lot of places in San Francisco." The décor verged on the tacky and most Italian restaurants in San Francisco were more subdued, but I added: "I could see it fitting in."

"Yeah?"

"Yeah." I paused. "Life's good here."

We drove under a railroad viaduct and emerged near the Hunt Foods processing plant. A freight truck pulled in front of us. Vince slowed as the eighteen-wheeler made its turn and headed in the opposite direction.

"So why don't you move back?"

"And do what?" I asked. The traffic quickened and we passed the municipal airport, Cessnas and Piper Cubs parked along the perimeter. A light Cirrus aircraft descended, waggling its wings as it neared the landing strip. "My whole life is books," I went on. "Nobody in Orange County reads books—except Tandoğan, and he's a Turk."

"I read Moby Dick," Vince said defensively.

"Bullshit," I retorted, laughing. "You read the Cliff Notes. I took that class with you. And you saw the movie."

"Gregory Peck was great as Ahab."

"Richard Basehart made a better Ishmael."

"Agreed."

* * *

Vince turned left on Stanton, crossed above the freeway; the fastmoving I-5 traffic churned underneath in both directions, then he turned left again on Eleventh Street. He pulled up to the driveway of my parents' house and shut off the engine. The garage door was up, propped open with a broomstick against the trim of the outer wall. My Dad was inside with his three parked motorcycles, sitting at a picnic bench and dressed in a blue checkered shirt and jeans, cleaning something. A small electric space heater nestled in the corner; its spiral of coils glowed.

I swung open the car door and got out and Vince did so as well. He waved to my Dad, who lifted his hand in brief acknowledgment. Vince unlocked the trunk lid with his key and pushed it open, then flipped up the lid of the cooler.

He turned to me. "Great day, buddy-boy. But it's been too long."

We shook hands warmly and embraced. He helped me retrieve my three bags of iced fish from the cooler.

"I'll let you know when I'm here next," I assured him. "It's been swell."

"Maybe we'll catch a Dodgers game the next time you're in So Cal."

"Sounds great."

"Say hello to your folks for me."

* * *

Inside the garage, two motorcycles were in parts; one had long cables hanging from the handlebars, drooping like flowers. The other had the seat removed as well as the rear wheel. My father used a small knife to scrape the carbon buildup on a spark plug, then ran a wire brush across the plug gap.

I showed him the three bags of fish. Their blackish heads and glassy round eyes stared at us from the ice.

"Black cod," he noted. "Put a couple in the fridge. I'll filet them later. We'll have them for dinner. The rest you can put in the freezer."

"We caught twenty-seven sablefish today—black cod—so we each took home nine."

"Fantastic."

I started up the steps to the access door and into the house.

"I'll broil them," he called out. "You should broil sablefish. You should never pan fry or deep fry them," he commented almost as an afterthought.

I entered the house and walked into the small kitchen. I wanted to show my mother the fish I'd caught, but she obviously wasn't home. Her car wasn't in the driveway and the house was silent.

I set two good-sized sablefish on a long tray and placed it in the refrigerator, then dumped the ice from the bags. The remaining fish I wrapped two at a time in brown freezer paper and sealed the fold with tape. One fish was left over, which I wrapped separately, then placed all four bundles in the freezer.

For all our differences, I enjoyed spending time in the garage with my Dad. When I was young, and he was in a bad mood or groggy from drink—or both, my mother used to send me out to the garage to cheer him up. "You're the only one who can," she would say.

His garage hadn't changed much over the years. The motorcycles might be different makes and models and he might have bought a new power tool or two, but the workbench was the same, with a vice at one end and a grinder at the other, a few hand tools scattered on the top, a shoplight, and pegboard nailed to the garage wall studs. Each tool had its proper function and place, and he had hung each one meticulously on pegboard hooks, then painted an outline of the tool so that he would always know where to replace it.

A travel poster was always tacked to the back wall—the last few years it showed a Spanish windmill with the word "Segovia" underneath. The green and white plastic tablecloth on the picnic table seemed perpetually the same.

I grabbed two cans of Brown Derby beer from the fridge, then used the can opener to punch two triangular holes in the top of each lid. I went back into the garage.

"Where's Mutti this afternoon? Church?"

"No," he shook his head. I handed him a can of beer and sat opposite him. "Thanks," he muttered. "She took her car in to be serviced."

"Today?" I sipped my beer. "Are they open?"

"Why not? Boxing Day isn't a holiday in the United States." He took a swig of beer. "It should be. Ignorant Americans don't even know the meaning of Boxing Day."

Even in his kinder moments he could be irascible.

"Cheers, Dad!" We tapped our beer cans. "To Spain!"

He barely smiled.

"To work at the Carriage House!" I enjoined.

We tapped beer cans again.

After a pause, he said: "You're lucky. You can come back here and see your friends. Go fishing. In Spain, we'd fish with nets and catch sardines, then grill them outdoors."

He let out what seemed to be a low sigh. "I thought when I came to this country I'd make good money and live well. Now, all I want is not to end up a senile old man in a government home."

"You're only fifty-six," I reminded him. "You could easily work another ten years."

"Hah!" he said skeptically. "That's what your mother says. You think you're the only one she nags? She used to have little children to scold. Now she only has me when you're not around."

We drank our beer in the garage. I went inside for two more. I didn't want the old man to become morose. When I re-entered the garage, I glanced at the travel poster. I sat back down and handed him a cold can of Brown Derby.

"I thought you wanted to work a few more years so you could travel to Spain a couple more times."

"That's another thing!" I realized I'd opened a can of worms instead of a can of beer. "I cannot even return to my hometown because of my disgrace."

I knew the story. He was an only child and had run off to join the British Army in North Africa when he was seventeen and had abandoned his widowed mother. When the French were forced out of Morocco, she was destitute and was sent back, as were most other Europeans, to their "country of origin"—which was ironic since many people of European descent had been born in French North Africa.

My grandmother had been born in Ceuta, a Spanish protectorate adjacent to Morocco, and was relegated to the "residencia," the poor house run by the government.

"She doesn't belong in Ceuta," my father explained. "She was only born there. Most of her life she spent in La Linea and in Casablanca. Your mother and I tried having her live with us in London, but that was a disaster. The two women didn't get along. Your mother said mi madrecita only wanted to smoke and drink and sit in a bathrobe all day talking to her son. I didn't want to be caught between the two women." He smoothed the plastic tablecloth, ran his hands across the imagined creases. "We sent your abuelita back after a year."

"I know." My beer can was almost empty. "Too bad she didn't stay longer. I would have grown up speaking Spanish at her knee."

"Hah! That's a joke. You wouldn't have learned anything good from her. She was illiterate. When I was in Morocco, I taught her how to write her name and a few other things. But you wouldn't have learned Spanish—only Andaluz. I spent years trying to forget Andaluz and learn a form of Spanish other people could understand."

"She's dead now, isn't she?"

"Probably. I don't get on with my cousin in La Linea. We stopped writing, but a few years ago she wrote me that my mother was in the residencia, half-blind and lost a leg to gangrene. That's why I can never go back to my hometown and introduce myself to my childhood friends—because I carry the badge of my own disgrace, because they say 'se fué a la militar y abandonó a su madre.'"

* * *

With the third round of beer the inevitable subject of my future came up.

"So," my Dad began. "You'll have a master's degree in a few months. Then what?"

I didn't say anything. I had a clerk's job waiting for me in San Francisco, a sometimes girlfriend who was as terrified of commitments as I was, a couple of evening classes in French and German I'd already signed up for.

"I don't know. I'll try to get some writing done. Maybe I'll get a lucky break."

My father shook his head in negation.

"I thought you were on a clear career path when you were studying film production. I thought you might become a cameraman or editor."

"It's all closed shop," I replied. "You have to be sponsored to join the union."

"So? You become a journeyman, like everyone else. You apprentice, get your union card. You have to start somewhere. I was in the culinary union."

"I *have* a career path."

"Studying books? How to write novels?" He shook his head more vigorously this time. "In Spain, writers are never respected until they're dead, and then they name a street after them."

"Okay, so maybe I'll write a novel one day—something decent. Something worth reading. But right now, I don't know enough."

I looked directly at him.

"If you really want to know what I'd like to do, I'd like to hang out in Europe for a couple of years, work odd jobs, learn about life, have some adventures."

We drank our beer and he seemed to soften. I'd told him about this dream before.

"I understand," he said quietly. "A man just wants to do something interesting, work as a taxi driver or a barman, but he takes on a big job to fulfill his wife's ambition. But you're not married. If you want to do something interesting for a couple of years, you do so with my blessing."

"Mutti will never understand."

"No, but she'll get used to it." He must have been thinking about my future for some time because after a pause he asked: "How's your German?"

I thought that was a strange question coming from my father. Over the years, he'd heard me speak German to my mother or to my cousins when we visited, or to one of my folks' German-speaking friends at the club.

"I'm not completely fluent. There's always more to learn." I considered my language skills carefully. "It's better than your Arabic."

"I can't read Arabic. I only learned it in the casbah."

"I know. Of course, my German isn't as good as your Spanish or French. Maybe something like your Italian."

He nodded but didn't seem to agree. "I think it's better than that," he mused. "Why don't you work in Germany for a summer?"

I listened carefully. What was he getting at? Did he know of a position?

"Doing what?" I asked.

"Working in a resort hotel in the Black Forest as a commi chef."

I was interested. "Which station?" I didn't want to be stuck in Pantry or Pastry.

"Probably Sauce."

"Go on."

"I told you Max has connections in Europe. His brother-in-law is the head chef at the Hotel Römerbad in Germany. He puts together a crew for the season around this time each year. I hope you don't mind. I spoke to Max about a job for you, if you're interested."

It certainly piqued my interest, but the news had come so suddenly that I was unsure what to say.

"Well . . . sure . . . this is worth exploring. When would he need my answer?"

"You'd have some time to think things through. You should let Max know that you're interested, but you wouldn't have to make a firm commitment until early March."

"What about a work permit?"

My father shrugged. He must have been investigating this and talking to Max in detail.

"You have a British passport. You can work anywhere in the Common Market. Those types of jobs in hotels often provide a room and meals. You meet people."

Don't tell me the next pitch would be that I could meet a "nice German girl."

He went on. "You make connections with the staff. When the summer season's over, they all work somewhere else. Maybe you follow one of them to another country, see new things."

He tilted his head. "It's not a bad life. You might like it. And it would give you a couple of years to sort out some things."

I tried not to sound overly enthusiastic, but I needed to sort out my life in San Francisco too. When I drafted my play, I sometimes wasn't sure what the next scene or act would be, and then there was a moment when things took on shape and became clearer.

"I'll talk to Max tomorrow, when we're back at work. I have a lot of questions, but I think I have some answers too."

* * *

When my mother came home, we said nothing to her about this possibility. She was in a good mood and was delighted I'd caught so many fish.

After dinner, I asked her if I could read out loud from Schnitzler's *Flucht in die Finsternis* and she could correct my German. I read for an hour and she seemed happy, commenting that my pronunciation was excellent.

* * *

In the new year, our work schedule was less hectic and there were fewer holiday parties and banquets. Max let some of the staff go or reduced their hours. I had spoken to him about my interest in the job in Germany; he said he'd let his brother-in-law know. I wouldn't have to sign anything until the beginning of March, but if I wanted the job I'd have to be prepared to report for work by May 25 when the resort season opened.

The timing would be perfect, I told him, because I'd have my degree in hand by then and could move on to other things. I thanked him and said I'd let him know as soon as I could if I could commit to the job.

With our reduced hours and revised work schedule, on the Saturday before I was to return to San Francisco, on one of my last days at the Carriage House, I only needed to work until noon, but my father wouldn't be done until three-thirty. I planned to hang around, sit in the breakroom and read a book I'd brought, but Denise said she could give me a ride.

"Come on, college boy," she insisted. "I live in Tustin. I'll drop you off."

I smiled. This might be fun. She'd been flirting with me for weeks, touching me or winking coquettishly in a way that gave me a tingling sensation.

"Sure," I piped up. I'd enjoy holding onto her on the motorbike. I missed the embrace of a woman and this might be as close as I'd get for a while.

I let my Dad know that I'd see him back at the house and he said simply: "Ten cuidado!"

I made it a point to shower in the cook's locker room and change into my street clothes quickly.

Denise waited for me in the parking lot. She looked fresh. Since she'd also finished early, she had time to change from her hostess outfit into a tan leather jacket and matching riding pants. I noticed she kept the jacket partially unzipped and wore a white blouse underneath. She had already straddled her Suzuki GS 550. When she saw me come out, she put on her helmet and kick-started the engine to life.

I pressed the snaps on my leather jacket, donned the helmet, and swung myself behind her. I was excited to sit close, but planned to hang onto the seat strap rather than put my arms around her. The temperature was in the low fifties. I felt warm and tucked my gloves into my jacket pocket, but Denise kept her gloves on. She revved the engine, then shot forward almost as soon as I was positioned on the seat, causing me to lean back. When she braked suddenly by the parking attendant, I fell forward against her back and put an arm around her waist.

"Come on, college boy," she yelled over the sound of the engine. "You know how to hold a woman."

I wrapped both arms around her and hugged her tight as we roared into traffic.

Denise opened up the engine and we went fast down the center lane of the Santa Ana Freeway, but after a few miles she exited on El Toro Road and turned onto Trabuco. We were going to wind our way through the countryside, maybe connect with the I-5 further north.

We roared through a tunnel of eucalyptus trees and passed

orange and lemon groves, the trees planted in neat rows that seemed to bend and wave as we shot by. The wind started to nip at my hands. With my helmeted head next to hers, I called out: "I should have worn my gloves."

"If your hands are cold, put them inside my jacket."

I reached up and placed my right hand inside, cupped her large, firm breast. I was hard almost immediately and I felt my breath catch. Denise wasn't wearing a bra; her full round tit jiggled against my palm from the motion of the bike. I undid a button of her blouse and slipped my hand inside. Her nipple was erect—I knew it wasn't just from the cold—and I curved my hand around her breast so that the nipple was notched between two of my fingers and I could exert a gentle pressure.

I tried to keep from sighing—I didn't want her to think I was weak—but my heart raced. Maybe this would lead to a kiss or two—maybe to some foreplay. Nothing much would happen, in all likelihood, but it gave me a thrill to fondle her.

I still had my left arm around her waist. She reached back from the handlebars with her left hand, grabbed my wrist, and moved my hand between her legs.

"Stay warm," she shouted, then closed her thighs around my hand, holding it tightly.

I kept telling myself this wasn't going to lead to anything, that she was just being a tease, as usual. And I didn't want to go too far or let things get out of control. Saloma trusted me; I didn't want to be with another woman, but my throbbing erection told me otherwise. It was almost painful, with the constriction of my pants, and I longed to get off the motorcycle and adjust my trousers for more room. But when Denise turned off the main road and down a rutted trail that led into an orange grove, the motorcycle bumped and bounced and my penis thumped within my trousers and against the seat. Holding onto her, her fat breast wobbled against my palm, her crotch jerked against my fingers. I thought I was about to come.

Denise made her way between the orange trees; moldy fruit was on the ground and a few shriveled oranges that hadn't been harvested still hung from branches. She slowed when she reached a clearing, pulled up next to an orange tree.

"That was some ride," I murmured when she shut off the engine.

She took off her helmet and shook loose her long blond hair. I took off my helmet as well and dismounted. I tried to adjust my trousers to allow for more room.

"*Was* some ride?"

Denise got off the motorcycle and pushed it back onto the kickstand. She placed her helmet on the gas tank. I moved next to her and set my helmet on the rear seat. As I did so, she reached over and touched my cheek, held the point of my chin, and turned my face toward hers.

She kissed me. It was nothing like the brush of her lips in the walk-in cooler, but deep, penetrating, openmouthed, with her tongue searching for mine. I thought when I got off the motorcycle my erection would lessen, but the opposite was true. She sensed it, broke off the kiss, and looked down.

"The ride isn't over unless you want it to be." She placed a hand on my bulging mound and squeezed. "I like your enthusiasm."

I glanced at the clearing, dappled with spots of sunlight and rotten fruit. We were about five hundred feet from the main road, but I could only see trees and a rusty smudge pot or two in any direction.

"We have to be careful," I said.

"Careful?"

With her slightly crooked nose and voluptuous mouth, she was very sexy. She was, what my father would call, a good-looking broad, and now she was unbuckling my belt. Maybe I should just stay in Orange County.

She pretended to look around.

"There's no one here," she laughed. "Oh . . . *careful.*" She pressed her face to mine. We rubbed noses then kissed lightly. I could smell her skin and her shampooed hair. "You mean birth control. A girl's best friend. Don't worry," she said, tapping my nose with her finger, "I'm on the pill."

* * *

It was too chilly to disrobe completely. We opened up our jackets; she fumbled with my shirt buttons while I undid her blouse. We pressed against each other so that we could feel the warmth of our bodies as we shimmied up and down. Her breasts rubbed against me and I held each one in turn, eagerly kissing them and trying to take one and then the other into my mouth. I tried not to think too much about the last time I had done this and with whom, but Denise took my mind off the past when she tugged my pants and underwear down to my ankles and worked me into her mouth for a few exquisite moments.

Denise knew what she was doing; her movements were slow and exciting. She kept me aroused without making me climax too soon and, when I was about to, she squeezed firmly so that I held off.

She stood up, kissed me again. I was breathless, flushed, and my heart pounded. She wriggled her tight leather pants and cotton panties down around her boots.

"Let's fuck. Now," she said, turning to face an orange tree and gripped the trunk with both hands.

I moved up to her. She took as wide a stance as possible with her pants down around her ankles. Her white round bottom was pushed up toward me and she swayed invitingly. I held her hips, let my erection press against her cleft and the rough curly hairs. I felt a slight natural resistance as I eased into her. I started to thrust and was surprised by how wet and slick she was and by how she contracted her muscles to form a tight grip. I was deep inside. She moaned as I thrust in and out of her, then made a cooing, yelping sound as I moved faster and faster inside her. She hugged the tree, her face buried against her upper arm, and I rubbed the smooth white curves of her buttocks and pushed her blouse and jacket up.

I could see a butterfly tattooed on her lower back, her spine, the sweat that started to bead on her flesh. I sweated as well and drops fell on her. My breath came chuffing, like a spent runner. I felt a few withered oranges shake loose and drop near us. She shuddered against me and cried out in a long gasp of pleasure. An old orange pelted us. I swelled and exploded inside her, then continued to thrust in and out of her wet, slippery canal.

* * *

When we were finished, we did up our clothes and got ready to ride the rest of the way.

"That was fun, Diego." It was the first time she used my name. "We'll probably never do this again, but I'm glad it happened."

Denise took me along Trabuco and Irvine Road, where we merged onto the I-5 for the rest of the journey to Buena Park. I held her snugly, but there was no more fondling or groping; only my arms folded around her waist.

She exited at Orangethorpe and I directed her to Beach and Eleventh Street, then told her to turn right and go halfway down the street to my parents' house. I was tempted to have her drop me off at the corner and I would walk the rest of the way, but my father probably wasn't back yet and my mother was probably at church on a Saturday afternoon.

We pulled up in front of the house. I got off the motorbike while she left the engine running. I took off my helmet and gave her a kiss.

"You're great, Denise," I told her. "The ride of a lifetime."

I looked up and down the street, then turned and smiled at her. She smiled back.

"I'll see you at work," I added. "Wednesday's my last day."

"I know that."

We kissed again.

"Luv ya!" she called as she rode off, wriggling her fingers in a wave over her shoulder.

When I turned to the house, I saw the lace curtain move. Someone was inside. My mother had been watching.

* * *

As soon as I entered the house, my mother related: "Someone's been calling for you. It must be a secretary from that ad agency you applied to—she phoned three times."

I started down the hallway; my heart pounded.

"Maybe they want to offer you a job?" she said hopefully.

"Yeah, maybe."

I started to sweat. There were three telephones in the house; a wall phone in the garage, a telephone on a stand in the living room, and one on a dresser in the master bedroom. I usually used that phone, if my parents didn't need the bedroom, for private calls.

I peeled off the leather jacket and tossed it on the bed, then sat on the edge. The dresser was full of perfumes and pins, a statue of the Virgin Mary, a crucifix, a chipped box made of abalone shells where my mother kept costume jewelry. I tried not to look at myself in the dresser mirror, but my hair was a mess, my clothes disheveled, and I thought I smelled of sex.

Saloma answered on the second ring.

"Are you okay?"

She didn't say anything.

"Did you get my letter?"

"Yes." Then, she added: "I miss you, Diego."

"I miss you too." She sounded upset. "What is it?"

She hesitated.

"I'm late this month."

I didn't want to sound obtuse, but "late" could mean anything. Maybe she was late with this month's rent, or she hadn't paid a water bill on time, or her tuition payment was past due. It could be any of a dozen situations, I hoped.

"What do you mean?"

"I missed my period." She started to cry. "Diego, I'm so frightened."

"Don't worry," I insisted, but I started to feel lightheaded. "I love you," I blurted out automatically, but an hour earlier I had pushed all thought of Saloma out of my mind so that I could concentrate on fucking Denise and coming inside her. "Luv ya!" she had said so casually a few minutes before, and now I tried to use those same words to reassure Saloma.

"Don't worry," I repeated. "Don't do anything. I'll be back in a few days. We'll talk this through."

CHAPTER TEN

1980

I felt as if I couldn't get off the train, that I'd been on one long, clanking ride or another, chasing, always chasing for so long that I couldn't remember what I looked for. It seemed hours before the train reached San Luis Obispo, with another two-hundred-and-thirty miles to go, and my stomach in knots the entire time. I tried drinking coffee, the weak, watery stuff they served on Amtrak, but it repeated on me with a sour taste of bile.

Taking the train had seemed like a good idea when I'd booked the roundtrip ticket: I was a graduate student, I had time and not much money; it was an intriguing itinerary because the tracks led through sections where the highway didn't go, and pulling into the railroad stations would be nostalgic, like scenes from an old movie—*The Lady Vanishes* or *North by Northwest*. Now, *I* wanted to vanish and wondered why I hadn't just flown roundtrip.

I'd told Saloma what time the train was due to arrive that Friday and she said she'd try to meet me at the Townsend Depot. That was two days ago, when I'd phoned a second time, and there was no news about her condition. I hadn't contacted her since. The train seemed to be hopelessly behind schedule—more than an hour by the time we left San Luis Obispo—and it rained; a thick, waving curtain that obscured most everything. I made out the shapes of a few houses, a water tower, a church, but the pellets of rain seemed to bounce high in the street.

We were headed up a steep, winding grade when the steel wheels screeched and shuddered to a halt. The train held still. We sat on the incline for more than half an hour. When, at last, the conductor sauntered through, someone asked him what was going on. The conductor, a man in his fifties with a waxed handlebar moustache and a gold watch chain, said: "We've only got the front engine. Not enough to pull us up the Cuesta Grade in this storm. The wheels and tracks are too wet."

"What's going to happen?" I asked. I felt the blood rush from my head; my throat throbbed. I needed to be with Saloma right away to find out what our destiny would be. I might as well forget about the job in Germany if she was pregnant. There were worse fates than being stuck in a suburb working a dead-end job, if you had a loving family—if.

"We're gonna have to back down this hill all the way to San Luis. We'll back into the station and add two more locomotives. That'll get us through."

He must have noticed the look of trepidation on my face. He patted my shoulder. "Don't worry, son. We'll be clicking along in no time."

* * *

As it turned out, we were more than three hours behind schedule by the time we reached the halfway point, then met another delay because we had to yield the right-of-way to a southbound passenger train that was on schedule. Consequently, we sat on a siding for what seemed an interminable amount of time until the southbound train shot past, klaxon blared, porthole windows flickered by like a deck of cards being shuffled. At least it had stopped raining.

I realized we had no hope of making up the time. I needed to phone Saloma, tell her not to wait for me at the Townsend Depot. There was no point in her trying to meet me. I might not reach the City for another several hours.

I asked the conductor where the next whistle stop would be because I needed to make a phone call. He told me I'd have about fifteen minutes in King City. He looked at his pocket watch.

"Should be there in eleven minutes. Now, there's a phone booth on the platform. Go toward the rear of the train. Just after the baggage car is the middle car and if you wait there, when we pull into the station, you should see the phone booth right in front of you. But don't be late, young man." He snapped the cover of his pocket watch shut. "When I call 'all aboard' that means 'all aboard'!"

Right, I wanted to say. We wouldn't want any more delays.

I made my way through three passenger cars and the baggage car, opened and closed the connecting doors and heard the whoosh of air outside, until I reached the vestibule and stood on the landing by the exit door of the middle carriage. A woman with a little girl dressed in a tiny coat and polished shoes stood there as well. The little girl held her mother's hand and clutched a teddy bear in her arm. The mother had a large suitcase by her feet.

As the train slowed, the woman smiled at me. I looked out the door window at the platform as it shook into view. We coasted to a stop and I could see the phone booth covered on three sides by an acoustic shield shaped like an eggshell. The booth was completely open on one side, with no door. I would be able to rush in.

I turned back and smiled awkwardly at the woman. "I have to make a phone call." I glanced at her suitcase sheepishly.

"That's okay," she replied.

But it wasn't.

The train jerked to a stop. I twisted the door handle and jumped out, then reached back to help the lady with her suitcase. She slid it to me with her foot and I grabbed it by the handle and tugged it down. I held my hand toward her so that she would have support as she alighted from the train, the little girl now cradled in her arms.

"You're very kind," she said when she reached the platform. She smiled at me. I smiled back and turned to the phone.

A surprising number of passengers deboarded at this small town, and an equal number waited to get on. I pushed through the crowd and tried to scoot my way toward the phone booth. A sailor lugged a duffel bag and got there first. He paused, lit a cigarette, and moved on.

I grabbed the handset, dropped a quarter in the slot, and dialed. Saloma picked up the phone on the second ring.

"Hello?" She sounded cautious, but not tense.

"Saloma? It's Diego."

"I know," she laughed. "You're coming back today." She seemed happy to hear from me; maybe that's just what I wanted to believe.

"How are you?"

"I'm fine." She paused. "I'm having my period. I was late, that's all." She laughed, dryly. "I was silly to be so worried—and to have worried you."

I wanted to reassure her but glanced back at the train. No one else boarded now. The platform was quiet. The conductor leaned out the open door and looked carefully in both directions, north and south, eyeing the near empty platform. "No, you weren't being silly. It's okay. It got me thinking about a lot of things."

I drew a deep breath. It started to sink in. Things were back to normal. Nothing had changed. Everything was just the same as it had been before I left for Christmas. She wasn't pregnant.

"Listen," I pressed on, "you don't have to meet me at the station. We'll be hours late. We probably won't pull in until after nine."

"I'll be there," she said with laughter in her voice. "I have more good news."

* * *

"You look happy," the conductor said to me as I got back on the train. "Did your girlfriend say 'yes'?"

"Not exactly," I hesitated, but when I walked back through the baggage car and thought no one could hear me, I burst into song, warbling "Miracle of Miracles" from *Fiddler on the Roof*. I danced a few steps of a paso doble, then hopped an Irish jig, jumped in the air and clicked my heels. I needed to burn through my ebullience before I reached San Francisco. I didn't want Saloma to think I was overjoyed that I still had options in life, but I was.

North of King City the terrain was mostly flat and the train made up some of the lost time. We pulled into the depot near China Basin several hours late, but about half an hour earlier than when I thought we would arrive. It was only a quarter after eight when I exited the train, swinging my suitcase and a carry bag.

The station was noisy, with the clatter of carriage doors opening and travelers heading down the long, awninged platform toward the turnstiles and the reception room.

Saloma had given me a fright, and she'd apologized for that. I'd spent six worried days, barely able to sleep or eat, worried sick, and the train ride had been the worst part because I thought I was finally moving toward a conclusion but felt stuck in time. In my more reasonable moments, I figured I should only be mad at myself for not taking precautions, but I wondered if she hadn't hit the panic button too soon. She was only a few days late; it wasn't as if she had missed her period two months in a row, but what did I know about a woman's reproductive cycle?

I reached the turnstile and pushed through. I didn't have sisters, my mother wouldn't talk about such things, and what little I knew about a woman's menstrual cycle came from a Sex Ed course taught by Father Maurice in an all-boys' Catholic school. The old priest, in a wheelchair, seemed more concerned with lecturing on the evils of masturbation than he did with explaining ovulation. Yuki had explained a few things, and the guys talked in college and swapped conquest stories, most of which probably weren't true.

I entered the massive reception area and waiting room. The cluster of travelers quickly dispersed, some headed for the luggage claim room, others for the parking lot, some greeted by friends or family. The Mission-style structure had been built in the heyday of rail travel, with elongated cathedral-type stained glass windows, thick ceiling beams, murals depicting the romance of Old California and the hacienda days, and long, padded benches with high backrests that could seat a dozen people or more.

Now, the waiting room was mostly empty; an old woman mopped the tile floor, a man in a business suit read the *San Francisco Examiner*, a Latino couple pulled an iron grate down in front of the snack bar and locked up.

I glimpsed Saloma at a distance and waved to her. I felt a

pang of guilt mixed with anger when I saw she wore a tight-fitting leather jacket and slacks. Denise had worn something similar, and I shouldn't have been playing around. But Denise knew what she was doing. She was a liberated woman who was on the pill. She was responsible for her own body. I'd had a near miss with Saloma, and I should probably get out while I still could.

But when she ran up to embrace me, I felt very differently. I set my bags down and hugged her. We kissed lovingly. I brushed back her hair with my hands, looked into her eyes, kissed her again. I could smell her warm skin, her hair, her perfume. I felt intoxicated, I was so happy to be with her. I kissed her once more.

"Are you alright, darling?" She nodded and I wiped the tears from her eyes.

"We have a lot to talk about," she whispered, and it was my turn to nod in quiet assent. I felt a lump in my throat and couldn't say much.

* * *

I retrieved my car from long-term parking and drove to the Pinecrest Diner on Geary. Saloma told me about her family's activities, the candlelight vigil at the church, how much she'd missed me. I said I'd missed her too and that I thought about her during the long train ride back. I told her about the delays and the trouble at Cuesta Grade.

Over dinner at the Pinecrest Diner, we spoke in greater depth about ourselves.

She lit up a cigarette. "I'm trying to quit." She held out an open palm. "Look! No little pill inside. Empty. I'm nervous all the time, but I haven't taken a Quaalude in three weeks."

"That's great." I held her hand.

"I thought I might be pregnant. I didn't want to mess things up with 'ludes."

"Of course not."

She stubbed out her cigarette.

"But I'm still nervous. I'm trying to deal with it in other ways. I've been seeing a therapist."

"Oh?"

She smiled at me.

"It's free. It's through the university. Oh—and did I tell you? I've applied to the College of Ed. I'm going to do a second master's—in Special Education." She pulled her hand away. "I'm going to teach little children who really need me."

"Tell me about the therapist."

She laughed lightly.

"You sound like a therapist. There's not much to tell. I've only had a few sessions. First, you fill out a questionnaire—all about your fears and anxieties. Then, you meet with the therapist and talk about them. Don't worry," she smiled. "I'm getting it together. A new Saloma for the New Year!"

We clinked our wine glasses. She seemed to be enjoying her chicken piccata. I pointed to my own dish. "The lamb curry's good."

She asked me about my trip to Southern California. I said I had a gift for her; she smiled and said she had something for me too. I told her about the pier fishing trip and about my parents getting older. I described the work environment at the Carriage House but left out the part about Denise and the orange grove. I even hinted that I might have an opportunity to work overseas if I wanted to follow up on it.

She set down her fork and looked at me.

"Maybe you should. You have so much wanderlust. I don't think you'll ever really be happy until you're traveled out."

I looked away. I didn't say anything, then turned back to her.

"Oh—on the phone you said you had more good news."

She gave me a big smile, hesitated; her smile grew broader. Even her eyes smiled merrily.

"My sister Ezzie will be in Washington D.C. the whole semester. She's doing an internship in public administration, but we're keeping the apartment because of the lease."

* * *

She invited me to stay the weekend, but because of the hour we decided to go to my room that Friday night. We were only a few blocks from where I lived, I hadn't been there in weeks, and we were young, healthy, and didn't want to waste any more time. Saloma had been to my room before, to bring Thanksgiving leftovers when I crammed for exams, but this was the first time she would spend the night.

I wondered if we were playing with fire, but she told me she was at her highest flow and there was no risk of her getting pregnant. Saloma was a very gentle person, vulnerable in so many ways, and I said I only wanted to do this if this was what she wanted too. She replied that she'd had three weeks to think about it and, yes, she wanted to be with me fully and completely, as my friend and as my lover.

I unlocked the front door of the building and we headed up the stairs. Saloma carried my small bag while I lugged my suitcase to the landing next to the hallway phone. Mr. Meriwether came out of his room wearing a lavender and turquoise striped bathrobe and mumbled something about "Welcome back." He gave Saloma an odd look, as if he didn't quite like seeing women in the rooming house.

"You've met before."

He ignored Saloma. "Your mail's in the front room, in a box." He must have thought I was dying to hear the rooming house news. He added: "Ferrano left. He walked off his job and moved back to Cleveland."

I cocked an eyebrow.

"I didn't know Ferrano had a job."

"He worked in a sandwich shop for three days." Mr. Meriwether seemed finally to discover that Saloma was still there. "The room's for rent, if you want it. I accept all kinds."

Saloma suppressed a smile, but I caught the laughter in her eyes.

* * *

Once we were inside my room, we embraced and kissed affectionately.

"He's an odd duck," she said, smiling.

"They're all odd ducks in this rooming house."

She kissed me again.

"Every writer has a story about oddballs in the rooming house. One day you'll write yours."

"I suppose so."

We tongue-kissed and sat on the narrow bed. The springs squeaked noisily.

"I'd forgotten about that."

She covered her mouth to suppress a laugh. "Everyone will hear us."

"Ferrano's in Cleveland–his was the room next to this one. Mr. Meriwether turns off his hearing aid at night. He can't hear a damn thing. The others are too far back or too stoned to pay any attention. No one will hear us–unless you're a screamer," I added.

She unbuttoned my shirt. "I'm not a screamer. I only let out little moans of pleasure."

* * *

The bed squeaked with every twist and thrust, and we made love tenderly, energetically, exhaustedly, until after midnight. I lay in a groggy haze with Saloma next to me. Her head rested on my upper arm, her hand moved every so often across my chest. It seemed an especially tranquil moment after a long session of lovemaking, and it seemed we were both fully satisfied, content, at peace. Light from the street fell through the window and the occasional siren wailed, then receded into the distance.

"What would you have done?" she asked me.

I turned slightly as she moved back to look at me.

"What do you mean?"

"What would you have done if I'd been pregnant?"

I took a deep breath. I thought carefully about what I would say, tried to sort through my feelings.

"I probably would have asked you to marry me." She had a completely blank expression on her face. I hesitated, tried to read some meaning in her eyes. "And what would you have said?" I asked.

She rolled onto her back, away from me and stared at the ceiling.

"I would have said, 'you should think about it.'"

I was taken aback.

"Not, 'I'd like to think about it?'" I questioned.

"No, *you* should think about it." She turned to face me. "I don't have a very good track record, Diego. I've been engaged twice and broke it off each time."

"I knew you were engaged to your father's business partner and it wasn't going to work out."

"I was engaged to him *twice*. The second time I'd gonc as far as selecting a wedding dress, but I couldn't go through with it."

There was a long pause as tears filled her eyes and spilled over. "I'm a terrible person. I can't make a commitment and just cause people pain."

"Don't say that," I implored. "You're a wonderful person, a very caring person, and I care about you."

I kissed her wet cheek, her mouth. I dried her tears. Her body was round and soft and firm where it needed to be. We caressed each other, snuggled against each other, and I felt her body rub feverishly against mine. We were both excited and her smooth hand ran the length of my torso, then reached down to grasp my erection. We made love again to the chorus of the singing bedsprings, and this time we were able to sleep.

* * *

In the morning, we had breakfast at the Happy Boy diner on Fifteenth and Market, with its clientele of elderly couples, immigrants, roadworkers, and gays, then drove through West of Twin Peaks and St. Francis Wood to her apartment, where I dropped her off. We agreed to meet in the evening, after I'd had a chance to organize some things, go through my mail, and find out if anything else needed to be taken care of.

Mr. Meriwether filled me in on the news, after he fiddled with his hearing aid to make sure it was turned up high. Nothing had changed and everything had. Lisa and Stephen, the couple from Australia, had left, saying they wanted to see what life in Vancouver was like; a new tenant, Wade, a sometime social worker, had taken the back room.

Ferrano had split for Cleveland, but he'd find nothing but disappointment there, Mr. Meriwether tut-tutted. "His father's a concert violinist, his brother's a professor, and his sister is a trial attorney. And Ferrano, well, he's—"

"A bit slow?" I queried. We sat in the common room, where the television set and magazine rack were. I'd entered to retrieve my box of mail but had fallen into conversation with Mr. Meriwether.

He tapped his temple. "He only comes across as stupid, but he's not."

"I always thought he was just a bit slow on the uptake," I offered.

Mr. Meriwether shook his head. "If he'd been born mentally deficient, he wouldn't have advanced reading skills and an extensive vocabulary. Do you ever see the books he reads—*Naked Lunch, Hopscotch*. I think he's brain damaged."

You probably needed to be brain damaged to understand those books, I thought to myself. "Ferrano told me about his acid trips," I said.

Mr. Meriwether clucked his tongue. "It's tragic, in a way. A good family, good education, and he would just lie on his bed all day long and stare at the ceiling."

"When he wasn't reading William S. Burroughs and Julio Cortazar or shooting the bull with Karl Hamburger," I put in.

"Well, I wouldn't be surprised if he ends up back here," Mr. Meriwether said. "If he does, he can have his old room back—for the same rent."

I met Wade Hoxsted, a burly, affable man in his early twenties, whose bushy black beard and thick head of hair seemed to sprout in all directions. He told me he worked part-time as a social worker but wanted to get more involved in political causes—he wasn't sure which ones, but he wanted to change the system.

"The way things are right now," he grunted, leaning against the door jamb of his room, "it's just one big rip-off, man! The system just wants to make money out of you and throw you away. The system doesn't see my job skills as marketable, so I just get ripped off." He laughed, exposing a big set of even teeth. "I get so depressed, it's all I can do to hang in there by taking pills at night and smoking weed."

At least he had a sense of humor, but I wasn't entirely sure he was joking. Even though he'd only been in the backroom a few weeks, a musty, acrid smell emanated from inside. The room reeked of dirty socks and smoke-filled air.

I didn't have much in the way of mail. A stack of rejection letters from publishers, a Christmas card from a cousin in Austria, a sweepstake offer that claimed I was already a millionaire. The most interesting piece of mail was a travel brochure advertising low-cost flights to Europe.

* * *

Karl was still around. After more than two years in San Francisco, he still lived on government assistance. He put in the minimum amount of time registering to collect his monthly check, but a more typical day began by him trying to scrounge up loose change. He told me about his modus operandi, how he kept himself entertained.

"See, sometimes I'll ask people if they have change for the bus, or I feel inside coin return slots at phone booths." He grinned when he told me how he hustled up change. "I really only need a couple of quarters to get started. A buck to keep me going on a bad day." He scratched his head. "A sidewalk near a bank's a good place to search for coins. If I'm desperate, I'll swing by a sidewalk café and scoop the tips from a table. If I'm really desperate, I'll ask someone for a handout, say I just lost my job and haven't eaten in three days. I try to pick a well-dressed lady out shopping or some business exec. Hell, they don't need it."

He beamed. Karl was a better-than-average pool player but a star, like Minnesota Fats, when shooting pool in some south of Market Street dive.

I'd seen him play, and he was right. He only needed a quarter to get started. For twenty-five cents, he could release a set of stripes and solids at Emmett's and play pool all day so long as he kept winning. Sometimes he'd wager a beer or a sandwich, if he thought he had a sucker.

"I usually win," he said. "I work hard at it."

In the evening, I drove over to see Saloma, as arranged. I hadn't driven my car in more than three weeks and it seemed to be acting up. The engine lugged whenever I went uphill. The brakes felt spongy. But at least the temperature gauge held steady; the needle pointed right where it needed to be.

At her apartment, Saloma greeted me with a warm kiss and took my coat. She wore jeans and an untucked blouse and her hair was pulled back. I kissed her again, looked into her eyes. I was afraid to tell her that I loved her because I wasn't sure how she would react. I couldn't recall her saying those words very often, as if she believed words cheapened our feelings. If we felt a certain way, we would show it through our actions. We would know it and wouldn't have to say a thing.

We sat down to dinner. She had made Shepherd's Pie and served it with a salad. I had brought a large bottle of Chianti, guessing that it would go well with most any meal, and we toasted as we wished each other a belated Merry Christmas and a Happy New Year.

"Shepherd's Pie," I enthused. "Perfect on an evening in January. It warms my English heart."

She smiled at me.

"You're more mixed up than I am. You're so many different nationalities. Which one are you tonight?"

"I'm all of them," I grinned. "And I'm happy when I'm with you." I ticked off the list. "I'm Spanish, Austrian, English, American." I paused. "And if we get married, I'll become honorary Filipino-Chinese."

"That won't happen," she said.

I feigned surprise. I knew neither one of us was stable enough for any long-term living arrangement, but it was fun to play at domestic bliss—the meal, the wine, the apartment, the shared intimacies. Still, it wasn't exactly an encouraging response.

"Why not?" I questioned.

"Because Filipino-Chinese isn't a nationality. And I'm American."

We cleared up after the meal, then sat on the couch to exchange Christmas gifts. She had gone back to Woolworth's to buy the leather-bound journal she had wanted to give me.

"It's lovely," I remarked.

"You can write down all of your adventures," she said. "Writers always do."

I also had a bound volume for her: a collection of Sylvia Plath's poems. The copy was used, but it was a first edition. I knew that ever since Saloma had read *The Bell Jar* she'd been interested in Sylvia Plath.

She seemed to blush then gave me a radiant smile. "I'll treasure it."

"Her husband was a bit of a bastard."

"Ted Hughes? I'm not surprised," she said lightly. "He was a man, wasn't he?"

A lot of women in San Francisco liked to beat men over the head with their brand of feminism, but Saloma wasn't like that. She wanted to be enlightened but dispensed with the agenda of grievance, even though she'd implied I was as unsavory as Plath's wayward husband, Ted Hughes. She must have read a look of disappointment on my face. She reached out and caressed my cheek.

"Not all men," she assured me. "You're not a bastard."

I hadn't made up my mind about Germany or about trying to stay in San Francisco to make a go of things, but whichever way I leapt, I'd let her know first and would tell her the whole story.

We were in bed by eight-thirty and made love under the covers. We were becoming more comfortable with each other's bodies, more proficient in the act of intercourse, and more knowledgeable about how we could give each other pleasure. Around midnight, we made love again, and this time Saloma bit my ear and dug her fingernails into my buttocks as I thrust faster and faster inside her. We slept exhausted in a tent of rumpled sheets and covers, our legs intertwined, our fingers laced together. I'd rolled onto my back sometime in the early hours of the morning; she had as well and I could hear her sleeping soundly, the even cadence of her breath, until that steady, reassuring sound lulled me to sleep as well.

We spent our Sunday at the Palace of the Legion of Honor Art Museum, at the top of a winding road on the northwest corner of Lincoln Park. I had visited the neoclassical-style museum once before, with a French language and culture class, and Saloma said she had toured the art collection on a few occasions.

It was a stunning collection for an American city the size of San Francisco. I was especially interested in the paintings by El Greco, Titian, and Rubens, and was in awe of the gilded Spanish ceiling from 1500. Saloma was more interested in the contemporary art collection and works by Jackson Pollock, Edward Ruscha, and Barbara Kruger.

It was a fine day, warm for late January, and we had lunch in the Museum café, overlooking the patio and with a view of Lincoln Park and the Marin Headlands. I had tomato bisque with a grilled chicken sandwich, while Saloma enjoyed a roasted cauliflower salad. We each had a glass of Chardonnay. It wasn't cheap eating in the Museum, and at this rate I could see myself burning through my holiday savings. But I was starting a new job on Monday and it seemed worth every penny to be in elegant surroundings with a beautiful woman I felt so strongly about. I held her hand and rubbed my fingers against hers.

On the drive back to her apartment, we stopped at a liquor store and bought two six-packs—one of Bass Ale and the other of Guinness Stout. We had decided to enjoy the rest of the afternoon over Black and Tans. I told her I had a way to layer the two beers, pouring the second beer slowly over an upturned spoon so that the pale ale and the black stout stayed separated.

We pulled the curtains back in her bedroom so that the late afternoon sunlight streamed in. We made love in the daylight and felt that we were out-of-doors. We dozed, then drank another Black and Tan and spent the rest of the afternoon touching each other and caressing, speaking of everything and nothing—mutual friends, past experiences together, my desire for travel, her love of children, our dreams and hopes and plans.

She told me Eddie had been dismissed from the creative writing program.

"I didn't know that." I turned to face her. Eddie from Hoboken. The guy who was always boasting about how great he was and how nobody else's writing measured up to his own. "I'm not altogether surprised," I added. "The last couple of times I saw him, he was in a tailspin."

"Not just the last couple of times," Saloma said. "He's been on the slide for years."

I smiled.

"I don't think I ever told you about this. Last summer, I was at a keg party with Eddie." I placed the half empty glass on my chest as I remembered Eddie, swaggering and guzzling the free beer. "He couldn't stop himself. He was already smashed, but grabbed two huge quart cups of beer." I paused as I thought of his thick fingers clawing the paper cups. "So guess what happened?"

"He fell asleep?"

"Not right away. When he tried sitting in an armchair, he dropped both quart cups right in his lap. *Then* he fell asleep. He spent all night in his soaked trousers, snoring as if he didn't have a care in the world."

We laughed despite ourselves. Eddie was a sad case and we should have felt sorry for him, but the thought of him being so greedy that he ended up looking like he'd wet himself had a kind of poetic justice.

"Poor Eddie," Saloma said when we stopped laughing.

I sipped my Black and Tan. "But for the grace of God, there go I."

She looked at me. "I worried about you for a long time. I thought you'd end up like Eddie."

I was touched that she'd been concerned, but I was also defensive.

"I hung out with him, yeah. But he always struck me as a bullshit artist."

"You hung out with him too much," she said, "but now I see you've figured out some of your own goals. That's good."

Did I want to be analyzed, mothered, told what to do? It was sweet of her to care, but I changed the subject.

"Cheers," I said. We clinked glasses and enjoyed our Black and Tans. "But you're doing well, Saloma."

She grew pensive.

"Yes, I've been working through a few things—with my therapist."

"You said you might do a second master's?"

She lay on her back and looked at the ceiling. The beer, the sunlight, the sex had made us relaxed and ruminative.

"My advisor thinks I'll get in."

"A second master's," I mused. "Special Ed on top of a degree in psychology. You can write your own ticket."

She didn't say anything for the longest time. When she spoke, it was in a soft but determined voice. "I don't want to write my own ticket. I don't want to go anywhere. You're the one who wants to go away."

I searched my mind for some line of poetry I might quote: the easy response, the quip, the philosophical reflection, but I had no answer.

* * *

When the light outside the window faded into dusk, then night, and we were hungry, we ordered Pasquale's pizza. We still had some beer, and when the doorbell rang I went downstairs with a towel wrapped around my waist and hurriedly accepted the box of pizza. I paid the deliveryman and tipped him the change.

"Thanks, pal." He tried to peek into the room, but I kept the door open only a few inches and shut it quickly, then went back upstairs to be with Saloma.

We didn't feel like getting dressed, we didn't feel like going out, we only wanted some quick nourishment so that we could spend as much time as possible together, naked and in bed, enjoying each other's bodies and the spots of time that would evaporate like teardrops on a hot day.

* * *

I left near midnight because I needed a few hours in my own room in order to be ready for my new job the next day.

"Call me soon," she said when I was leaving.

She stood by the door, hair tousled, with only a coverlet around her. I kissed her lips.

"Of course I'll call you. I'll call you every day, if you want me to."

She questioned me with her eyes, her smile tight, but we kissed again.

CHAPTER ELEVEN

The first day on the job I could barely get up from my desk to walk to the file room. I was assigned to the Occupational Safety and Health Administration as a clerk/typist for thirty hours a week, which was ideal because while I earned benefits I would still have time to pursue other endeavors, principally language study and writing. But I was so sore even the touch of my underwear on my genitals hurt like hell.

Mr. Weaver, a short man with a crew cut and horn-rimmed glasses, must have noticed I limped. When I had applied for the job, he had interviewed me in the Federal Building on Seventh Street and I had glided into the room to shake his hand. Now, I favored my right leg. Mr. Weaver seemed to be staring. He was my supervisor and was going to show me the ropes. He said: "You look a bit stiff."

I extemporized.

"I guess I overdid it," I suggested with a weak smile. "I spent the whole weekend playing pick-up games of basketball." He raised an eyebrow. "Full court," I added. As if that wasn't convincing, I went on: "With a bunch of undergraduates."

"Yes," he said and looked at me over the rim of his glasses. "Well, none of us are as young as we used to be. Basketball," he mused. "Full court. With undergraduates." He shook his head and led me down the hall.

What was I supposed to say—I just came from a marathon sex weekend with my girlfriend? I wondered if Saloma was as sore as I was. I'd have to phone her in the evening to see how she was doing.

As he opened the door to the file room, Mr. Weaver turned to me: "It must have been a rough game. Somebody bit your ear."

Despite the sarcasm, it didn't take me long to learn the office routine. As a clerk/typist, I was responsible for typing letter-perfect, multiple copies of memos.

"Speed is less important than accuracy," Mr. Weaver lectured me. "No more than one corrected word per page."

That meant if I made two mistakes I'd have to start over, even if I was at the bottom of the page.

For some of the memoranda, I needed to make several carbon copies at the same time. Each copy was on a different colored carbon paper—one green, one light blue, one pink, one lavender—and the sheets had to be stacked and aligned, then fitted tightly into the roller of the typewriter. Again, I was only allowed one corrected word per page, but since I had to change copy with different colored correction fluid—there were bottles for the green, the light blue, the pink, and the lavender sheets—and I had to wait for the pages to dry before I could realign them, it almost wasn't worth it. I'd start over even if I'd only made one mistake.

The content of the memos didn't make for compelling reading; they were usually about who would go on vacation when or the dates for the issuance of new photo I.D.s.

Because San Francisco and Oakland were major seaports,

our office investigated numerous shipbuilding and ship repair accidents, as well as commercial shipboard casualties that took place in the Bay. I was responsible for collating and filing the fatality reports, which *did* make for compelling reading in all their grisly detail. I hadn't known there were so many ways a seafarer or workman could meet his end. Falling overboard and drowning was the obvious demise, but a person could also be crushed by heavy equipment, tumble down a shaft, suffocate in an enclosed space, lose consciousness from chemical fumes or toxins, be incinerated in a shipboard fire, or blow oneself up welding too close to an acetylene tank.

The fatality reports were almost always accompanied by photographs. One poor bastard who'd died in a fire looked like a charred log except for the soles of his feet, which were intact because he'd been standing when a ball of fire roared through the gangway and turned him into instant charcoal.

Maybe it was best that I didn't get a job on a ship. I might cut or burn myself cooking if I went to Germany, but a sliced finger or blistered hand healed rapidly enough.

The afternoon-commute the dozen blocks home on the BART train was a flurry of umbrella and newspaper-toting office workers, the whoosh of train doors opening and closing, and a blur of muralled stations and spiraling staircases that led to the street. Headed home after my first full day, I negotiated the steps of the Mission Street station with some difficulty, then hobbled the rest of the way home. What normally should have been a ten-minute walk took me almost twenty. I phoned Saloma from the hallway of the rooming house.

She sounded tired.

"How are you feeling?" I asked.

"Happy and content. And sore," she added.

"Me too," I laughed softly. I looked down the hall. Wade's door was open, but his room was all the way in the back. "I think we overdid it," I said.

"It was worth it."

"For me too."

I told her I would try to stop by Wednesday evening after my German class, if she was in. "Just for a drink," I added.

"You'll have recovered by then," she teased, but I wasn't so sure.

* * *

Over the next several weeks, I fell into the pattern of the morning and evening rush-hour commute, typing and filing throughout the day, and then trying to do some writing in the evening or on the days when I didn't work at OSHA. My writing seemed circuitous and tortured; if I reread a passage a day or so later I concluded I'd wasted my time. But I really hadn't. As a young writer full of ideas and ambition, it was good to try everything—to write using different points of view, different voices and styles, different genres and techniques. Those failed attempts were attempts, not failures, and they all added up to experiences and a repertoire I could use in later years.

Those weeks were also filled with thoughts of Saloma, seeing her at least one evening a week after my French or German class, talking to her by phone most nights, and often spending a long weekend with her if she wasn't busy with her family. We were very careful and either paid close attention to her cycle and calculated the safe days of the month or I used a condom. Sometimes, we used both methods, though Saloma said she was never really comfortable with contraceptives because of the Church, but the rhythm method was fine. It was the old saw, I told her; the Church didn't allow contrivances, but contrivance was okay. I reassured her: she didn't have to use a contraceptive—*I* would, since I wasn't a practicing Catholic, and that seemed to settle things.

Office work was office work. I came to understand the office as a place of tedious tasks and endless ennui, but also the locus of internecine intrigues and intimate relationships. Half the office workers seemed to be sleeping with the other half, and everyone seemed to have a story. There was the office flirt, who had been divorced three times; the office drunk, who could be relied on to fall asleep after his three-Martini lunch; the ex-merchant seaman, the reformed drug addict, the suburbanite, the Puerto Rican who told everyone he was gay, the rate-breaker whom everyone despised because she produced too much work. It was a government office like any office anywhere. We were on the fourteenth floor of the Federal Building on Seventh Street in San Francisco, but I told myself we might have been at the Hague.

When the weather grew warmer in late February, Saloma and I decided we would drive to Baker Beach for a cookout. Baker Beach was at the foot of Golden Gate Park, about fifteen minutes by car from Saloma's apartment. But that Saturday we drove first to the Safeway on Taravel to buy pork chops, the vegetables we'd want to cook, beverages, charcoal briquettes, paper plates and plasticware, and whatever else we thought we might need for an outing. We returned to her apartment briefly to dice and marinate the vegetables, mix a separate marinade for the pork, then pack the cooler and load the car.

My car gave me trouble; it seemed I had to top off all the

fluids before driving anywhere. Sometimes, I had to add a second quart of oil for the drive back. But so long as I didn't have to go for a long drive out of town—no further than Oakland or Berkeley—I didn't worry overly.

We spent the early evening grilling at the beach, enjoying the stiff breeze and the view of the Golden Gate Bridge and Marin Headlands. It was almost perfect, the vivid and crisp colors of the hills and the sea, the sailboats, the rust-red pylons of the famous bridge. We had the beach almost to ourselves, it seemed; in the distance, fishermen in rubber waders cast into the surf. They were brave souls, as were we; it was really too early in the year to enjoy an evening at the beach.

But Saloma looked beautiful with her sable hair blowing back in the wind. We were foolhardy in more ways than one, trying to eat outdoors as the sun set and the temperature dropped even lower. She sat on a log the entire time, wrapped in a thick blanket. I wore my Army surplus jacket as I cooked and left it zipped up. We laughed about how cold it was, ate hurriedly, and got back into the car.

That night, after making love under the warm covers in her bedroom, she told me about her abortion.

"You knew I had an abortion, didn't you?"

I hesitated. She was lying on her side next to me, looked at me intently. I didn't want to say too much in case Ezzie hadn't informed her of our conversation.

"My sister told you, didn't she?"

"Yes," I admitted. "I think she wanted to frighten me away." I turned to Saloma. "That didn't work—obviously."

She offered a wan smile, then rolled onto her back.

"I was only sixteen. I was forced to have an abortion. I didn't have any choice."

"No one would blame you. I feel sorry for you—at that age, having to go through that."

I didn't want to trespass on her privacy. She could tell me as much or as little as she wanted to. I wondered who the father was. I assumed it was the man she'd been engaged to twice—her father's business partner.

"It isn't a sin if you have no choice, is it? Sort of like 'the sins of the father.' They shouldn't be passed on to the children." There was a lot in what she didn't say that had me thinking, and I could tell a great deal from her tone of voice.

"I'm the last person you should ask about sin," I replied. "I don't know anything about it—what's right or wrong for a woman, what she should or shouldn't do in that situation."

We lay together side by side, in silence. Then, she continued: "I felt so miserable for a long time. I felt betrayed, abandoned by the one person I thought I should be able to trust. I didn't want to go on living."

She spoke more rapidly, and a quick breath seemed to punctuate each sentence.

"Whatever feelings of affection I had turned to hate. Leaving the Philippines was a blessing, but I haven't been able to love anyone—or trust anyone—ever since."

She turned and gently rubbed my chest. She spoke thoughtfully: "That's why it took us so many months, Diego. I was afraid."

I let out a deep breath. "You know I'll leave one day. Maybe soon."

"I know."

"It doesn't matter?"

"It doesn't matter."

We listened to the sound of the night traffic, a siren in the distance, a ship's foghorn out at sea. After a long while, she said: "Now I've told you my sad story. You'll have to tell me yours. You look so sad and serious sometimes."

We bared everything—our bodies, our souls, our past. But some things I wanted to keep from her.

"Why should I tell you my sad story?"

"Because you're my friend."

That struck home.

"Yeah, I guess so. No great tragedy or loss," I shrugged. "Just all the disappointments and humiliations and rejections—the little sadnesses—that add up to something larger." I'd had my own suicidal moments—what thinking person doesn't consider the prospect of self-slaughter—but I didn't want to compare my unhappiness to hers.

"No great loss in my family," I said. "—so far. You've had it a lot worse."

"What about your brother?" she probed. "You never talk about him."

For good reason, I thought to myself, but she wanted honesty and trust and was revealing all her vulnerabilities to me as another form of penetration.

"*That* character," I said. "The Golden Boy." My chest constricted and I gritted my teeth. "He could never do any wrong in my parents' eyes—until he did. And even then, my mother tried to overlook everything." I paused, took a deep breath. I felt my temples throb, my jaw muscles clenched. "Oh, he was the wunderkind, the big man at Stanford," I went on. "My father thought he should have gone to West Point to be an Army officer."

"And then?"

"Two-eighty-eight P.C. Ever heard of it?" I must have sounded angry because she didn't say anything for the longest time. I wasn't upset with Saloma, only enraged with all that had happened in the past, the lost opportunities, the misplaced affection. "That's California Penal Code 288—the 'Short Eyes' charge. Child molester, sexual assault of a child . . ."

I breathed heavily now. I was ashamed of what had happened; I was ashamed that my eyes filled with tears; I was ashamed that Saloma was about to see me cry over something I had tried to suppress for so long. "Have you heard enough?" I asked her.

"It's up to you." She stroked my chest. "Sometimes it's good to talk, to let these things out."

I took a deep breath, held it, then exhaled slowly.

"My mother tried to excuse everything," I said in a choked voice. I shook my head in anger, tried to fight back the tears. "She paid his bail. She wanted to pay for an attorney. He—" The words felt like chunks of dirt in my throat: "—asked her for five thousand dollars . . . then took off for good."

Tears streamed from my eyes and ran down my cheeks. I stifled my sobs but shook against the bed. "I'm sorry," I said fitfully. I wiped my eyes hard with the back of my hand.

Saloma pressed herself against me and kissed my wet cheek. She nuzzled her face against my neck; I could feel her tears as well.

"I'm the one who should be sorry—for asking—and for making you relive so much pain."

"It's okay," I answered, but I wasn't entirely sure it was alright. People always said this sort of thing didn't reflect on the family, but it did. My parents had been heartbroken. It had taken me years to forget about my brother, to pretend he didn't exist. "It's okay," I repeated. "He's out of my life now—I hope forever. The last I heard he was living in Honduras."

I tried to say something clever.

"Maybe he's become a priest."

And despite ourselves, we were able to laugh through our tears and see the absurdity of life mixed with sorrow.

* * *

In the middle of the night, Saloma asked if my brother had ever tried to molest me. She spoke clinically, as if she were analyzing a case study in one of her psychology classes. "Many instances of child sexual abuse are with adults who are known to the victim—sometimes a family member, but generally a trusted adult who is already close to them and is known to them. In that sense," and Saloma's voice was cold, toneless, seemingly devoid of emotion, "child sexual abuse may share situational similarities with incest. The trusted adult may be an older brother, an uncle, a father," and this time her voice trailed off.

Saloma had more or less confirmed what I had suspected—that she had been impregnated by her own father, but she was probably never going to reveal any more than that to me. Why should she? It wasn't going to change the way I felt about her. I felt disgust, revulsion at what her father had done, but only deeper compassion for Saloma. I lay next to her with my arms folded, staring at the ceiling. "No, my brother never touched me." A vivid memory came back to me, my brother and I walking to St. Pius V Catholic school dressed in our blazers and ties. He asked me about my school friends, wondered if all of us showered together after gym. It was a strange question—in the elementary grades, we went straight back to class after recess. He knew that.

I hesitated. "He went off to Stanford when he was seventeen. I didn't see too much of him after that." I remembered another strange question he'd asked me. I was probably ten years old and he would have been sixteen. He wanted to know if I had a female side. I was too young to understand what he meant, but I must have looked at him in an odd way. "I do," he said smugly. "I have nothing from Bartolo—everything from Mutti. She's the one who made me."

I was old enough to understand he must owe something to

my father, even if my Dad didn't always live up to my mother's aspirations. Instead, she lived her aspirations through Hidalgo.

"Nothing from Dad?" I'd asked.

"To me, he's nothing but a Spanish peasant. His idea of happiness is being drunk with his pals in a ditch." I rolled onto my side and looked at Saloma. "My brother is a messed-up guy —my mother poured all her ambitions into him and praised him to no end. I think he thought he could get away with anything. But we make our own choices too. We had the same parents, we went to the same school, were raised in the same religion. We even speak the same languages."

"He's lucky."

I propped myself on an elbow, stared at her in the half light. "What do you mean?"

"It's tough living in Honduras if you don't speak Spanish."

Ferrano returned to San Francisco after only a few weeks in Cleveland. He was able to get his old room back. I saw him on a Thursday afternoon sitting in the common room, staring listlessly at a television set. I was on my way to my German class but took a few minutes to say hello.

The Undersea World of Jacques Cousteau was on and Ferrano told me he enjoyed watching the shapes and colors.

Ferrano had his lucid moments, but this didn't seem to be one of them; I wondered if he'd dropped a tab.

"You tripping, man?"

"I just got back from a trip," he snickered. "From Cleveland."

"How was it?"

"Same old, same old." He paused; his glazed eyes widened

as he stared at the blobs of jellyfish moving on the television screen. "Same cold. Same old tired bullshit."

"I'm surprised you're back," I replied casually.

Ferrano's wavy brown hair looked a bit longer, but he was still clean-shaven and square-jawed. He wore tooled cowboy boots, blue jeans, and a tee-shirt that read: Cavaliers.

"Thought things would be better with my family," he spoke up, "but it's just the same."

Maybe he could hear me, maybe it registered. I couldn't be sure, but I asked: "Yes, but why come back here, to San Francisco? Why not try your luck somewhere else?"

What ran through my mind was that Ferrano had been miserable living in that small room, with no girlfriend in town, no job, and no prospects—and he returned to the same.

He looked at me. "I like the shapes and colors. It must be fascinating to go to the bottom of the sea. I wonder what it's like there. Do you think there's intelligent life?"

* * *

I'd been studying French on my own and through evening classes for a little over a year and had layered additional knowledge on top of whatever I had learned at home or through travel. Still, I was much less proficient in French than in German; I could read newspaper articles or young adult literature readily enough but struggled with the pronunciation. When I watched French movies and deliberately ignored the subtitles I missed a great deal of what was said. I also had trouble wrapping my mouth and tongue around the vowel sounds—at least to the satisfaction of our French teacher, Madame Gilbert, a slender, lean-faced woman who was from Bayonne. Yet I knew that if I had an opportunity to work in

France, or for that matter in French Canada, I would come back reasonably fluent.

I'd grown up hearing Spanish and German. For the longest time, I was the immigrant kid embarrassed to be different. If my mother spoke to me in German, I'd answer in English, afraid that other kids my age would think it strange if they heard me speaking "the old country language." When I entered high school, with its requirement of four years of a foreign language, I selected Spanish, took an interest, spent two summers in Mexico as an exchange student, and maintained my oral skills either speaking Spanish at home with my father or with the kitchen help in restaurants.

I also took two years of German as an elective in high school; I pled my case with the principal, Father Koperski, that I would be going into the Humanities and that additional knowledge of foreign languages would be of greater benefit to me than Physics and Calculus. He relented, saying: "I knew your brother. He was a good boy. He's at Stanford now, isn't he?"

Unlike most other students in my high school German class, I had endless opportunities for reinforcement, if I wanted them, and the occasional family trip to Austria allowed me to put my knowledge to greater use and to practical application.

By the time I took "German for Reading Knowledge" at San Francisco State, I was comfortable with the spoken form, had a reasonably extensive vocabulary for everyday purposes but could see the benefit of advanced readings in a range of topics: German history, sciences, psychology, theater history, and selections from famous literary works. The course was designed to prepare graduate students to pass their foreign language proficiency exams, if they were going into doctoral programs, or to read scholarly articles in scientific journals if they were working in industry.

Because I was already at a higher level in German than in French, I enjoyed the reading class more. There were plenty of "skills and drills" in the French class and we seemed to answer such questions as "Ou est le gare du Nord?" ad infinitum, though I recognized that a basic ability to respond rapidly to simple interrogatives was a survival skill I would need if I ended up in France.

Some of the readings in German, on the other hand, struck me as profoundly interesting and relevant. I was fascinated by Hugo von Hoffmannsthal's classic "Letter from Philip Lord Chandos," and on first reading was completely fooled into believing it was a German translation of an Elizabethan document rather than an early twentieth-century expression of existentialist doubt. It seemed to encapsulate everything I felt about failed literary goals and the inadequacy of language. Equally compelling, for me, was a passage from Harold Clurman:

"There will always remain a yearning for something else: the unknown, a different home, even at times a different country. Still, one must choose what is compatible with the most consistent reality of one's nature and situation."

I hadn't yet chosen, and I was running out of time.

* * *

That weekend, Saloma and I decided to drive to the Noe Valley Ministry, a wooden Presbyterian church on Sanchez Street that resembled a large Victorian home, but with a steeple and a cross added on. A special Saturday afternoon screening of the 1924 silent film *Greed* was to take place in the community room, preceded by a lecture. We were both interested in seeing Erich von Stroheim's opus, which originally came in at more than eight hours of screen time but had been edited down by "insensitive" movie moguls to a still lengthy two-and-a-half hours. Considered a landmark in movie history, it was one of the first major productions to have been filmed entirely on location, and much of it was shot in San Francisco and Death Valley.

I was interested in the movie because I had seen parts of it in film school. Saloma wanted to view images of the San Francisco her mother had inhabited, since she was born the same year the film was made. We planned on having an early dinner afterwards.

She dressed elegantly in high-waist slacks, a blouse with a wide collar, and a sleeveless crocheted vest. The weather was still cool and she wore a belted camel-colored cloth coat on top.

I thought we still looked good together and my outfit—a tweed sports coat, corduroy waistcoat and trousers, and an open collared dress shirt—didn't seem at odds with hers. I wasn't expecting rain but carried a trench coat in case it got cold later.

In the church community room, we hung our coats on wooden pegs, then sat on a long bench. About a dozen other aficionados were seated around the room, which had a small stage in front with a piano to the side and a screen pulled down from the ceiling.

Behind us was a 16 millimeter projector on a cart. A busty woman with round glasses and white ringlet curls of hair had already threaded the first reel into the projector.

The guest speaker took the stage. He had been billed as the grandson of the famous filmmaker and he looked something like Erich von Stroheim, minus the monocle and cropped Prussian military haircut. He spoke without a foreign accent and didn't strut the stage arrogantly, as his grandfather might have.

He spoke briefly about the importance of the film, his grandfather's obsession with "realism" and adherence to the source novel, his use of San Francisco locations that many of us might recognize. He concluded that it was a great shame that crass studio heads, concerned only with the bottom line, had wrested artistic control from an obvious genius, and I thought to myself: they all say that, every director who brings in a film over-budget and overly-long—Sergei Eisenstein, Orson Welles, Michael Cimino— "it was a masterpiece until the moneymen cut it to shreds."

When the lights dimmed and the movie started, the projector rattled and whirred behind us, and the black and white images flickered on the screen. A pianist improvised music to accompany each scene, pounded out something threatening when McTeague scowled and skulked and looked angry, then segued into a tender melody when he gazed at Trina and fell in love.

I appreciated the use of the deep-focus cinematography, almost two decades before Orson Welles was praised for the same, and the "Soviet-style" montage editing that cross-cut for ironic emphasis.

Saloma sat very close to me, and we held hands. During some of the more dramatic moments, she gripped my upper arm and was excited when she recognized a locale, whispered into my ear: "That's Polk Street" or "That's St. Paulus Lutheran Church." She'd lived in San Francisco much longer than I had, but I recognized the Ferry Building, Market Street, and the Cliff House, though the exterior had been extensively remodeled since the film was made.

I recognized the intersection of Hayes and Laguna but was surprised by how many power lines and cables hung above the streets in those days. Nothing seemed to have been buried underground and it was fascinating to see images from more than fifty years ago of a place where I lived.

We both enjoyed the movie, talked about it afterwards, and

found the highly stylized silent movie acting sometimes hard to watch and the frequent intertitle card "Such was McTeague!" risible.

"Such was Diego!"

"Such was Saloma!" we joked as we walked arm in arm to the car.

"Such was McTeague!"

* * *

We drove the five miles from the Noe Valley Ministry to Santorini Fish Market on Mason and Bay, passed Russian Hill, where we had first kissed. It was late afternoon, and the colors of the Bay were lush and resplendent. I was able to park a mere two blocks from the restaurant.

"Grad students know all the good places to eat," Saloma said.

We entered Santorini Bakery and walked through to the small seafood restaurant.

"We share notes," I chuckled. "We know all the little hideaways where it's 'bring your own bottle' but good eats." I held the door for her. "But this place actually has a wine list."

The room was narrow, with a few booths running along the two facing walls, a cluster of tables near the street window, and four long tables pushed together in the middle of the hardwood floor. Most of the tables were taken by couples and families, and a group of teenagers wearing Galileo High School sweatshirts sat at the center tables.

The young people seemed to be eating gyros with fries, but the older couples had ordered seafood dishes or traditional Greek roasts.

We were lucky to get a booth on a busy Saturday night. It

was noisy and we had to wait while our table was being cleaned.

I pointed out the celebrity photos on the exposed brick walls—all of them pictures of famous Greek-Americans: Pete Angelos, the basketball player; Daphne Athas, the writer; John Cassavetes, the movie director. There was even a photograph of the former Vice-President, Spiro Agnew, who had resigned in disgrace. A disclaimer was tacked next to it: "This establishment expresses no political opinion but acknowledges that Mr. Agnew was a prominent politician of Greek descent."

When our table was ready, our waiter, a man in his forties who wore a bow-tie and long apron, showed us to our booth. He set warm pita bread, a cruet of olive oil, and a small dish of kalamata olives in front of us.

"Drink?" he said, not making eye contact.

We both asked for Ouzo, and I ordered Loukaniko—charcoal grilled sausages—as an appetizer. I noticed Saloma didn't light up and didn't pop a pill. Her therapist must have helped her work through a few things.

We laughed a lot that evening, the weather was beautiful, the movie had been fun, and we toasted each other: "Such was Saloma! Such was Diego! Such was McTeague!"

The entrée, Garides Giovetsi—prawns baked with feta and tomatoes—came in an earthenware casserole dish and served two. We ordered a bottle of retsina and toasted each other again. We held hands and looked at each other lovingly.

"I'm very happy," she said.

"I am too."

She grew pensive and rubbed the knuckles of my hand with her thumb.

"For however long this lasts, Diego, you've made me happy."

* * *

We left the car parked near the restaurant and walked with arms linked down to Fisherman's Wharf and along Embarcadero. It was the low season, and even though it was a Saturday, the waterfront seemed uncrowded. We paused near the commercial fishing fleet, the small boats with names like Lucky Lady, Pico, and Angelina, and with trim around the cabins a bright red or blue or yellow paint. The boats creaked against their moorings, dipped and rose gently in what looked like a green glaze. We could hear the cry of gulls, the sound of a musician playing a Joan Baez song on a guitar, a trolley clanging on the tracks behind us.

"I love coming here," Saloma mentioned, and I knew that even for people who had grown up in the City the waterfront had its charm.

We strolled along Embarcadero, held hands, passed a mime dressed in a beret and striped shirt, a small group that watched, a juggler who tossed oranges in the air, a souvenir shop that sold seashells and dried starfish in wicker baskets.

"It's not too touristy for an old San Francisco hand?" I asked.

"It's not touristy—it's tacky," she said with a smile. "Delightfully so!"

We reached an old pier that jutted into the Bay and walked slowly to the end, where we sat on a wooden bench. I put my arm around her and she placed her head on my shoulder.

"This couldn't be more perfect," I remarked, and she nodded.

The air had cooled with the evening, but the light was at its most magical. The hills across the Bay stood out sharply, the long span of the Golden Gate Bridge seemed an arc connecting two worlds, and I admitted: "This reminds me very much of the day I arrived in San Francisco, a year-and-a-half ago."

She looked up, lifted her head from my shoulder. She straightened her back and sat facing the Bay.

"What have you decided, Diego?"

I took a deep breath.

"I'm going to take the job in Germany," I said.

She nodded.

"I knew you would." She wiped her eyes with her fingers. "I want you to. Otherwise, you'll never be at peace."

"It doesn't mean," I started to say, but she cut me off.

"You made up your mind a long time ago."

Again, I wanted to protest, but she spoke over me.

"I've known since you came back from Southern California that you'd made up your mind. You may not have known it, but I knew."

We sat in silence, side by side, the beauty of the setting unable to cheer us. I sensed how miserable she was, and that made me miserable too.

She started to cry, noiselessly. Her body shook and I was afraid to comfort her. She fumbled in her handbag for a tissue, tossed her head back and tried to smile. She dried her eyes. I didn't know what to say. At last, when she spoke, she seemed to have gotten her emotions under control.

"What we have is only temporary. I know that. We could never make each other happy in the long run. Neither one of us is ready for a life together, and we're too different."

"But we're so compatible," I protested. At that point, I was so jarred and my emotions were so raw that I almost wanted her to talk me out of leaving.

"No, Diego." She shook her head, vehemently. "The timing isn't right. Maybe if I'd met you ten years from now, after you'd had all your adventures and seen everything you wanted to see, it could have worked out, but you're still confused and angry and struggling and trying to find yourself."

I had no answer for what she said. She was right, and I sat with my hands folded in front of me and my forearms on my knees, leaning forward.

"I want children," she went on. "You know that. And I'm running out of time. I need to find someone who—" Her voice trailed off. She sobbed heavily. "I don't even know—" Her sentence was punctuated by a gulping sound: "—if I can have children," she blurted out, "after what happened in Manila."

I put my arm around her, tried to kiss her wet cheek, but she pushed herself up from me and stood by the railing, peered out. I got up as well and moved next to her. I held her gently.

"You're right, darling," and I kissed the soft hair near her temple as tenderly as I could. "I'm not the right man for you."

"And I'm not the right woman for you."

"Don't say that," I implored, turning her to face me.

"No," she said, placing her index finger against my lips to silence me. She'd calmed down, seemed not only assertive but aggressive when she spoke: "You don't need me. You only think you do. The kind of woman you're looking for doesn't exist in America—and probably not in Germany either."

"What do you mean?"

She took a deep breath and laughed lightly. She seemed to want to tease me and herself into a better frame of mind. She said: "You'll end up in Asia. I know you will. You might find a nice Asian woman you can love and who'll be what you're looking for."

"But you're Asian."

"No, I'm not anymore. Not in the way you mean. I'm American." Her face grew stern, and then she said harshly: "You're looking for a woman who questions the Church but doesn't question male authority. You're looking for a woman who's sexually permissive but conventional in every other way. You're looking for the kind of woman who hasn't been born in this country for the past fifty years."

I was hurt, and I told her so. I reached down and took both her hands, held them gently. I looked at her tear-reddened eyes.

"I may not find anyone else like you again. I may end up in Asia—maybe I will, but I'll always be looking. Maybe I'll grow old searching for what we have right now and never find it. Maybe you'll stay forever young and beautiful in my memory as I grow older and older." I started to cry and barely got the words out as I recited: "I wither slowly in thine arms, here at the quiet limit of the world, a white-haired shadow roaming like a dream, the ever-silent spaces of the East."

CHAPTER TWELVE

We continued to see each other and remained intimate, but Saloma placed an ever-greater distance between us, which I understood. I phoned Max Manfredi at the Carriage House and told him I would be delighted to accept the job in Germany. He seemed pleased and said he would send me the required paperwork.

The next phone call, I feared, would not be as easy. I informed my mother of my plans, but she took the news remarkably well. My father must have primed her. She tried to sound very positive, saying: "You'll be fluent in German when you get back and then can enter a doctoral program." We spoke about the arrangements for graduation weekend, what day my folks planned to arrive by car and where they might stay. I asked if, in the meantime, I could ship a few boxes of my things to their house for safekeeping since I would be leaving for Germany directly from San Francisco.

That year, Easter weekend was the first weekend in April. The Iranian hostage crisis had escalated; the U.S. had cut all diplomatic ties with Iran and had imposed an economic embargo, but I mostly focused on my personal concerns. I wouldn't be able to see Saloma over Easter weekend or stay at her apartment for a while. She had a full schedule of Easter-week activities at the Filipino church, and her sister was back from D.C. for ten days.

I discreetly removed my toiletries kit from the apartment before Ezzie's stay and returned it afterwards. I wanted to make the best of a difficult situation so used Easter weekend to sort my stuff into three piles: items I would take to Germany; things I would give away or throw away; possessions I either needed to ship or have my parents take back with them in the car.

I boxed up most of my books; they would have to be loaded in the trunk or on the backseat of the Buick. Breakable items, such as my typewriter and cassette player, would also need to be loaded in the car, but I decided that a lot of the lighter items —posters in a mailing tube, shirts I wouldn't need in Germany, even some of my cassettes—could be bundled up in parcels or thin cardboard shoe boxes and mailed to my parents' address.

I didn't work at the Federal Building on Wednesdays, so I used the morning to take six parcels to the main post office downtown to have them weighed. I shipped them at the cheapest rate, but it was still expensive.

All morning long, I heard sirens wail across the City as a police motorcade escorted Iranian diplomats and their families from the consulate in Presidio Heights to the airport. At noon, I still heard the sirens, but by three o'clock only the scream of an ambulance or the honking of a fire truck rose and fell, and I knew I probably wouldn't hear police sirens for a while and that the last members of the Iranian mission had been expelled.

My birthday was the following weekend and I wanted to go out. I turned twenty-five that month, and Saloma was already twenty-seven. I was supposed to be an adult by then, but I wasn't always so sure.

My parents phoned me on the day itself to wish me a happy birthday. They had sent me a card and a gift—a check for fifty dollars. I thanked them and said I looked forward to seeing them in just a few short weeks.

I then phoned Saloma. We had agreed to go out that weekend and I suggested Le Montmartre, a French-Algerian hangout on Broadway. But I knew Saloma had two friends from her schooldays in the Philippines in town.

"They're both from Spain," she began. "Their father worked in the Embassy in Manila. You'll like them. Can they join us?"

I hesitated. It wasn't exactly my idea of a romantic evening on my birthday, but I was afraid if I said "no" Saloma would say she needed to be with her friends. She must have sensed the hesitation in my voice. She added brightly: "Why don't we go to Le Montmartre first and then they can join us later. We can all go somewhere else after that."

I was still reluctant but said it was a good plan. If three is a crowd, I thought hopelessly, four is a mob. And I worried that the evening would turn into sorority sisters on the town with me just an embarrassed witness.

* * *

Le Montmartre was near Columbus in North Beach. The restaurant was decorated outside in the French café style with an awning and sidewalk seating, and inside with a patterned tile floor, long wooden bar, and chairs and square tables around an open dance floor.

Saloma and I enjoyed ourselves, ate a simple cous-cous and

lamb stew dinner, and drank Algerian red wine. Three musicians were to the side of the dance floor: a keyboard player, who provided percussion on his electric piano as well; an acoustic guitarist; and a vocalist. The combo performed familiar hits from the 1960s by Gilbert Bécaud and Charles Aznavour. In fact, the vocalist, who was short and lithe and wore his dark hair over the ears, looked a bit like Charles Aznavour. He must have wanted to emphasize the resemblance since he wore tight black trousers, a 1960s suit jacket, and sang with the same gravelly intensity as Aznavour.

Saloma wasn't particularly communicative during dinner, which I attributed to her probably having spent a couple of late nights with her friends. Still, when we danced, she was responsive to my touch. We slow-danced to "Et maintenant," a melody which Elvis covered as "What Now, My Love," and to "Hier encore," which Sinatra and many other performers had sung as "Yesterday, When I Was Young."

Saloma wore a silky purple dress that fanned out into a pleated knee-length skirt, and as I held her in my arms I could feel her curves through the thin fabric, her lips pressed against my jawline, and I could smell her luxuriant hair and her perfume. As we danced, she ran her palm across the back of my neck and shifted her face so that her cheek was against mine. I yearned for her, and we danced as if we were one.

The song ended and we walked back to our table. I was filled with feelings of affection for her, and love. I knew she wanted us to embark on a physical and emotional separation, but at that moment, I didn't know how it would be possible—especially on my birthday. I hoped she felt the same, and I smiled at her.

Within a few minutes, we were joined by her two friends—sisters, from the look of it, of about equal height and similar olive-skinned complexion. They were dressed expensively and wore bracelets and gold necklaces that matched. I stood up and so did Saloma, squealing with delight as she embraced the two women in a scrum, kissing them on each cheek and hopping up and down. Happiness at seeing old friends is one thing, but I thought the emotional display was a bit much, especially since Saloma had told me they'd had lunch the day before.

Saloma introduced me to the two sisters—Pilar and Marisol. We sat down and the three women babbled brightly while the musicians were on break. Pilar was the elder of the two sisters, with a sharp Spanish profile and a hooked nose. Marisol was prettier, with an infectious smile and bright brown eyes, but the women were obviously rich, talked about all the shops they'd been to over the past few days and where they were going next. Pilar mentioned that in Spain, the shopping scene had improved since Franco died, but in every other way the country had been better under "El Generalissimo." Her sister nodded. I gritted my teeth. My father and all his kin had been against "el Bandido General," but I wasn't going to say anything.

I started to be annoyed in other ways as well. I noticed that the three of them had silly schoolgirl nicknames for each other. Marisol was "Meenie," Pilar was "Beanie," and for some reason Saloma was referred to throughout the evening as "Bong-Bong."

Pilar turned to me. "I'm going to call you 'Chaco' tonight."

"Why?"

She waved her hand dismissively. "Diego sounds too stuffy. Like a saint. Chaco—there was a character in an Argentinian movie called Chaco. You look like him. So I'll call you Chaco."

Marisol pulled a packet of Benson & Hedges from her handbag, and the three women lit up. Marisol offered me a smoke but I declined. I looked over at Saloma, tried to catch her eye. I wanted to indicate mild disapproval, but it was no use. She puffed happily and blew smoke rings in the air. The sisters laughed. Even if Saloma knew I didn't like her to smoke, I had no real claim on her anymore, or whatever claim I had was fast slipping away.

I turned to Pilar.

"I may have seen that movie," I said in Spanish.

She glanced at me in amusement.

"You speak Spanish?"

We chatted amiably for a while and her sister joined in. They spoke with Castilian accents, which I was familiar with, but they were also from Madrid and their words rattled out like shots from a chattering machine gun. When they spoke to each other, slang terms peppered their talk and I had difficulty following.

"Where did you learn your Spanish?" Marisol asked me.

"In Mexico," I answered in that language. "Also, my father is from Spain. From Andalusia."

Pilar snickered. "You speak good Spanish—for an Andaluz."

And Marisol laughed.

Pilar and Marisol had no interest in staying at Le Montmartre, so we left before the next set. They wanted to go to a place called the Fu-Bar. I'd been past the place; it was on Geary near Arguello, not far from USF and the former Iranian consulate. Of course, I drove and the three of them piled their jackets on the front passenger seat and sat in the back, arms linked, Marisol directly behind me, Saloma squeezed in the middle, and Pilar to her right—or should I say, Meenie, Bong-Bong, and Beanie in a Hear No Evil, See No Evil, Speak No Evil pose.

It was going to be a long night, and as I drove to Presidio Heights, my car sputtered up one hill and down the next. The three girls giggled from the back or laughed uproariously, sang school songs from their days in Manila, or teased each other with a smattering of Tagalog. I glanced in the rearview mirror from time to time and tried to smile. I wanted to be a sport, but the effort was wearying.

I pulled up to the Fu-Bar to let the women out. A long line of people in their teens and twenties waited to get in. A bouncer checked I.D.s and used a rubber stamp to mark the back of patrons' hands. A thin woman sat on a barstool by the doorway and collected the cover charge.

"Don't be long," Saloma said, peering in through the passenger window.

I glanced at the crowd lined up outside.

"Who knows?" I tried to sound cheerful. "I may be back before you're even inside."

"We'll hold a place for you." She gave me a reassuring smile.

As it turned out, it took me more than half an hour to rejoin them. I had to park my car on a hill four blocks away, walk back to the bar, then stand in line. Ahead of me, the bouncer checked I.D.s and either stamped the back of the left hand with a symbol in red ink, meaning the patron could enter but couldn't consume alcohol, or stamped the back of the right hand with a mark in black ink, meaning the person was over twenty-one. Enforcement must have been a nightmare, but it looked like the Fu-Bar made a hefty profit off both age groups.

When I reached the bouncer, he gave me a surly look and said the photo on my driver's license didn't resemble me. I told him it was taken four years ago. "Okay," he muttered, then stamped the back of my right hand with a black-ink insignia. I handed over a five-dollar bill to the thin woman. She gave me a toothy smile. I waited. I said: "I thought the cover's three dollars." She slowly handed back two.

When I finally entered to a loud blast of music, I looked up to see a full-sized hot rod hanging upside down from the ceiling. I surveyed the room, searched for Saloma and her friends, but it was hard to spot anyone. Heads bobbed up and down; the floor space was extensive, with booths and tables along the perimeter, and a sunken area in the center with more tables. A large dance floor was in an adjacent room, just behind the bar that filled most of the back wall, and I could see the flash of strobe lights and purple, blue, and red streaks that pulsated in rhythm with the dance songs. I didn't recognize the music, but it was loud and pounding, with a repetitive hammering beat.

Most everyone seemed a good five or six years younger than I was, and I saw several men and women sitting together wearing USF tee-shirts and sweaters, which made sense: we were just down the road from the private university. Two pool tables were over to the left. A man in a flannel checkered shirt chalked his cue. I moved through the crowd, scanned the room for Saloma. I guessed she and "the gals" would be somewhere near the bar, smoking, laughing, and having a good time.

I swam upstream, passed waiters and waitresses who slithered rapidly between tables to deliver large pitchers of beer. At the far side, I saw the bartender working non-stop to fill clean, empty ones. I inched past a pillar pasted over with advertising flyers: *Wet Tee-Shirt Nite on Wednesdays, Ladies Nite on Thursdays*, and *Every Nite College Nite with I.D.* I hadn't been in a place like this since the night I turned twenty-one and passed out in a bathroom stall in Westwood.

I looked up and down the bar and finally saw them. Saloma stood near the middle of the bar with her two friends. She was facing out, with her elbows resting on the bar top. I watched her lick salt from the back of her hand, toss her head back to swallow a shot, then bite into a wedge of lime. Great, shots of tequila, I thought. I wondered who was buying. Pilar, probably.

I walked up to them.

Pilar eyed me up and down: "Buy you a drink, Chaco? I mean, buy me a drink, big guy?"

Saloma laughed and I told myself I could only take so much of this. I needed to find a spot where I could sit and brood and nurse a beer or two, pretend that I was having fun and just delighted to be out with the gang.

Eventually, we scooted into empty seats next to a group of college students. Saloma sat with me for a while, drinking beer from a Pilsner glass, smoking one cigarette after the next, before she jumped up with Pilar and Marisol to go to the Ladies Room, have another shot at the bar, or shimmy into the next room to dance.

I put on a brave face and grinned glassily. I gazed over the room. I was tired of this scene and of being a college student—even a graduate student. I wanted to get on with my life. Watching Saloma talk with her friends, put away too many, smoke constantly, I knew she wanted to get on with her life as well, but it seemed to me she was regressing. I toyed with my cocktail napkin, watched it turn wet from the moisture on my beer glass. I was unhappy for her and for myself. She probably wanted to get smashed tonight and let loose because she felt as if she'd broken up with her boyfriend; in a way, she already had. I drank my beer and had trouble swallowing. The beer tasted stale.

* * *

We left when the Fu-Bar closed that night and I had to drive Pilar and Marisol to some address in the Marina where they stayed with a friend. Saloma sat in the front passenger seat this time, slumped against the side door, her coat in a pile near her feet. Behind me, Pilar and Marisol were also quiet, sprawled at opposite ends with their heads resting on the seat back. Pilar looked up from time to time to give me directions.

She explained that she and her sister were leaving in two days to join their father in Washington D.C., where he was posted to the Spanish Embassy. "Maybe we'll come back this summer."

Wonderful, I thought, but didn't say anything. I'd be gone anyway.

I pulled up in front of a high-rise condominium building not far from Fort Mason Center. Pilar shook her sister. When Marisol woke up, the two women stumbled out.

"Don't wake Bong-Bong," Pilar whispered, then looked at me. "She's the best. Take good care of her—tonight and forever."

A lump rose in my throat. I nodded. Pilar waved her hand dramatically as if to say "Go! Go!" then took her sister's arm. The two of them staggered toward the building.

* * *

It was nearly three a.m. when I parked in front of Saloma's apartment. I turned off the engine and set the brake, then walked around to the passenger door and opened it. I caught Saloma as she slumped from the seat. She woke up and murmured groggily: "What time is it?"

"It's late."

I helped her get out of the car and stand, then gripped her upper arm firmly. Her head sagged against my shoulder; her damp hair reeked of cigarette smoke. I could smell dried sweat from her frantic dancing. I decided to leave her coat in the car.

"Saloma?

She looked up.

"We're going inside now. I'll help you to the door. I'll get you back."

She nodded, but I was worried. I managed to nudge the car door shut with my hip and helped her move forward. We swayed up the walkway toward the front door, negotiated the first step, then stood on the cement landing.

"Don't worry," I said. It hurt me to see her this way. "I'll get the key from your handbag."

As I fished in her handbag searching for the key, she swooned, her head thrown back and her eyes closed, then lurched to the side and bent doubled over the iron handrail. The contents of her stomach gushed out in a stream; she coughed and a second jet spewed into the bushes. My hands shook as I held her; I told myself there wasn't much I could do except let her retch and gasp and heave until her system settled.

"It's okay, Saloma," I insisted, but I wasn't sure. Her body convulsed as she purged on an empty stomach; I tried not to look as she wiped the bile hanging from her mouth. "I'll take care of you." I patted her on the back. "You'll be okay."

She tried to stand straight, her eyes still closed. I put my arm firmly around her waist and half-lifted her up on her toes. I found the key, managed to unlock the door and tugged her over the threshold. I closed and latched the door from the other side.

"I want to sit down," she gasped.

"No," I answered. "We're going upstairs." I was afraid if we stopped she'd spend the night on the couch or the floor and I wouldn't be able to get her undressed and in bed for hours. I considered lifting her in my arms and simply carrying her upstairs, but I wanted her to walk it off a bit, go upstairs more or less on her own power. I looped her left arm over my neck while still gripping her waist tightly with my right. We moved gingerly toward the stairs, but she sagged. I held her up and urged her: "Just place one foot in front of the other. We'll get there."

She nodded.

We reached the base of the stairs. We took each step slowly, paused, then stepped up once more. We made clumsy, cumbersome progress. I gripped the banister rail on my left and pulled hard, getting us to the landing. We turned, made it up the first three steps. One of her shoes had come off. I had to drag and lift her the final two steps. Her other shoe came off as well. I kicked it to the side.

When I managed to guide her into the bedroom, I flicked on the light. I placed an arm behind her back and one behind her knees so that I could hoist her into my arms and try to place her on the bed. Saloma was only five-foot-four and a hundred-and-ten pounds but felt much heavier. As I placed her on the unmade bed, her mouth fell open, she drooled, and let out a moan.

"You'll be okay, darling," I whispered. It came out like a prayer, and I wasn't sure to whom. The bedsprings creaked as her weight settled into the mattress. She breathed regularly, and I must have sighed in relief. I calmed down; I was in control, I told myself. I knew what to do. I just needed to be methodical and clearheaded.

I turned on the light in the bathroom and filled three Dixie cups with water. I placed them on the nightstand, next to the portrait of her deceased cousin Tommy. I also wet a washcloth and wiped her face, cleaning the sickness from her mouth and chin. Her forehead was cold to the touch and I felt her shiver. I made her sit up. I had to place my arms behind her back and pull her into a sitting position and hold her there.

"Here, darling," I coaxed. "You need to drink something."

I held one of the Dixie cups to her chapped lips and she drank. She held the second cup with her own hands and finished all the water. She drank most of the water in the third cup, opened her eyes and smiled weakly.

"I feel better," she said, but she was still limp in my arms.

"I need to undress you. You need to get out of this dress."

"Why?" she slurred.

I looked down at the sleeve. It was wet with vomit, as was the front.

I unzipped the back of the dress. "Come on." I got her to stand up momentarily so that I could pull the dress up and over her head. As soon as it came free, Saloma sank down heavily on the edge of the mattress, then fell back onto the bed. I decided she could sleep in her slip and underwear but not in her bra and pantyhose, which would be too uncomfortable.

She didn't object when I reached under her slip, tugged her forward and unfastened the bra, removed it from her body gently and felt her heavy breasts on my arm. But she opened her eyes and smiled when I gripped the waistband of her pantyhose and unrolled it across her hips, down her thighs, and freed it from her legs and ankles.

She wagged a finger slowly.

"Naughty boy," she said in a hoarse laugh. "Sex, sex, sex."

I loved her, but we certainly weren't going to have sex. I loved her, and just wanted to make sure she'd be okay. I dumped her beautiful dress in the shower stall and ran hot water. I found a fresh washcloth and wet it thoroughly, added a bit of soap, and returned to the bedroom so that I could wipe her hands. She said something about my being rough, but I wanted to make sure her hands were clean in case she rubbed her eyes at night.

I tossed the washcloth in the shower stall and turned off the water. I removed my own clothes. I'd sleep in my shirt and underwear but would take off everything else. I flicked off the bathroom light, got in the bed next to her, and pulled the covers over us. She must have been feeling better because she snuggled against me and rubbed her hand on my chest. She tried to kiss my mouth, but I turned instinctively from the stench of sickness and cigarettes.

She kissed my cheek instead. "Happy birthday, Diego."

"Just go to sleep."

"You're a good man, Diego." She patted my chest then placed her head on my upper arm as if it were a pillow. "You're a good man," she repeated sleepily. "You take care of me."

I was exhausted from events and wasn't sure I was good for anyone, but at least we'd gotten through the evening and she was safe. I was angry at her for getting so drunk, but sensed I might be at fault in some way. It was very late; very early, and there was no point in tormenting myself or her.

"We'll talk in the morning," I suggested, but she was already asleep and I could hear her snore.

* * *

We slept until eleven a.m. and when she stirred, I woke up as well. I lay on my back with an erection, and I reached across the bed to find her side empty. I wasn't feeling my best but at least I hadn't gotten sick the night before. I looked up. Saloma was in the bathroom; I heard the shower run and then she cried: "Oh, my god!"

I threw off the covers and in two strides was inside the bathroom. With her hands at her mouth, she stared down into the stall.

"What happened to my dress?"

"You don't remember?"

"No."

"Do you remember leaving the Fu-Bar?"

"No." She paused. "Oh, god. It's ruined!"

"Never mind. We'll send it to the dry cleaners." I still had an erection but it was starting to abate the longer I talked to her and worried about her. I lifted the soaked dress from the shower stall and placed it in the bathtub.

"How do you feel?"

"I feel awful." She tried to laugh but it was more of a low exhalation. She certainly looked awful, I thought. Her hair was a tangled mess, her skin a chalky yellow with shadowy bags under her eyes. She rubbed her face with both hands as if to restore circulation or to hide her shame. "Did I act like an idiot last night?"

Then, she looked at me.

"How did I get undressed?" She thought about it. "You must have undressed me." She was still making connections, thinking things through. "My panties are still on. That's a good sign," she laughed, then rubbed her hip. "I feel sore all over." She lifted up her slip and tugged down one side of her panties, revealing an ugly purple lump. "How did I get this bruise?"

I shrugged. "Probably when I wrestled you through the doorway—and up the stairs."

She still looked at me inquisitively. I took her in my arms and kissed her on the forehead. The skin was damp and clammy.

"Listen, are you okay to take a shower by yourself?"

She nodded. The water still ran, but I reached in to turn off the hot water so that it just ran cold.

"Take a nice cold shower—and brush your teeth. Come down when you're ready. I'll fix breakfast."

"I don't think I can eat."

"You'll feel a lot better if you do."

* * *

In the kitchen, I rummaged through the refrigerator and found what I was looking for—a round of Gouda cheese. I would have preferred a hard Italian cheese like Romano or Parmesan, but Gouda would have to do. I removed the shiny wax rind and cut the cheese into wedges, boiled four eggs and got the coffee going. I'd never liked to mess with percolators but managed, pouring water into the lower chamber and adding coarse ground coffee to the brew basket. I added extra scoops because I wanted the coffee to be as strong as possible. I plugged in the percolator and let it do its work while I turned my attention to the pièce de résistance—burnt toast.

I'd burnt a few things in kitchens over the years, including my hands. I put four slices of white bread in the toaster and twisted the dial to "eight"—the highest setting. When the smoking, hot bread popped up, I pressed the lever down again so that it would toast a second time.

Saloma entered the kitchen wearing a bathrobe. She looked sheepish and sleepy and her wet hair was tied up. "This smells terrible. What are you making?"

"Burnt toast," I smiled.

"Should I open a window?"

The bread popped up and was thoroughly blackened.

Saloma sat down heavily at the breakfast table. I poured her a glass of orange juice, which she sipped. The coffee was ready and I poured a cup for each of us, then arranged the food items on two plates, served her, and set my plate across from hers.

"What's this?"

"Burnt toast, a wedge of cheese, and a hardboiled egg. I'm having the same. It's the best cure there is for a hangover."

She looked at me. "How do you know this?"

"A wise old man told me. He worked as a ship's cook for the British merchant navy for several years. He said it gets rid of a hangover every time. He would know."

* * *

Saloma admitted she felt better after "the sailor's cure," and color had come back to her cheeks. Her eyes were less bloodshot and the skin underneath started to take on a normal complexion. We sat on the couch and drank coffee. She asked me several times what had happened the night before and I filled in a few of the details. I tried to be reassuring.

"You were just having a good time," I put in. "You were just overjoyed to see your friends."

"No," she shook her head. "I overdid it. I was upset. I was trying to—" She stopped and turned to me. "I'm not going to drink and smoke like that again. That's it. I'm going to take it easy."

"That's right," I said, stroking her arm. "You should rest today. You shouldn't go anywhere." I looked at my watch. It was almost one o'clock. "I should probably get going."

"You don't have to." She smiled over her cup of coffee. "You can shower and we can get into bed and sleep the rest of the afternoon."

"And throw the curtains open and lie in each other's arms in the sun?"

"Just like in the old days," she agreed happily.

"And when we get hungry we'll order Pasquale's pizza and have it delivered?"

She laughed this time, and my mood brightened.

"Like in the old days," she said, setting her coffee cup on the end table. I reached over and took her hand and brought it to my lips. I kissed her palm and the soft inside of her wrist.

"Only better," I replied.

And it was better because we didn't feel compelled to make love or to possess each other physically; we could do what our bodies told us to do that afternoon, which was to lie close together in the bright sunlight and rest and comfort each other and say that nothing really mattered except this moment.

* * *

I gave my three weeks' notice at work and needed to inform Mr. Meriwether that I'd be vacating the room shortly after graduation. I found him sitting in the common room, his back to the Bay window, huddled in an old armchair with a blanket over his lap and reading a copy of *Life* magazine from the 1940s.

Two large cardboard file boxes were stacked on top of each other; the lid of the topmost box was tilted back and a large stack of *Life* magazines had been sorted through. Several of the magazines fanned out like playing cards, exposing the stark black and white images of the covers.

I knew Mr. Meriwether was a collector, but he seemed completely absorbed as he thumbed through an old issue. I called to him twice and when he looked up through his glasses, he reached to adjust his hearing aid, a banana-shaped device wrapped behind his ear, and turned a small dial.

"I almost have a complete set," he smiled.

"Of all *Life* magazines?"

"No, no, no, no, no!" he sputtered. "Of course not. I only collect issues from the nineteen-forties. I'm still missing a few, or want to replace some copies that aren't in very good condition. It's the war years I'm mostly interested in." He proudly showed me a few of the issues: most of the covers had head shots of glamorous movie stars—Katherine Hepburn, Ingrid Bergman, Lauren Bacall.

"Here's one of my favorites." He dangled an issue from November 1945 delicately between two fingers. The cover showed the boyish face of a handsome young sailor in a Cracker Jack uniform, staring straight at the camera as he held an ice cream soda and sucked through a straw. The caption read: "The Fleet's In."

I didn't say anything about the cover, then thought to myself Mr. Meriwether would have been an adolescent during the Second World War.

"Why didn't you save the issues when you were a kid?" I asked. "It would have been a lot easier."

He stared at me in bafflement.

"My mother subscribed to the *Saturday Evening Post*," he related. "Besides, I enjoy hunting for these. You never know what turns up at a flea market or an attic sale."

I sat down in the armchair opposite him and sank heavily into the soft cushion and broken springs. "I wanted to let you know I'll be leaving right after commencement—in case you wanted to advertise the room."

He set the magazine carefully on top of the others in the box. "I suppose you expect me to prorate the rent."

"Well, yes," I added. "That would be nice."

He paused, clucked his tongue against his cheek as if physically calculating, then said: "I can do it."

I thanked him and started to rise when he asked me: "So where are you going next? Hollywood?" He grinned happily, then belted out the first lines from "Hooray for Hollywood!"

"No," I interrupted. "I'm taking a cook's job in Germany."

He looked puzzled. I thought he was going to say something about a waste of my education, but he blurted out: "Germany? *Germany?*" then clucked his tongue again. "Well, the war's over, I suppose."

He seemed interested.

"Where in Germany?"

"A village called Badenweiler. It's in the southwest corner, not far from Mulhouse in France."

"Which sector?"

"Sector?"

"Military sector."

Germany was still divided into East and West, and the Bundesrepublik was further subdivided into Allied occupation zones.

"I think it was French right after the War, but the zones were reorganized. It's probably in the American zone now." I shrugged. "I'm not really sure."

"You'll know once you're there," he replied, sitting back in his chair.

"I *have* been reading up about that part of Germany," I acknowledged, "and about the village where I'll be working as a cook. It's probably best known as the place where Anton Chekov, the Russian playwright, died."

"I hope not from the cooking."

I smiled.

"No, he had tuberculosis. Badenweiler is a Kurort—a health resort with spas. People have been going there for generations for the fresh spring water and the fresh air."

Mr. Meriwether looked out the window at Duboce Park, with its broken swing set and smashed bottles on the pathway. "Sounds like a healthier environment than here."

"There are even Roman ruins in Badenweiler—old Roman

baths. The hotel where I'll be working is called the Hotel Römerbad. That means 'Roman baths.'"

He turned from the window and looked at me. "You sound enthusiastic. You must really be looking forward to it."

"Yes, I am," I said. "But I have mixed feelings."

He took a deep breath. "Yes, your sweetheart, I suppose. That lovely creature you brought here a few times. You look at her like she's your high school sweetheart."

Mr. Meriwether was gay, eccentric, and about as odd as anyone I'd met in San Francisco, but he was an older man with some life experience.

He said: "It's never really easy, is it?"

CHAPTER THIRTEEN

I took Saloma out to dinner and a play one last time before I left for Germany. She phoned me and said there was an avant garde production of Ibsen's *Hedda Gabler* at the Zodiac Theater in Berkeley. The performance was part of the May Day International Workers Celebration. Would I be interested in seeing it? she asked, since I'd studied Ibsen.

"Sure," I replied. "We can take the BART or I can drive. I'm selling my car next week. I might as well get a bit more use out of it."

She hesitated.

"Unless you think it'll break down again and we'll get stuck like we did in Davenport," I tried to laugh.

"No, it's not that. I think you should know. The event is a fundraiser for Angela Davis. All the proceeds go to her campaign."

I thought about it. When I'd been in high school, there had been all that controversy about the Black Panther movement, Davis' tacit support of armed insurrection, her anti-Vietnam

War activities, her getting fired twice from UCLA—once for Communist Party affiliation, the second time for incendiary language. The list went on: firearms she owned had been used in an armed takeover of a courtroom in which four people were killed. And now she was on the Communist Party ticket for Vice President. What a piece of work. But it might be the last time I'd be with Saloma, and I always had difficulty saying "no" to her.

"If that's what you really want," I said mildly. "Who knows? It might be fun."

Saloma sounded delighted.

"Angela Davis is even supposed to be there. She's scheduled to speak at the event."

* * *

The performance wasn't until eight, but I picked Saloma up at six so that we'd have time for a light dinner somewhere near the theater on Telegraph Avenue.

We were probably both overdressed for a night out in that part of Berkeley. The last time I'd been there, Telegraph Avenue was awash with old hippie hangers-on and druggies, street vendors, Rastafarians, tarot card readers, Hari Krishnas, teenage runaways and Black Power activists—and I didn't think it had changed. I probably didn't need to wear a corduroy sports coat with a turtleneck sweater. Saloma had put on a flared, multi-colored skirt with beadwork that looked slightly gypsy. She covered her hair with a bandana tied in back and wore a single earring.

"Sort of the gypsy-pirate look," I told her. She gave me a tight smile. "This will be fun," I persisted.

Although the drive was only a short seventeen miles, I was concerned about taking my eight-year-old rattletrap with four bald tires across the long, connecting spans of the Oakland Bay Bridge.

"I plan to sell my car next week," I repeated.

"That'll be a relief."

"Yeah, the last thing I need is for the car to break down again."

I should have kept my mouth shut. Saloma probably didn't need to be reminded of how precarious a ride in my old beater could be or that I arranged to leave soon. She sat quietly, her hands folded in her lap, as the bridge took us high above the water, then downwards to Treasure Island and another long, connecting span to the East Bay.

"We could have taken BART," I admitted.

My right hand was on the stick shift, which vibrated in my palm as I drove. Saloma patted my right forearm.

"It's okay," she said, and smiled at me. "I know you always top off all the fluids before you go anywhere."

I smiled back, grimly. It was my turn to be reminded of something I'd just as soon not think about.

As we rode across the next long, curving bridge, the water two hundred feet below and crinkled into sharp wavelets, I stayed in the right-hand lane, close to the pedestrian walkway. But at that height, my car shook with the wind. I didn't relish the thought of walking across the bridge in a stiff breeze if my car broke down.

The panorama ahead of us in the early evening light was stunning. "Look," I remarked. "I think that's the Berkeley Campanile in the distance."

The conical peak of the bell tower was illuminated, and we could see it against the darkening hills, almost like a beacon. I hoped to take our minds off the chuffing of my car engine.

"I don't think UC Berkeley is in my future," Saloma said quietly. "I've been accepted into the Special Ed master's program at SF State, and I'm staying where I am. My sister's back at the end of May and we're keeping the same apartment."

"That's great news," I tried to say cheerily. "I knew you'd get in."

* * *

We found a vegetarian café on Telegraph Avenue, just across the street from the Zodiac Theater. The walls of the café were plastered with advertising flyers for musical events: *The Lewd Sponges—Admission .50, Nik Down Under at California Hall, Eye Protection at the Back Door.*

We ordered chicory coffee and avocado and alfalfa sprout sandwiches on unleavened bread. It might have been tasty with a couple of slices of ham and cheddar cheese, but I was learning to keep quiet.

* * *

We argued about the merits of the production on the drive home. I was stuck at a traffic signal. I kept running my tongue along my back teeth, feeling the sharp edges. When the light turned green, I shot through the intersection and told her what a wretched performance I thought that was.

She sat in silence as I drove through Berkeley. She had removed the bandana at the end of the play and her black hair fell long and flowing. She stared straight ahead. We approached the onramp to the bridge.

"I thought it was good," I heard her say.

I accelerated, headed up the bridge ramp. The motor pinged. I tried to tell myself everything was fine. The rhythmic puttering of the engine seemed to follow a regular beat.

I spoke in a low voice. "The acting was okay." I tried to

regulate my breathing. "I have no problem with the set design," I went on. "Some of the lighting effects were interesting." I paused and held my breath, then blurted out: "But what was the director *thinking*?"

"He was trying to bring it up to date," Saloma said firmly. "Make it relevant."

I drove on. The Oakland Bay Bridge curved like twisted tracks over the expanse of water. Ahead of me, a stream of red taillights ascended in a long arc.

"I'm all for connecting with an audience," I continued. "That production of *Macbeth* we saw—where everyone wore U.S. Army fatigues and the castle was a fort in Vietnam? I got it. The audience got it. It wasn't subtle."

She didn't seem convinced that I agreed with her—up to a point. She still stared at the windshield; she drummed her fingers on the armrest.

I turned to her briefly as I drove. "But they didn't change the *ending*. Macbeth still dies in Act Five and gets his head cut off."

"So?" She finally looked at me. "What was wrong with this *Hedda Gabler*," she paused, "since you're the expert on Ibsen."

I noted the sarcasm.

As we curved toward Treasure Island and the bridge span that took us home, the oncoming headlights on the eastbound side looked like diamonds on a conveyor belt. The traffic churned in both directions; my car hung on; everything should have been fine, but I was becoming increasingly agitated and didn't know why. I responded: "I'll tell you what was wrong," and I looked at her. "They changed the bloody ending."

I was annoyed now. The damage they had done to a great play offended me. "Hedda doesn't commit suicide in this production—nooo," I sneered. "She triumphs over Judge Brack and makes a grand speech about the new world order."

"They made it real," Saloma said bitterly. "Otherwise, it's just a museum piece."

"Right, and if that wasn't enough, the whole cast comes out—and not for a curtain call—and they link arms and sing the Internationale with the audience—all six verses, with the chorus each time. I thought we were never going to get out of there."

I glanced at the dashboard. My heart pounded but the needles on the gauges were where they needed to be. Neither of us spoke, and I thought maybe I should just let things settle down, simmer for a while. I didn't want this to end badly. I started to calm down. Then, Saloma said: "I'm just disappointed Angela Davis didn't show up."

I told myself not to say anything, but this was nuts. Saloma's friends from Spain thought Franco had been a great leader, she took money from her father who was pals with Ferdinand Marcos, and she wanted to vote for Angela Davis. Only in the Bay Area could her inconsistencies seem to make some sense. It was about as illogical as what Wade Hoxsted at the rooming house had said the other day: "I'm in a rush. I've gotta run down and buy a pair of prewashed Army jeans, get my hair frizzed, and then hang out at the Marxist bookstore."

At least Wade had been joking; Saloma spoke in earnest.

I retorted: "Well, I'm sorry Leon Trotsky didn't show up. But isn't he down in Mexico getting a haircut? A parting in the middle is fashionable this year." I assumed she got the reference to Trotsky getting his head split open by an ax.

"You think you're so amusing."

She got it.

"I try."

"You'll never understand my politics."

I struck a conciliatory note.

"Look," I pressed on. "I agree that major reform is needed in this country . . . sweeping change, but—"

"You're too stuck in the past to believe in reform," she cut in. "We need new ideas too."

I was taken aback, wounded even, if I thought she implied everything I tried creatively was imitation. I didn't want to say much more. It was as if we were manufacturing an argument so that it would be easier to break up. We were halfway across the final span; the City looked magical at night, a sheen of shimmering lights against the water. I tried to soften my tone even more.

"Okay, so there's an old-fashioned streak in me, but that's why we get along. There's an old-fashioned side to you too—the Spanish princess."

"Don't call me Spanish," she snapped. "The Spanish did nothing for the Philippines except exploit us."

We drove in silence the rest of the way as I wound through the City and back to her apartment.

* * *

I pulled up to her building. The two-story duplex sat squat among even rows of identical townhouses, like stumps in a forest.

I kept the motor running, listened to it putter and throb while we sat wordlessly. I wasn't sure who was going to speak first. I tried to sort out my emotions, and I sensed that her feelings were conflicted too.

"I'd better go in," she said.

I looked at her soft profile.

"Saloma," I began. "We shouldn't argue about politics. It's silly. We shouldn't argue about anything. I just—"

She got out of the car and shut the door. She rushed up the

walkway to her apartment. I turned off the engine and hurried after her.

Saloma had reached the front steps, struggled with her keys and unlatched the door. I caught up with her.

"Saloma," I pleaded, cupping her elbow gently. "We've been through a lot together."

She faced me with a blank, almost expressionless look. Wisps of hair had fallen across her forehead; her eyes studied me.

"Is this your big farewell speech?" she asked.

"No."

I placed my hands lightly on her hips and inched closer to her. We almost embraced. She arched her back and her face turned up toward mine. Her mouth was slightly open. She brushed a strand of hair from her eyes, and I leaned forward to kiss her.

"No," she stated firmly and opened the front door. Then she turned back to me. "You act as if we're still a number. We're not."

"Okay." I stepped back. "If that makes it easier for you."

"Yeah." She reached up and combed her hair back with her fingers. "It makes it easier."

But it didn't look easy for her. She started to shake, bit her knuckle, and turned to look at the road.

"My therapist told me I need to protect myself emotionally." She took her fist away from her lips and rubbed her eyes with the back of her hand. Her eyes had reddened and were wet. "He said I shouldn't see you again."

I realized that tears ran down my cheeks as well. I tried not to, but emitted a painful sigh. Saloma moved close to me, gasped my name in a sorrowful moan, and embraced me.

I felt her body pressed against mine. Our lips met and our mouths opened against each other. I sensed the beautiful contours of her face, felt the wetness of our cheeks as our bodies heaved with emotion. I wanted to change everything, rewrite the course of my life, tell her everything would be different from now on.

Saloma broke off the kiss and hurried inside. I tried to say something, but the door closed shut with a click and a turn of the deadbolt.

* * *

The next week, I sold my car. I tried advertising it for six-fifty and had no takers. I raised the price to eight hundred and sold the vehicle right away.

I think I got as much as I did because it was a Japanese car and consumers were concerned about fuel economy. I wouldn't have gotten as much for an eight-year-old Ford Galaxie 500. I felt flush with eight hundred dollars in my pocket and a one-way plane ticket to Frankfurt.

I thought I might see Saloma in the lead-up to graduation or perhaps at the ceremony, but escorting my parents for the three days they were in town kept me busy, as did the explosion near the Stanhope Park Hotel.

Commencement was on Saturday, May 17th at 1:00 p.m., with my parents scheduled to drive up the day before. I had made a two-night reservation for them at a restored Victorian hotel close to Golden Gate Park, not too far from where I roomed and in a safe neighborhood. In fact, it was across the street from the Cole Valley SF Police Station.

My parents were driving the 101 and would phone me when they arrived in town. With my wheels sold, I would take over the local driving duties and show them the sights and some of the out-of-the-way finds I'd only learned about in the past two years.

That Wednesday evening, two days before they were to arrive, an explosion ripped through the police station, knocked out windows, overturned chairs and desks, and killed two officers. A pipe bomb, filled with ball bearings and roofing nails, had been laid on the window sill of the squad room, timed to explode during a shift change when the greatest number of officers would be in the assembly hall. According to the *San Francisco Chronicle*, a number of officers had lingered in the locker room; otherwise, the tragedy would have been worse. The Weather Underground was suspected because the method and the target were similar to other attacks perpetrated by the terrorist group in the early 1970s, though according to the paper their activities had been tapering off.

The blast had rocked nearby buildings. A multi-block area was cordoned off pending the investigation. In consequence, I cancelled the reservation at the Stanhope Park and booked a room at the Travelodge on Greater Highway in the Outer Sunset. It was farther away, by about five miles, but closer to the university. I decided not to say anything to my parents in case they asked me what kind of city I lived in.

They arrived in the early afternoon on Friday, May 16th. Of course, they'd heard the news on the radio but I told them Cole Valley was a long way from where they would be staying and that the Outer Sunset was safe. After I got them checked into the motel, I drove them to the Palace of Fine Arts, then along Embarcadero to the foot of the Transamerica Pyramid Building, where I parked. We made it a point to see Chinatown and we took some photos in front of a row of shops and restaurants with pagoda roofs, not far from where we had posed in 1967. We asked a passerby to take a snapshot of the three of us.

My father looked distinguished in a navy-blue suit with narrow, chalk-grey pinstripes, a white dress shirt and a red power tie with small pale-blue and yellow squares. His steel grey moustache was tightly trimmed. My mother must have had her hair permed the day before because it rose like an elaborate nest, with each curl and wave in place. She wore a mottled tan and white pants-suit with a forest-green scarf and carried a chestnut-colored handbag that matched her shoes.

I was happy they were nicely dressed since it indicated they were proud of the occasion, but I had decided to save my best outfit for graduation day itself and was dressed more casually, with an open-necked polyester shirt, flared light-blue trousers, and a denim sports coat.

We would probably pull out all the stops for dinner the next night but still wanted a restaurant with charm and atmosphere that Friday. Good value wouldn't hurt, as my mother was wont to say, so I took them to the Gold Spike, a family-owned and operated Italian restaurant on Columbus that still offered five-course meals for under eight dollars. The Gold Spike was also known for its décor: a long bar rested on an uneven floor, a moose head and a marlin hung from opposite walls, with most of the remaining wall space papered over with business cards and dollar bills tacked by customers.

"Looks like a fun place," my father commented as we sat down at a wobbly table. I could almost predict what my parents would select: My mother ordered veal scaloppini because it was similar to Wiener Schnitzel; my father asked for Osso Bucco because it was one of his favorite dishes to cook in the London hotels. As for me, I had linguini with white clam sauce, maybe because I'd enjoyed that dish with my pals in college.

But I don't think my parents had expected the meals to come with garlic bread, minestrone soup, salad, a side of pasta, and dessert. We called for a bottle of Tuscan Red to complement the entrées. On the way out I asked my mother what she thought of the place.

"It looked so dirty." She forced a prim smile, then added. "I was afraid to use the bathroom."

From there, I took them to two bars, just for fun: the Spitfire, with a lot of RAF memorabilia, tartans, and British ales; and the Dortmunder, which my father said reminded him of a bar in Hamburg.

One of the patrons at the Dortmunder wore red suspenders and, with a face almost as red, had trouble sitting on the barstool and kept sliding off. Each time he got up, he gave a Nazi salute and shouted: "Deutschland!" and "Heil Hitler!"

An older gentleman at the bar, who wore a sports coat and drank beer from a Hefeweizen glass, called him "Schweinhund" and told him: "Halt die Klappe!"

My mother looked embarrassed, my father appeared bemused, the bartender yelled at the drunk patron: "Kasi, halts maul! Du bist ganz besoffen!"

My mother frowned when the bartender told Kasi he was completely soused and should shut his trap. My father chuckled: "Why don't they send Kasi to that RAF bar two doors down. They'll take care of him."

But at that point, the gentleman in the sports coat had his arm around Kasi's shoulder and called him "Mein Freund." Kasi replied: "Du bist ein guter Kamerad."

They bought each other drinks and clinked glasses.

I leaned back in my chair.

"That's the great thing about San Francisco," I remarked. "Just on this one street, you have a bar full of Scotsmen, another full of Germans, a Korean café, and a joint called the Irish Castle."

"Only in America," my mother noted. "London in my day was never so mixed."

My father looked at me with a raised eyebrow. "And now you're leaving."

I thought about it, then found myself saying: "If life were nothing but going to bars and nightclubs, San Francisco would be the greatest city in the world. But there's got to be more to life than that."

"I'll drink to that," my father agreed, and the three of us toasted.

My mother seemed reconciled to my leaving America to work in Europe as a cook. Later that evening, she even said: "Depending on how long you stay in Europe, we may have a family reunion. Your father and I plan to visit Spain and Austria in a year or so. Maybe we can travel together to visit relatives."

* * *

The Seventy-Ninth Annual Commencement was held in Cox Stadium, outdoors and in the hot sun. I sweltered in regalia, a cap and master's degree hood. I hoped to catch a glimpse of Saloma, wave to her, maybe say hello, but there were close to five thousand graduates listed in the program, and probably close to that number of us seated in folding chairs on the football field in front of the draped platform stage. The stands held another five thousand people and looked full of family members. All around me on the field was a sea of black caps and gowns; we were seated by college and program, and the informal receptions hosted by each college dean later in the day would be in different buildings. I didn't think I had much chance of finding her.

The mass graduation ceremony with its thousands of graduates and mob of family members in the stands seemed interminable, as did some of the speeches. A distinguished alumnus from each college was invited to offer remarks, and the phrases and sentiments sounded identical: "The future is in your hands

. . . the attainment of your goals . . . hard work, sacrifice, perseverance . . . the debt of gratitude you owe to your supportive family members . . ." et cetera, et cetera, et cetera. I thought of Yul Brynner in *The King and I.*

In the oppressive heat, wearing a necktie and woolen gown, I wouldn't have minded being garbed like Yul Brynner in that movie—bare chested, with breeches that ended at the knee, and cloth sandals with pointy tips. Even his shaved head I considered appealing.

The "Address to the Graduates" was offered by the Australian Ambassador to the United States, Sir Nicholas F. Parkinson, whose speech struck me as a string of foreign policy clichés punched up by a lilting emphasis on key words: "Our two *Nations*, linked by mutual needs in trade and commerce, mutual heritage and *Traditions*, and a common love of freedom and *Democracy*," et cetera, et cetera, et cetera, as Yul Brynner's King Mongkut would have said.

Ambassador Parkinson spoke of the Soviet threat and the dangers facing the *Modern World*, proxy wars fought by geopolitical rivals, the Malthusian curve and *Massive Dieback*, OPEC and the EEC, the *Commonwealth* and the *Commonweal*, and I looked for the mute button, but the remote control was back in the *Common Room* of the *Rooming House* on Granger.

* * *

After the combined commencement ceremony, I met my parents at a spot we'd designated beforehand, then made our way to the Humanities College reception in the Terrace Room. We stopped to take photos on campus with different buildings as backdrops: the Library, the Humanities Building, the Conference Center. My mother looked tearful, my father shook my hand. I wanted to introduce my parents to Saloma, but there was no sign of her.

* * *

My parents drove back to Southern California the next day, and we said our farewells. I was due to fly to Germany on Wednesday. I told my parents I'd write regularly.

I stood for a long time in the parking lot of the motel, waving goodbye as they headed south on Greater Highway, then turned and walked slowly to the bus stop.

I spent most of the afternoon cleaning my room, which I would vacate in a few short days. It felt strange with most of my things gone; no wall hangings or books, no cassette player, a few items still in a drawer and three packed suitcases in the corner.

I watched the tv news in the common room. The local station updated viewers on the Cole Valley Police Station bombing. The newscaster stared into the camera and intoned the names of the two dead policemen; large headshots of each of the two victims appeared again and again on the screen. The newscaster stated gravely that Sergeant Mulcahey was a twenty-two year veteran of the force, was well-regarded in the community, and was dead at age forty-six. Patrolman O'Keefe was only twenty-four, the newscaster related almost in a hush, and had left behind a wife and two small children. At the time of the broadcast, no arrests had been made and no group had claimed responsibility, though the newscaster mentioned the usual suspects: the Black Panthers, the Weather Underground, even the IRA.

In the event, no one was ever apprehended and the Weather Underground—the likeliest perpetrator—always denied involvement.

It had been a busy weekend, and I didn't feel like going out.

I made a Spam and cheese omelet for dinner, with toast. I wanted to use up my remaining food, including breakfast items in the fridge. I opened a can of whole potatoes and heated them.

I went to bed early but woke up at dawn in time to look out the Bay window of my room and see the orange globe of a full moon, cratered and hanging low, before it disappeared.

* * *

I didn't have much to do the next day. I'd said my goodbyes to classmates and professors at the college reception, and there had been a farewell luncheon for me at the Federal Building on my last day of work. I spent most of the day walking the City, reflecting on my experiences over the past two years and on what I'd achieved, if anything.

If a goal had been to take in the arts, I certainly managed that, visiting all the major museums and returning for special exhibitions, such as the one on Dutch art of the Golden Age. I'd taken in Chekov's *The Cherry Orchard* at the ACT and had also caught Shakespeare's *Macbeth.* As for opera, I'd stood for three long matinee performances, seeing grand performances of *The Magic Flute*, *Turandot*, and *Otello*, with the title role in the Verdi opera sung by Placido Domingo, whom I'd never heard of at the time.

I'd earned my degree and had read widely and voraciously, and I'd made some inroads with publishing, though what anyone would term a "break" would elude me for several years.

And I'd loved and laughed, as the Sinatra song goes—or was it loved and lost? It was both, in my case, and in part it was my own fault. When I thought about Saloma, I felt like crying. We loved each other—at least, I knew I loved her, but we constantly stumbled over barriers of our own making.

I walked around Hallidie Plaza for a while, then out to the Ferry Building where I watched the commuter boats dock and re-cross the Bay. Eventually, near dusk, I caught the MUNI back down Market and walked the last few blocks to my neighborhood. I planned on cooking something cheap and simple for dinner; I still had some cans of tuna and peas and could fry an onion. I stopped at the Lebanese grocery store across from my rooming house to buy a packet of egg noodles and a can of mushroom soup. I could prepare a simple tuna casserole, which would last me two nights. I wouldn't have to go out much.

Going anywhere in town would only bring back memories of Saloma, and I wasn't sure I could deal with any more remorse. Staying in probably wouldn't help either, but at least it wouldn't cost much and I wouldn't be squandering money I'd soon need for travel.

But in the kitchen sat Ferrano and Karl—one short, one tall, both with goofy grins on their faces, waving cigarettes as they blew out smoke, a pack of Chesterfields on the table between them.

"Diego! What's cooking?" Karl Hamburger asked.

No doubt, he'd invite himself to a hefty scoop of tuna casserole if he knew that's what I planned to prepare.

"I'm not sure yet." I remained standing, kept the egg noodles and the can of mushroom soup hidden in the brown grocery bag and placed it on my designated shelf in the larder.

"Just make sure you don't eat pork," Ferrano cautioned. "Pork's no good for you." He took a thoughtful drag on his cigarette, exhaled slowly. "It's because of that Chicano worm. You got to be careful. That Chicano worm can get in your muscles and eat them up."

"Is that so?" I said.

It was warm in the kitchen. The window to the airshaft was up and I smelled a riot of spices and fried foods from the different apartments, competing to create a rancid odor. But the smell of cigarette smoke was worse.

I started for the hallway.

"You leaving?" Karl asked.

"In two days," I replied. "For Germany."

"I know that," Karl shot back. "For a job. I'm surprised. You had a job here."

"That's right," Ferrano concurred. "And a girlfriend." He shook his head, took another long draw on his cigarette. "I had a job. In a sandwich shop. But it was beneath me. I'm looking for something better."

I thought about that. In my own way, I looked for something better too—but what had Pilar told me? Saloma's the best. Take care of her, now and forever. I was a fool in so many ways, but was curious about what Ferrano had just said. He was looking for a job? Ferrano and Karl had been on government assistance the entire time I had known them.

"What kind of job are you looking for?"

"Why, there's the fishing boat fleet at the wharf—Fisherman's Wharf." He stubbed out his cigarette. "I figured I could get a job as a deckhand. I'd feel free. Out there on the ocean blue. At least I wouldn't come back smelling like pickles, onions, and tomatoes, like I did at the sandwich shop."

Karl grinned at me. I thought he was going to say something about coming home smelling of fish guts, but instead he barked: "The wide-open spaces. That's the life! That's why I'm going up to Napa this summer to get a job picking grapes. The harvest! What could be better?"

I'd heard enough. Ferrano as a deckhand on a fishing boat? He'd have to get up at two in the morning, which was when he usually staggered home. Karl picking grapes? Not unless he was going to put them in his mouth. Suddenly, I didn't feel like cooking dinner. I'd been walking most of the day but I decided another twenty minutes on foot headed somewhere—anywhere —was in my best interest.

* * *

I strode down Sanchez Street to Eighteenth, not really sure where I wanted to go. I passed two men arguing at a bus stop. From a distance, they were shapes gesticulating in the gloom but their voices penetrated above the screeching brakes and door whoosh of an arriving bus. When the bus drove off, the men were gone, as if erased from a blackboard.

I followed Eighteenth Street east to Mission, with its wedding gown shops, jewelry stores, pawn shops, and movie theater marquees advertising *Amor en Tierra del Fuego* and *La Chiquita a Fuentes*. Each telephone booth I passed had its handset torn out. Someone had spray-painted "Despierta Pueblo" and "Born to Lose" across a brick wall, and I felt as if I couldn't win, no matter what I did.

Saloma must have loved me very much to have overcome her fears, the past sexual abuse in the Philippines, her conflicted feelings about her father, to have given herself to me, and I was too much of a horse's ass to have accepted that. Instead, I wanted "experience."

I looked north and south on Mission: candy-colored cars cruised by; a group of teenage girls with high-gloss lipstick and fake snakeskin jackets entered a dress shop; a man tugged along by a German Shepherd on a leash crossed at the intersection. A sign above me read: "EL JALISCO . . . . FE," the first two letters of "Café" probably burnt out long ago. I pulled on the heavy door and entered to the warmth of steam and cooking, the aroma of spices and stews, the sound of norteño music from a jukebox where a couple danced, and the sight of old couples and families taking up the booths and tables on the mosaic tile floor.

Experience lay at my feet, and all I could think of was Tennyson's line: "Yet all experience is an arch wherethrough gleams that untravelled world whose margin fades forever and forever as I move."

Whatever I sought would always recede like that margin—like that horizon—that I could never reach.

I sat at the bar. A man next to me ate Birria de Chivo—goat meat stew in a thick red sauce; farther down, someone appeared to eat Caldo de Siete Mares—a seafood soup. Soups and stews must have been the specialty of the house. I glanced down the bar into the kitchen; an agile cook flipped a frying pan onto the stove; his gold teeth glistened when he laughed.

The bartender came over. He was a round-faced man with a moustache and wore a floral shirt. I spoke to him in Spanish. Joking to myself, I almost wanted to ask him if there was a cook's job for me at "EL JALISCO . . . . FE." Why not? That would be an experience too.

Instead, I told him I'd like to see a menu. He jerked his thumb at a chalkboard above the bar, next to the image of the Virgen de Guadalupe and a poster of Robert Kennedy.

"Anything to drink, cuñado?"

We continued to speak in Spanish.

I asked for a Negra Modelo, changed my mind and called for a Beck's, then told him whatever he had on tap was fine.

The bartender seemed to study me. He gave me a big smile.

"Corona en barril," he said cheerfully as he turned a spigot and filled a tall beer glass.

I could think of a dozen reasons why my relationship with Saloma hadn't worked out. It wasn't just my restlessness or the tumult of my unfulfilled ambitions. We were compatible in so many ways, but our backgrounds were so different that our attitudes toward all the big subjects—politics, religion, children, the nomadic or the sedentary life, were at variance. And neither of us really believed we could make it work; we both feared a life together would be undone by an underlying instability.

It didn't matter. It was over. I was leaving in a couple of days.

The bartender set the beer in front of me, and I drank half of it at a gulp. He asked me if I wanted anything to eat. I looked at the menu board, ran my eye down the list. I told him I'd have the Pozole, changed my mind and ordered the Carne Asada.

He said he wasn't sure there was any left.

"Okay, make it the Guisado de Puerco." I really didn't give a damn and drained my beer.

When the bartender returned from the kitchen, he asked me if I'd like another draft.

"Why not?" I shrugged. "I leave for Germany in two days."

He mulled it over.

"Germany?"

The bartender worked a towel into the mouth of a glass and dried it carefully.

"Yeah," I muttered.

He grinned knowingly.

"Have you said goodbye to all your novias?"

I thought about it.

"Not yet."

CHAPTER FOURTEEN

I phoned her the next day. After a long pause, I heard her say: "I was wondering when you'd call."

"I'd like to see you for a while—today," I put in. "Before I leave." I added: "Just for a short while."

She agreed to meet me on campus, when she finished work. We were only a few days from Memorial Day weekend and it was warm for the end of May. I wanted to look relaxed and wore a Hawaiian shirt with a palm tree and coconut pattern, sneakers, and Bermuda shorts. Maybe the look was a bit too relaxed, but I was supposed to be taking a few days off before starting work again in Germany on May 25th.

I took the bus down Irving to Judah, then got off at Fischer's Books. I knew the store well: used paperbacks stacked on shelves and on the floor, but also hardbound first editions, the occasional rare book, and used collector's facsimiles in glass-door bookcases. It didn't take me long to find what I was looking for.

I selected a book and paid at the counter. Fred Fischer, the owner's son, was already in his mid-forties, with curly greying hair and wire-rimmed spectacles. I borrowed his pen so that I could write an inscription.

"Inside cover only," he grunted without looking up. "Never write anything anywhere else in a book."

I had limited time. I wrote quickly and without hesitation. I wrote what was in my heart, then gave him back his pen. "Do you gift wrap?" It seemed a logical question.

He handed me a sturdy twelve-by-twelve-inch brown paper carry bag with twine handles. That was just as well; I didn't want Saloma to think this was some grand farewell ceremony, and I wasn't sure how she would take a parting gift.

I caught the southbound bus on Nineteenth and rode the rest of the way. I was early. The campus was as still as a photograph. I walked for a while, enjoying the warm, cloudless afternoon. The last time I'd been at the university was for commencement, when all the parking places were taken, the grounds were thronged with families and cheering graduates, and festivity and excitement filled the air.

As I walked past some of the places where I'd been so many times with Saloma—the Library, the quad, the Humanities Building, the knoll—a strange feeling overcame me because the campus was nearly deserted. It was intersession and only a few days before the Memorial Day holiday.

A grounds crew worked at the far end of the quad. A man with a pruning-pole cut branches and stepped expertly out of the way as they fell. Another man walked behind a self-propelled lawn mower. I could see the crisscross pattern on the grassy square where he'd cut back and forth and could hear the steady moan of the mower. When he reached the backside, he killed the engine and it coughed into silence.

I watched him load the mower onto a trailer and drive away.

I looked at my watch. It was almost four-thirty. I entered

the Humanities Building and headed down the hall in the direction of Dr. Papandrakis' suite. I could smell paint. At the end of the hallway, men in white overalls and painters' caps pushed rollers up and down a wall.

Saloma came out. She was dressed in a cotton summer dress and rope sandals. Her hair hung over one shoulder and was tied in a bow.

"Hi." She crossed her arms and fingered the tip of her ponytail. "You look cool."

"So do you." I gripped the twine handles of the brown paper shopping bag and kept it behind my thigh so that she wouldn't spot it immediately. "Thank you for seeing me."

She gave me a half smile. "I *wanted* to see you," she assured me. "You leave tomorrow." She reached up and kissed me on the cheek. "Don't be silly."

We walked down the hallway and outside to the bench where we'd sometimes had a sack lunch together. The air was refreshing, with a light breeze, and we sat close together on the bench, but our hips and thighs didn't touch. I placed the paper shopping bag to my right, next to the armrest.

We talked about the weather. I said it was always very pleasant in San Francisco in May. I asked her when she would start her graduate program in Special Ed. She said in the fall.

I could feel the warm breeze across my face, like a hand closing my eyelids. I closed my eyes, kept them shut, could sense Saloma next to me sitting in silence, could hear her gentle breathing.

When I opened my eyes, nothing had changed; the criss-cross pattern still created a checkerboard on the grassy square, the pruned trees were still at the far end, Saloma was still next to me.

"We'll write," I said, only half believing it. I looked across the quad, at the Library, at the steps where a blues band had once played.

"What are you thinking about?" she asked.

I smiled. "I'm thinking about the future."

She took my hand. "What's the hotel like—where you'll be working?" She tried to sound positive, but I could hear tension in her voice.

"It's a grand place, of course," I said matter-of-factly. "It looks like a chateau, but it's been used for different things." I could feel her rub my knuckles, and I moved my hand carefully away from hers. I leaned forward and folded my hands in front of me, my forearms on my knees. "During the War, it was used as a field hospital," I continued. "I guess any place with that many beds was going to be requisitioned."

"And the village where you'll be staying?" Saloma feigned nonchalance, but her voice cracked.

I hesitated for a moment. I didn't want to make it sound too exciting, and I guessed it wouldn't be.

"Well, it's a village," I shrugged. "There's a church, a graveyard, some shops, a town square from what I've seen in the tourist brochure. There's a war monument, of course. I suppose every village in Germany has a memorial listing the names of the young men who died in the two World Wars."

We were making small talk, avoiding what we needed to say.

"What about you, Saloma?" I asked, looking at her. "Are you going anywhere for Memorial Day?"

"No," she replied quietly. "We always stay in town. Do the family thing—cook out, go to the park, go to church." She paused thoughtfully, and I leaned back on the bench. "My uncle was with the Philippine Scouts in the U.S. Army," she went on. "On Memorial Day itself, we always go to the National Cemetery in the Presidio and visit his grave."

She gave a slight smile. "We place a small flag on the grave and attend the ceremony at the parade ground."

"I didn't know that."

Our conversation wasn't headed where I wanted it to go. We were saying everything except what we needed to say.

"Listen, Saloma . . . I have something for you." I reached over into the paper bag and brought out the book. "It's a small something, but I thought you might like it."

I handed her a leather-bound Classics edition of *Anna Karenina*. Saloma's smile brightened, and she kissed me on the cheek.

"It's beautiful, Diego," she said, accepting it. She ran her hand along the spine, across the embossed gold and brown leather cover. She kept smiling, and I smiled as well.

"Open it," I coaxed.

"I don't need to," she laughed, then quoted: "'All happy families are alike. Every unhappy family is unhappy in its own way.'"

I laughed as well, drily. "I wrote something inside. Go ahead."

She opened the book. Underneath the date, I had written a simple inscription: "To My Dearest Saloma – With All My Love—Diego."

She tried to smile, but her lower lip quivered and tears filled her eyes. A lump came into my throat and I realized my eyes were wet too.

"Saloma," I began. She shushed me.

"Don't say it." She held up a hand. "I know what you want to say." She was wiser than I was. She knew I was about to tell her I wanted to be with her but couldn't; that I would have wanted to marry her if circumstances had been slightly different. She was right. It was best left unsaid.

Ahead of me lay a two-year sojourn in Europe, a first novel, a teaching job in Indonesia, a doctoral degree, marriage to a Balinese dance teacher, a house in a leafy suburb, a vacation home.

I turned to her that May afternoon. She had opened the book at random and her fingers ran along a line of print as if she were reading.

I saw a drop of fluid on the page spread open like a flower, then another. She tried to wipe the tears from the page but more fell.

"I'll always love you, Diego," she said.

"I know."

"Come back one day."

"I will."

EPILOGUE

1992

San Francisco hadn't changed, though the Loma Prieta earthquake had knocked out the Embarcadero Freeway, which was demolished and removed. Another mass shooting in the Financial District had left eleven people dead and sixteen wounded, with the berserk gunman throwing himself from the thirty-fourth floor when the police closed in, and the 49ers had won the Super Bowl four times since I'd left, though I didn't much care for professional sports.

I was attending an academic conference at the Fairmont and was scheduled to present a paper on "Dryden and Derangement." There was a good chance it would be published in a scholarly journal once I'd gathered feedback toward a revision.

My panel presentation wasn't until Saturday. I had two days to attend other sessions, network at the publishers' fair, and hobnob at the social events. And I had one night to see Saloma—Friday night.

When I talked to her on the phone from my house in

Michigan, I suggested we meet at Santorini's in North Beach—"For old time's sake," I added.

I could almost hear her smile over the phone.

"It's been gentrified," she said lightly. "You won't recognize it."

"No more sawdust on the floors?" I joked. I couldn't remember it ever looking like a saloon. It had been an out-of-the way mom and pop Greek restaurant behind a bakery. As I recalled, it was mostly gyros and souvlaki on the menu with a few lamb and seafood dishes.

"I'll see you at six," she said, and hung up.

* * *

I was early. I didn't want to wear a business suit, even though I'd brought one along. Instead, I wore the uniform of the academic: a herringbone tweed sportscoat, open-necked dress shirt, and slacks. I was hoping Saloma would say I hadn't changed. My hair was still dark, if thinning, and I still sported a moustache and goatee, though it was nicely trimmed. I needed eyeglasses from all the reading, but I probably needed glasses twelve or thirteen years earlier when I was too vain to use them.

I waited for Saloma outside the restaurant. Santorini's Bakery was gone—or rather, it had been converted into a bar and waiting area, and there was a doorman now—an imposing African-American in a light blue tuxedo who smiled affably.

A sign read: "Valet Parking." As I waited, I watched two teenage carhops jockey vehicles to the parking garage and then trot back uphill.

Saloma arrived. I kissed her lightly on the cheek and she smiled. I wanted to see her as I remembered her, and I did: her clear skin, luminous brown eyes, her dark hair that fell across her forehead, though she had cut it short and wore bangs.

"You look great," I grinned. "How are you?"

"Hungry," she chuckled.

"Then let's go inside."

The doorman extended a long arm and pulled the door back for us. We walked through the bar, past a knot of conventioneers yelling at a ball game on the television screen, and into the restaurant. I admired Saloma's graceful movements as she entered; when she turned to face me, I took in the pendant earrings and matching necklace, the navy-blue dress with an open jacket, and the polished shoes. Mid-October could be cool in San Francisco and she wore a russet-colored coat with brown faux-fur trim.

"Let me help you." I slipped her coat from her shoulders. Saloma thanked me and smiled.

I hung her coat on the rack and waited with her by the hostess' station. I barely recognized the place, which was probably just as well. The exposed brick was gone, covered by red-felt patterned wallpaper. Full-length, gold-leaf mirrors faced each other, no doubt to make the room seem larger. The cushioned booths were gone; round tables with floor-length cloths fanned across the floor, like waltzing couples. The décor was gaudy, rather than refined, and the space reminded me of the lobby of a movie palace that had seen better days.

"What happened to the photos of famous Greek-Americans?" I quipped.

"They went the way of Spiro Agnew." Saloma hadn't lost her sense of humor. She must have remembered there'd been a portrait of the disgraced vice president on the wall.

The maître d' came over. He wore his black hair long and slightly over the collar and his dark suit was as shiny as his hair. He showed us to our table. I held the chair for Saloma and inched it forward as she sat down.

I hadn't seen her in more than five years—seven, to be

exact, when I was last in San Francisco during a long layover on my way back from Asia to begin a doctoral program in Chicago. Saloma had driven to the airport to see me, and we had lunch at a nearby hotel. At the time, she was engaged to be married —"So I can have children," she told me. I didn't think that was much of a plan—to marry someone only to have children. The more she'd revealed over lunch that time, the less promising the arrangement had seemed. Her fiancé was in the Coast Guard; he spent much of his time deployed near the Bering Sea and was six years younger than she was. But I didn't have anything better to offer her, so I'd told her I was happy for her and wished her well.

I glanced at the menu: "Santorini's – Specializing in Seafood Dishes from the Greek Isles," it announced boldly. There didn't seem anything Greek about the menu except the coffee and some of the lettering. Chilean Sea Bass, Arctic Char, Fresh Ocean Perch—it sounded good, but not too authentic.

I ordered the perch and Saloma had the sea bass. I decided not to drink too much because I didn't want to become too sentimental. We decided to order wine by the glass.

"So now I'm divorced," she related during dinner. "But I have the two children I told you about. Would you like to see their pictures?"

"Of course."

She reached into her handbag and pulled out a small red wallet. She unfolded it and showed me photos of a little girl who looked about three and a little boy who seemed a year or two older.

They looked mixed-race—Asiatic and Caucasian, which Saloma was—but a bit on the fairer side, almost with blond hair. Then I remembered her fiancé had been named Linman or Lindemann and had been as blond as a Viking.

"They look lovely," I remarked. "You must be very happy."

She told me their names—Tina and Ramon. "He'll be starting pre-school next year—and Tina—I'll have her at home for a few more years."

"But you have help," I said.

She smiled and nodded. "I took a leave of absence from the school, but I still have a part-time practice."

She was a licensed clinical counselor, and the last time I'd seen her she'd been teaching special ed at a middle school.

She asked me about my parents, and I told her they'd been retired for a few years and had moved to Lake Elsinore.

"What about your family?" I added. "How's Ezzie? Is she out changing the world?"

Saloma gave a rueful smile. "She goes by Esmerelda now. She's a legislative aide in Sacramento." Saloma set her knife and fork at an angle on her plate, in the European way, showing that she was finished with the entrée. "Ezzie helped get some of the insurance fraud bills through the Assembly," she put in.

"Well, it's a start," I said philosophically. "We change things in small ways."

We were concluding the meal and I asked Saloma if she'd like any dessert.

"Just coffee," she replied. "Maybe the specialty of the house." She paused, then looked at me directly. "How about you? You seem to be doing well."

"Yes. I'm up for tenure and promotion next year."

The waiter came over and I said we'd each like a demitasse of Turkish coffee. I corrected myself: "Greek coffee," I told him, and he managed a thin smile.

I turned to Saloma. "And you know I'm married."

"Yes, you told me. To a dance instructor. What kind of dance?"

"Balinese, but these days mostly jazz and aerobic."

The coffee arrived and Saloma sipped hers thoughtfully. She pursed her lips and blew gently across the top of the cup. "Does she make sure you get lots of exercise?"

I felt myself blushing. "In a manner of speaking, yes."

"And still no children? But then again, you never wanted any."

I tried to laugh. "No, I didn't." I set my coffee cup down and it clattered lightly in the cup. "It's better that way. Not everyone should have children—and I'm one of those."

I gave her a tight smile. "Instead, I have time to research arcane subject areas such as the literature of the Protectorate and the Interregnum. I'm presenting a paper tomorrow."

"On what?"

"Dryden and Derangement."

She tried not to laugh but broke into a broad smile. "You'd know a lot about the derangement part."

"I was certainly crazy about you."

"That was a long time ago, Diego."

"I know."

* * *

After dinner, in the wan light before sunset, we found our way down Mason to Embarcadero, past the fishing fleet and the wharf, out to the old pier. We walked side by side, silently, out to the end as a gull soared above us, also in silence, and we could hear the quiet lapping of the waves against the pilings.

Ahead of us was the Golden Gate and the bridge, the shoreline of Marin and the gateway to the Pacific Ocean and beyond.

We stood wordlessly side by side. Our hands hung close to our hips, close to each other, almost touching.

ACKNOWLEDGMENTS

My thanks to the Melvin J. Zahnow Library staff at Saginaw Valley State University in Michigan for their invaluable help in accessing historical documents and to the Theodore Roethke Home Museum for providing a venue for authors to read works-in-progress.

RIZE publishes great stories and great writing across genres written by People of Color and other underrepresented groups.

Our team consists of:

Lisa Diane Kastner, Founder and Executive Editor
Cody Sisco, Acquisitions Editor, RIZE
Benjamin White, Acquisition Editor, Running Wild
Peter A. Wright, Acquisition Editor, Running Wild
Resa Alboher, Editor
Angela Andrews, Editor
Sandra Bush, Editor
Ashley Crantas, Editor
Rebecca Dimyan, Editor
Abigail Efird, Editor
Aimee Hardy, Editor
Henry L. Herz, Editor
Cecilia Kennedy, Editor
Barbara Lockwood, Editor
Scott Schultz, Editor

Evangeline Estropia, Product Manager
Kimberly Ligutan, Product Manager
Lara Macaione, Marketing Director
Joelle Mitchell, Licensing and Strategy Lead
Pulp Art Studios, Cover Design
Standout Books, Interior Design
Polgarus Studios, Interior Design

Learn more about us and our stories at www.runningwild-press.com

Loved these stories and want more? Follow us at www.runningwildpress.com, www.facebook.com/runningwildpress, on Twitter @lisadkastner @RunWildBooks @RwpRIZE